The LAKE House

JEFF LAFERNEY

THE LAKE HOUSE

Copyright© Jeff LaFerney, 2023

ISBN-13: 979-8398756241

Published by:

TOWER
PUBLICATIONS

Contents

Acknowledgements 1

Prologue 2

    Pickett County, TN, Twenty-three years in the past 2

Chapter 1 6

    Present time, twenty-three years later 6

Chapter 2 11

Chapter 3 16

Chapter 4 20

Chapter 5 24

Chapter 6 30

Chapter 7 37

Chapter 8 42

Chapter 9 49

Chapter 10 56

Chapter 11 64

Chapter 12 72

Chapter 13 78

Chapter 14 84

Chapter 15 92

Chapter 16 97

Chapter 17 104

Chapter 18 108

Chapter 19 117

Chapter 20 124

Chapter 21 129

Chapter 22 137

Chapter 23 142

Chapter 24 149

Chapter 25 157

Chapter 26 164

Chapter 27 170

Chapter 28 179

Chapter 29 192

Chapter 30 202

Chapter 31 212

Author's Note 218

Acknowledgements

As with all of my previous books, I always have help. I'd like to thank Ashley Fontainne for all the formatting work she does and for another cover I love. She's an awesome friend. Thank you to Neesha Hosein, Ada Lape, and Nya Ando for doing content editing for me. All three gave me some great suggestions and help and are amazing people. Thank you to my friends, Eric Duncan, Bill Hansel, and Renee LaRocque for proofreading for me. They found errors I would have been embarrassed to have left in the book. Thank you to my brother, David LaFerney, for helping with realty questions. I'm grateful to Ada Lape for straightening me out on some of my police material (she's an expert from all the research she does on her amazing books). Nya Ando knows psychology and medicine better than I do and gave me some good insights (her terrific books demonstrate her vast knowledge). Neesha gave me the plot idea that got my writing juices flowing, so thank you for that. Thank you to my sister-in-law, Shannon LaFerney, and niece, Kylie Miulli, who gave me an additional plot idea I used in the book. Thank you to my wife, Jennifer, who patiently listens to me when I'm stuck or excited or feeling some other emotion and is understanding when I'm holed off in my office for hours on end for three or four months. Thank you to my readers, as well. I'm grateful for all the people who give my books a chance and support me. I hope I always come off as appreciative as I feel.

Prologue
Pickett County, TN, Twenty-three years in the past

Police Detective Reese Carlton entered the captain's office. Carlton, after six years in the Pickett County Sheriff's Department as an officer, had been promoted to detective less than a year earlier.

"Sit down, Detective," said the captain with a wave of his hand toward the padded folding chair in front of his desk.

Detective Carlton nodded his head at Captain Chester Kennedy, whose Irish last name meant helmet headed. Kennedy displayed many of the stereotypical characteristics of the Irish—red-haired, lover of a "pint" after a work shift, quick-tempered, and religious. A transplant from New York State, he was fair and friendly, but when he made up his mind about something, he was the most "helmet-headed" person Reese knew.

"I got a memo today from Chief Rogers. Says for you to stand down on your investigation."

"That can't be right." Reese leaned forward, his blue-green eyes penetrating the captain's.

"There's a fatal car wreck off Parker Road at the bridge over the Wolf River. I'm sending you to investigate the scene as soon as we're done here."

"Why take me off my case?"

"Because it's a nowhere case going nowhere. We need you to work on cases that can be solved."

"Is that you speaking or Chief Rogers?"

"It's me speaking because I follow orders just like you will."

"Captain, after sixteen months of building Dale Hollow Dam, three men from the town of Willow Grove still refused to sell their land—land scheduled to be submerged to create Dale Hollow Lake. The dam was built, but without those sales, the project would have been terminated indefinitely—

3

maybe permanently. At the last minute, all three contracts were signed, but the men are missing now. None of the three wives will speak to me about the sales, but, as you know, I got that anonymous tip saying one of the men was murdered."

"Yes, we've talked about that before. Have you learned who sent you the tip, Carlton?"

"Not yet, Captain. It was a kid—a girl—but all three men are still missing, and their wives refused to talk to me. They all have girls, but none of them would let me talk to the kids either."

"I'm well aware of all of that, so what evidence have you found of foul play?"

"I already told you."

"What you've told me is not evidence. Do you have murdered bodies? How can there be a murder if there's no victim? Do you have a murder weapon for any of the so-called murders? Any physical evidence at all?"

"The town is already flooded. The flooding began within three days of the last sale. How can I get evidence? What I have is a suspect."

"A suspect for murders you can't prove were committed and with no evidence pointing at him."

"I have a physical description."

"From your anonymous caller? If you don't know who the witness is, it's just hearsay."

"The caller said a man came to get some papers signed, but her dad wouldn't do it. The caller said the man pointed a gun at her and threatened to kill her. She said her dad struck the man with a fire poker. He turned and shot her dad in the chest. That's what the caller said. The man carried her dead father away after her mother signed the papers. You *do* realize, I hope, Kingston Phipps, the owner of Pickett County Real Estate, the company that bought all the land from the Willow Grove families, would've lost millions of dollars if those families hadn't sold. He was under contract with the state to sell the land so the lake could be formed, and as owner of the land, he's reselling the properties and building lakefront homes at greatly increased property values. Without the sale of those final three homes, he may have even been sued by the state for the twenty-eight million dollars it cost to build the dam. He had major motivation to harm the three missing men."

"But as your reports have stated, he doesn't fit the child's description of the shooter...and Phipps has an alibi for the time of the so-called shooting."

Reese sat still, breathed in and out to still his frustration. Finally, he said, "But we found the man who fit the description, Paul Miller, dead at his home two days later. He even had a gash on the side of his head."

"Suicide, Carlton. Miller killed himself in his garage. He hung himself from a rafter."

"There were fingernail marks on his neck. He tried to get free."

"Sometimes people regret their decisions. But it's too late. There was a stool in the garage that had been knocked over. He stood on it and kicked it aside."

"There are other irregularities, Captain. The knot tying the rope to the beam was a clove hitch, and for some reason there was a different knot—a figure eight knot—around his neck. Both are boating knots. Miller had no boat."

"People can learn to tie a knot from a book."

"There were no rope fibers on the palms of his hands. Only on his fingernails where he scratched at the rope on his neck. If he tied those knots, especially if he perspired from nerves or climbed to the beam to tie the knot, there would be fibers on his palms."

"Unless he tied the knots and hung the rope at a different time and then washed his hands sometime between then and the suicide. It was two days after the so-called murder. Maybe he planned it all out beforehand."

"There were frayed rope fibers on the rope going both directions, like someone hauled the body up with the rope and then the body weight dragged the rope back down—possibly more than once."

"Was it a new rope, Carlton?"

"No, it was an old, used rope."

"So the markings could be from something else also."

"Okay…since I'm getting nowhere, why was the knot at the side of his neck instead of the back if he took the time to kill himself? He'd put the knot part behind his head, right?"

"Unless it was hanging to the side when he climbed up on the stool and he didn't bother to turn around. Think about it, Carlton. Someone was strong enough to lift him to kill him and then while he hung there, tie a knot ten feet off the floor? Seriously, all your questions prove you're a good detective, but they don't prove someone murdered Paul Miller."

"Maybe there was more than one person who hung him. Do you think he committed suicide out of guilt for the murder he committed?"

"That would be a logical conclusion…*if* we had any evidence he murdered the caller's father."

"He was an employee of Kingston Phipps. Phipps could have had him killed for screwing up. The other two men disappeared with no witnesses. Maybe that was the plan for the third man too, but Miller screwed it up and was witnessed killing him….Miller had a gun in his house, Captain."

"The gun was thoroughly cleaned, and there were no fingerprints. We couldn't even tell if it had been shot recently."

"But it might be the murder weapon. If we find the body, it might match."

Captain Kennedy slammed his fist on his desk and then rose, his face reddening by the second. "Do you have a dead body shot by his gun? You have no physical evidence, Carlton! Circumstantial evidence at best. Logical suspicions maybe, but no evidence, so it's time to move on. Chief Rogers says you're done. *I* say you're done. Get your rear end out of my office and head to the accident scene. You have some detecting to do. Until there's some evidence, your wild goose chase has come to an end."

Chapter 1
Present time, twenty-three years later

Reese Carlton screwed in the last of thirty cabinet and drawer pulls and took a drink from a water bottle. Reese, a sinewy six-foot, one-inch man, worked part-time on residential remodeling jobs when he wasn't at work for the Pickett County Sheriff's Department. He replaced the bottle cap and put a toothpick back in his mouth.

Grayson Phipps, his employer and the owner of Phipps Construction, stepped out of the bathroom where he worked on some backsplash above the vanity. "Reese, could you help me with the mirror in here?" Phipps, the thirty-four-year-old heir apparent to his wealthy businessman father, was showing flecks of gray in his close-trimmed beard and at his temples. At six feet tall with a muscular, toned frame, he should have looked like a young man, but he looked tired beyond his years as he took a sip of his Coke and set it back on the counter.

Together, they lifted the mirror off the floor and set it on the vanity with a groan. "We're a couple of sorry-looking guys," Grayson said. "When're you gonna give up your police job? You look exhausted."

Reese had a clean-close-cut haircut. The few wrinkles at his eyes and on his forehead were easily explained by a thirty-year police career. "You sure you're lookin' at the right dude in the mirror. Bloodshot eyes, traces of gray, slumped shoulders. You've aged ten years over the last few months, but to answer your question, two weeks. I'm retiring in two weeks. Then maybe a long vacation. How's your son?"

"A week...maybe two is all he has." Grayson wiped a tear from the corner of his eye, taking in and letting out a deep breath. "Brain cancer sucks. No child should have to go through it."

"You could use a vacation too when this is all over. How's Angie handling things?"

"Not good, and she's in constant conflict with my dad. He wants to control everything, like always, and she wants

7

nothing to do with him. They fought yesterday, and she told him when Noah passes, we're leaving Pickett County."

Still looking in the mirror, Reese sighed. "And here I thought I would be your right-hand man. Fifty-two is too young to spend the rest of my life in a recliner, watching news on the TV all day." He rubbed his eyes and pinched the bridge of his nose, a lingering headache still bothering him. "You on board with that?"

"You know…my happiest times in life, besides hunting, were the two years of high school I spent with Mom after the divorce and the five useless years I spent at college, wasting Dad's money. The only valuable thing I got out of college is Angie. But then Dad gave me part of his construction business and all the clients I could hope for. He expects me to take over his other business interests. I'm not sure what to do."

"I'm struggling with the same sort of questions," said Reese. "I've been a cop for thirty years. What'll I be after that? Will I be happy living here still, or will I want to get away and start something else?" He paused, sighed, and added, "Do I want to be lonely the rest of my life?"

"You can have my company if Angie has her way. We'll be out of here and never look back, and Dad will be furious. He's still trying to groom me and teach me the ins and outs, but I can't be around him all the time. It's why I went to college. It's why I hunted and fished when I was a kid. It's why I've been content with this career. Don't be running over to make any arrests, but I think my dad is shadier than a palm tree. Do you think I'd be busting my butt in a construction company if I wanted to work for him? Trust me when I say my mom left him for good reasons."

Reese raised his eyebrows, sneaking a peek at the creased lines in his face in the mirror. He *was* tired. Pickett County wasn't a bad place to be a police detective. With a population around 5,000 residents, he was one of eleven police officers and the lead detective for twenty-four years. In the past decade, only three murders occurred, all of which were solved, but it was the supposed murders from twenty-three years earlier that caused him to lose sleep at night. And the thought of retiring with no solution left him thinking Angie had a good plan—leave and never look back. He also felt a twinge of guilt for finagling his way into Grayson's business because of his obsession with Gray's father. Gray was a friend and a good man—nothing like his father.

Together, they set the mirror in place and fastened it down. Grayson inspected his handiwork before catching his reflection in the glass again. "Angie has always called me Gray. Who would've ever thought I'd be turning gray at the age of thirty-four?"

"There's a lot of stress in your life. You'll get through it."

"I won't until Noah dies, and when he dies, our hearts are going to be broken."

"And then you can leave if you want...and heal. Start over." Reese swept up some dust and tile chips from the vanity and dumped them into a trash can as Grayson continued to gaze into the mirror.

"Do you think my father will simply give me his blessing to leave? I don't. He'll manipulate things to try to keep me here, and if I don't break away, I might lose Angie too. She despises him." Grayson's phone buzzed. He took it from his toolbox and answered, "Angie? Is everything okay?...Okay, we're done here for the afternoon anyway. I'll head for the hospital now."

"Bad news?" Reese placed a hand on his friend's shoulder.

"My dad is fighting with Angie again. He wants to check Noah out of the hospital. Dad wants Noah at his home where he can be more comfortable. He doesn't understand it's not his decision to make, but he wants control of things. I have to run. Can you clean up and lock the house for me?"

"Sure, Gray. Go."

Gray finished off his Coke in three big gulps. "Have a good afternoon, Reese...and get some rest. You really do look awful."

They bumped fists, and Gray hustled to his truck.

9

***

Ella Dixon stepped off the elevator onto the pediatric ward of Cookeville Reginal Medical Center. Nurses, doctors, and nurse practitioners like Ella busily carried out their duties. She waved and half-grinned at her friend, Stacy Howard, who carried a lunch tray to room two, the room of a cute eight-year-old girl who had had a scary allergic reaction and was on the floor for testing. Ella turned left and headed for her office.

"Hey, Ella," said Doctor Sam Garrett. "Where have you been today?"

Tapping her satchel full of information from her trip to Monroe Carell Jr. Children's Hospital at Vanderbilt, Ella replied, "Vanderbilt. Meetings." Ella wore her white lab coat, her long, straight, brown hair hanging past her shoulders. A five-foot-nine-inch-tall athlete, she had a pretty face with full lips, long eyelashes, and penetrating brown eyes, but she dressed plainly and rarely wore make-up. As far as the staff knew, she didn't date and had no known interests outside of the hospital. Her only real friend at work was Stacy, and she either naively never noticed the attention of Sam or she genuinely didn't care about his obvious interest in her.

Voices sounded down the hall, and both Ella and Sam turned to look. A man stepped out of room five, his face reddened from arguing, Ella assumed. They made eye contact as the man hesitated and then proceeded down the hall to the waiting area, taking a second look at Ella on the way.

"That's Noah Phipps's room," Sam said quietly. "I've heard they're talking about releasing him and taking him home. Are you familiar with his case?" Sam followed Ella to her office.

She didn't say anything until they closed her door. "He has an intracranial glioblastoma, taking a rapidly fatal course. By the time it was diagnosed, it had already grown into the brain tissue, so surgery wasn't possible. Radiation and steroid therapy didn't help. The cancer is too aggressive. He's going to die soon, so all that can be done is try to ease his symptoms and suffering. The poor child is only five years old."

10

"Is he one of your patients?"

"No, but I consulted with Dr. Anthony once the tests were run. I haven't even met the parents."

"Well, according to the nurse gossip, an argument broke out between the mother and grandfather about where he should spend his last days. I think they're waiting for the father to arrive."

"They're under a lot of stress. We *all* are, but getting away from here seems like a good plan. I'd do it myself if I could." She blew a stray hair from hanging over her eye and sighed. "I have work to do, Sam. Those meetings put me behind."

Sam stared at her a second too long, but when Ella looked up, he turned away. "I'll see you later, Ella."

The only response he got was clicking on computer keys. She was back to work before the door closed.

11

Chapter 2

When Grayson Phipps arrived, he walked directly to Noah's room, ignoring his father in the waiting area, and put his arms around Angie. "Are you okay? Is Noah okay?"

"Thanks for coming so quickly, Gray. No, I'm not okay, and neither is Noah. Look at him…so helpless…so much suffering." Angie looked like she always did; professionally dressed; make-up applied; brown, curly, off-the-shoulder hair prepared perfectly; and mascara highlighting her brown eyes. At five feet eight inches, she looked like a runway model. She owned her own tax business and since Noah's hospitalization, did a lot of her work at the hospital.

Noah looked up and forced a grin when he saw his father.

Then his grandfather entered the room. Angie stepped away from Grayson, backed up against the wall, and crossed her arms. What he saw in her eyes wasn't anger, like he expected, but rather, it looked more like hatred. "Son, we need to talk." After a long pause, Grayson looked at his wife. Finally, he turned to his father, but he said nothing. "Noah needs to be comfortable. My house has room for everyone. Get him out of here with all these strange people and noises and smells and awful food, and let's give him his last days in the best environment possible."

Again, Gray looked at his wife. Surprisingly, she gave a slight nod of approval. "Let me talk to Angie, Dad. Give us the room, please."

Kingston glared at Angie but left the room without argument and closed the door behind him. "What did he say to you, Angie? Something's not right here."

She hesitated. "He's right. I can't stand him, Gray, but he's right. It's the best place for Noah and us right now, and there's room there, including room for a hospice nurse." She started crying and moved toward Grayson, drawing him into a hug. "I don't want him to die here. Let's get him out." She squeezed her husband tightly for another long moment and then moved away without looking at him. "I'll go and start making arrangements." She walked out of the room without looking back, leaving her husband to stare helplessly at the door and then at his son.

Kingston re-entered the room. Dressed as always in a suit and tie, he gave off the air of wealth suitable for a multi-millionaire. Divorced, his mother said, because of his narcissism and drinking, Grayson suspected it was for far less scrupulous things than those. Long gone after her divorce settlement, she had never met her grandson. Kingston, a real-estate mogul turned entrepreneur after making a fortune on the sale of the property around Dale Hollow Lake, had a full head of gray hair and a red, splotchy, bloated face from drinking. He looked older than his 64 years, but though he'd aged physically, he remained the same cocky, demanding, inflexible man he'd always been. He always got his way, and Grayson wondered how Angie, who stood up to him on most occasions, was persuaded to agree with him.

A nurse came in…checked things…didn't say a word. A doctor came in…reviewed Noah's chart…stared at him for a moment and walked out without speaking. Finally, Kingston spoke. "I don't like her, Son."

"Why? Because she's strong and independent? You should respect that."

"She doesn't respect *me*."

"Should she?"

"I'm trying to help."

"You're trying to control…get your way. Maybe you're right, Dad. Maybe your place is best, but it was *our* decision to make, not yours."

"She's the problem, not me, but I'll head home and get things ready for you. You're making the right decision, Grayson….And when this is over, we need to talk about your future with the business."

"There's nothing to talk about right now. Noah is our top priority."

Kingston gave a slight nod of his head and left his son in the room with Noah. He took out his phone to make a call but hesitated when he saw Ella Dixon for the second time, delivering a file folder to the nurses' desk. He stopped and watched her hand the folder to a nurse, say a few words, and then head back to her office. He followed curiously, and from a distance noted the door's nameplate—Ella Dixon, ARNP. He opened the note app on his phone and punched in the name, put his phone back in his jacket pocket, and left the hospital, an idea formulating in his mind.

He straightened his tie as he exited the building, walked across the street, and climbed into his $100,000, fully loaded, bright yellow Ford Super Duty F-350. It was an impressive vehicle for a man who cared mostly that people thought he was impressive. He took his phone from his jacket pocket, pushed the home button, and spoke. "Call Beau." When his right-hand man, Beau Struthers, answered, he said, "Make sure the house is ready. The boy and his parents are moving in."

As he exited his parking spot, Reese Carlton observed from a space across the lot. Knowing Kingston Phipps was at the hospital, he had driven from the construction site after locking up the house. Watching his suspect and tapping his fingers on his steering wheel, he wondered if the one case that ate at him most of his career would ever be solved.

***

Beau Struthers worked for Kingston Phipps his entire adult life. No one was more loyal. At 6'4" and 230 pounds, he was an imposing figure. His nose bent from being broken multiple times in fights and his cauliflower ears from wrestling made him look like a goon. He dressed in a suit every day like his boss, but his muscular body still looked imposing. He wore a short, trimmed beard and mustache, had a big chip in one of his front teeth Kingston offered to fix, but Beau refused. It happened riding as a teenaged passenger with his brother during a motorcycle accident which resulted in his brother's death. Kingston took the place of Beau's brother, but the chipped tooth remained as a trophy, reminding Beau of the brother he lost because of his recklessness. Beau strived to never be reckless, but he also rarely smiled because of the broken front tooth—or because he was mean. That's what Gray and Angie Phipps would have said.

Nevertheless, Beau stood outside Kingston's home, his black Toyota Tundra pick-up truck parked in the driveway. Once Noah arrived, he carried both the boy and his wheelchair inside as if they were weightless. Angie and Gray carried in his personal effects and medical equipment. They returned to the truck to get their luggage for an indefinite stay. When everything was out of the truck and settled into a guest bedroom, they went to look in on Noah. Beau already had him in his bed with his monitors and IV set up.

"Mommy, I don't feel good."

Angie had been worried the drive would be difficult, and Noah confirmed it. "I know, sweety. It was a tiring drive. You need to rest, and you'll feel better."

"When will I feel better?"

Tears welled up in Angie's eyes as Gray, Beau, and Kingston looked on. "The pain will be gone someday soon, honey. I don't think it'll be long. God has his eye on you."

Noah smiled. He tilted his head. The tumor sometimes affected his vision, and he had to find a better angle to see. "God loves me."

"Yes, he does. He loves you very much."

"Almost as much as you do, right, Mommy?"

"More. He has the biggest love there is."

"Mommy, I'm tired. Will you stay with me?"

"I'll stay until you sleep, and then Daddy and I will move into our room in Grandpa's house. We'll always be right here." Angie sat and held Noah's hand, and he drifted off into sleep within a couple of minutes. She covered him carefully with his blanket and tiptoed out of the room behind the three men.

Out in the hallway, Kingston spoke first. "Why do you always have to bring God up?"

"Because I speak the truth to my son. I don't hide things from him."

"Are you talking about me now?" Kingston's splotchy face turned a darker shade of red.

"Not everything's about you, Kingston. But since you think it is, does *your* son know what you do? The crimes you've committed? I've lived in Byrdstown since birth, and you've been the most notorious person in this county my whole life. And Beau here is second. You earn respect by your deeds, and you lose it the same way."

"People look up to me here," Kingston nearly shouted. The small, red bumps and splotches on his face seemed to grow with his anger. "I do good deeds. I've given people money. I'm paying for Noah's hospital bills. I'm letting y'all stay here, for Heaven's sake."

"Does that boost your shaky self-esteem? Does it make you feel like you're better than other people? Because everything is all about you, Kingston, including bringing us here."

Grayson eyed his wife and father, his pupils darting back and forth while he tapped his toe anxiously on the floor. Beau stood completely still, no emotion reflecting in his face.

Again, Kingston blurted out angrily. "You're here because I'm a good person!"

"No, we're here because you want something. It meets *your* needs. We're here now, but your manipulating of me and my family ends today. And when God takes my beautiful son home, I'm leaving this town, this county, this state. Hopefully, *we're* leaving, Gray, if you have the courage to be a man." With that, she stormed off into her new bedroom, leaving Gray to consider the implications of what she just said.

Beau watched her all the way into her room. Kingston walked away to pour himself his typical drink, and then Beau glared at Gray. "You'd better get her under control, Grayson. Your father has plans for you, and I'm sure it's best she don't interfere." The glare he gave Grayson sent a shiver down his spine.

Chapter 3

It was late morning on a beautiful Friday, August day on Dale Hollow Lake. The crystal-clear water's temperature registered at 86 degrees at the surface. Bob Weathers, employee at Rhea's Diving Services, steered the dive boat across the lake. Randy Harper, his paid client and diving partner for the day, finished putting on his wetsuit. After cruising past the dam, Bob drove toward the favorite diving destination of most visiting divers, the Willow Grove Schoolhouse foundation.

Randy spread defog gel on his mask after checking his regulator, scuba tank, and buoyancy control device. The mountain trees, numerous inlets, sparkling sun, and clear turquoise water gave Randy much to admire as they skimmed toward a destination.

"Would you like to dive at the Willow Grove Schoolhouse?" Bob asked. "It's a popular diver destination. Or you could try Diver's Rock. The water is clear, and there're loads of fish."

Randy paused before answering while admiring the homes up in the trees above the water's banks. "I practically spent my life savings on this diving gear and dive training, and I have to wonder what people with homes like that make?" He pointed to a beautiful home with huge, glass windows on the mountainside overlooking the lake.

"Yeah, that one belongs to Kingston Phipps, a bazillionaire. He owns or owned everything not water or dam or public park around here. Businesses like ours, we lease the property from him, but the marinas, the boat launches, three restaurants, and most of the businesses on the lake are his."

"He has a dock and a boat. Why can't I see any others?"

Bob let the boat idle. "There are restrictions on private boat docks and even on tree removal from the shoreline in hopes of maintaining the aesthetic beauty of the environment. Phipps sold all the lots and wrote the association regulations under the advisement of the Tennessee Valley Authority. There are a few other docks besides his, but they belong to people with influence like the governor and the attorney general."

"Well, let's stop here for the dive. Maybe some of his riches have settled here. Maybe we'll find a pot of gold." Randy began putting on his fins.

"That's good with me." Bob displayed a "Diver Down" flag and dropped an anchor overboard. "The depth here will be about eighty feet today." He went over all the safety precautions for Randy. They reviewed how much oxygen and how much time they had, and then they made sure all the gear was on properly and working.

Randy checked his dive knife, his digital compass settings, and his dive light. He put his mouthpiece in his mouth, nodded to Bob, and they fell over backward into the water.

Because of the denseness of the water, it supported Randy's weight, allowing him to move freely in any direction. But the density also caused pressure changes on his body, so as he swam deeper into the water, he paused to regulate his pressure using the buoyancy control device. Bob, as his more experienced diving partner, waited and gave a thumbs-up in encouragement. Underwater, Bob looked larger than life, but when Randy reached out to touch him to get a sense for the distance, he couldn't reach. Bob was farther away than he looked.

When Randy was comfortable, they descended deeper. The lake was clear, but as they swam farther from the light above, everything looked blue green. Action transpired in all directions as fish darted near to and then away from the divers, and Bob appeared and disappeared in unexpected locations in the darkened waters. Water pressure and temperature changed throughout the swim, but finally, they reached the bottom of the lake. As they stilled their movements, sounds seemed to come from everywhere. His breathing made him sound like Darth Vader, but incredibly, the fish nibbling on plants made noises he could hear in the deep-water environment. His dive light lit up rocks, plants, and aquatic creatures.

As he kicked his feet to move horizontally above the lake bottom, Bob swam along beside him, keeping a close eye on his digital compass and the time underwater while Randy explored. About twenty minutes into the dive, Randy noticed something odd lying in the silt. He shined his light on the strange material and swam to take a closer look. He had difficulty reaching it with his hand as he kept misjudging the distance. Finally, he grasped the object. It was heavy and looked like a barbell from a gym. Out of curiosity, he lifted it to see if it was lying loosely on the ground. As he lifted, he noticed the weight was attached to a strap by something that looked plastic. A zip-tie? He waited for the silty cloud to disperse, and he gave the strap an aggressive yank. A huge, white bag lifted partially from the ground, allowing him to see four gym weights zip-tied to two bag handles.

Figuring the weights were what was making the bag heavy, he slipped out his dive-knife. After several futile stabs at the zip-ties, he finally zeroed in on their location and carefully cut each tie, allowing the weights to fall free. When he got his fingers on the bag's zipper slider, Bob bumped into him while trying to get a closer look. Randy's hands flew off the bag, and he gasped, holding in a yelp. His heart pounded in his ears. Once he got his breathing under control again, he unzipped the bag. He and Bob both shined their lights, and what they saw startled Randy once again. Bones. Human bones. About a quarter unzipped, he saw two skulls. Out of panic, he zipped it closed again and backed away.

Bob grabbed a handle and lifted while pointing for Randy to grab one on the opposite side. Randy lifted and realized it was much too heavy to bring to the surface. Bob motioned for Randy to start his ascent. He made Randy go slowly while adjusting his buoyancy control device. It was part of the training, so as anxious as Randy was to get to the surface, he did as he was directed.

When they emerged, they were twenty-five yards from the boat. Bob ripped off his mask to speak. "We have to mark this spot and call 911. I'll get the boat. Stay here, so we know exactly where to drop anchor. I think we have evidence of multiple murders."

The 911 phone operator dispatched Bob's call to the Tennessee Department of Safety and Homeland Security, who had to organize a dive team. News of the dead bodies also reached Detective Reese Carlton, who managed to board the dive boat and be on location for the recovery of the bodies. Dale Hollow Lake was within the Pickett County Sheriff Department's jurisdiction.

Bob and Randy spent most of the day waiting as per instructions from the 911 operator.

"It's a body bag," said Bob in answer to the officer from TDSHS. "Randy opened it, and we saw two skulls."

"We dropped anchor where we came up," said Randy. "The bag's directly below us. Weights were attached—four of them—but I cut them off. I had no idea bodies would be inside. It's plastic, I think...and white."

"We'll bring the weights up with the bodies," said the officer from TDSHS to Detective Carlton.

They used an inflatable airbag to get the bag to float to the surface, and then a rope and pulley were used to lug it to the boat. The fact Randy had allowed water to nearly fill the bag made it tremendously heavy when added to two dead bodies. Each of the weights rose to the surface, hooked to airbags as well in case they could be forensic evidence, and they were towed in with ropes.

Randy and Bob headed back to the dive shop once Reese finished his questions, and the police dive boat met an ambulance back at the main docks. After talking to the coroner, Reese made the decision to completely unzip the bag so the water could drain out. With much difficulty, the body bag was hoisted to the dock, and then Reese unzipped it. Water flowed out. Reese gulped, fighting the urge to throw up. Two skeletons lay upon a sickening goop, presumably decomposed skin and organs and congealed blood and body fluids. The bag must have been watertight until Randy opened it, and over a long period of time in cold water under tremendous water pressure, the bodies decomposed but had no way to evaporate or turn to dust. He saw bones on a mucky, gross sludge.

The bag was rezipped and, with much difficulty, loaded onto a gurney and heaved into the ambulance for delivery to Pickett County's medical examiner located in Nashville.

Chapter 4

Ella Dixon and Stacy Howard sat in Grandma's Pancake House in Cookeville late in the morning. Ella played with her Kijafa Cherry crepes with her fork as Stacy devoured her mushroom omelet with three pancakes. "You're a pig," said Ella, a grin on her face. Stacy wasn't a pig. She turned heads wherever she went with her wavy blonde hair, athletic physique, gorgeous smile, and sparkly sky-blue eyes.

"It's nearly noon, and I haven't eaten since some nachos after my shift ended yesterday. I'm starving. If you can't finish those crepes you're playing with, I'll help you."

Ella slid one onto Stacy's pancake plate. "You ever wonder if there's something more to life than steady work shifts at the hospital? This is my first morning off all week, but I work second shift today and a morning shift tomorrow. That'll be my sixth Saturday in a row I've worked."

"We could go to Nashville tomorrow evening. Go to one of the bars. Listen to some good music and maybe dance."

"You know I'm not comfortable in bars...and besides, I get jealous when guys hit on you and leave me alone."

"You might as well have a sign on your forehead saying 'I'm not interested.' Guys pick up on that." Stacy took a bite of Ella's crepe. "Ooh, this is good. Want some of my omelet?" She licked cherry sauce from her lip.

Ella shook her head no. "I don't have time for romance, and I don't have the energy either. I need a vacation...far away...by myself...in a lake house. That's a reasonable short-term goal, don't you think?"

Stacy looked at Ella seriously. "You've mentioned that before—a lake house."

"I used to live in one. Well, at least that's what my dad called it. It was more of a house on a wide stream. But it would flood sometimes, and it seemed like a lake. That's where I have my happiest childhood memories, so yes, someday, I want a big house on a lake where I can look out when I'm tired and overstressed and busy...and simply relax."

"But by yourself? You know Doc Garrett crushes on you, right?"

"One goal at a time, but Sam isn't in my plans. He's a workaholic. I want my life to slow down, not get more hectic." Ella pushed her unfinished plate toward Stacy. "I'm so full I might barf. Thanks, but no. I'm going to my parents' place for supper tomorrow, so I'll overeat two days in a row."

"I thought you suggested Nashville tomorrow. You can't even go yourself."

"I would change my plans for you. Say the word, and I'll call Mom and Dad and cancel."

Ella shook her head. "No, you do your thing. You're lucky to have family to spend time with. Maybe we'll do Nashville some other time."

"You're right. My mom would pitch a fit if I canceled again." Stacy caught the waitress as she walked by and asked for the checks. She witnessed Ella sigh as she began gathering her things to leave. "Is there something else bothering you?"

"I don't know….I've spent my whole life preparing for a career in medicine, hoping to do something good with my life. To help people. But when I see things like the little Phipps boy dying of cancer, and I can't do anything about it, I wonder if I'm doing what I was meant to do."

"You care more than anyone there, Ella. You can't save 'em all, but no one tries harder than you do."

"Yeah, well, I don't give up. There's that. Thanks for breakfast…brunch…whatever this is. I need to head home and change for work. Have fun at your parents' house this weekend." They hugged, Ella dropped a twenty-dollar bill on the table, and she left.

***

Kingston stood at the back window overlooking Dale Hollow Lake. After installing a new lock on the bedroom door of Noah's room, Beau joined him. A crew of men, including several divers from a police diving unit, worked in front of

Kingston's property. A boat with the Rhea's Diving Services logo on the side also anchored in the water. The house, nestled over 200 feet behind and above the water, had windows stretching all the way across the back to give amazing sight lines to the lake. Kingston used binoculars to get a clearer picture of what was going on.

An inflatable airbag popped to the surface of the water, and then some divers went to work attaching ropes to whatever was being recovered. A system of pulleys was used to reel in the prize, which turned out to be a large, white bag. Calm as he always acted, Beau breathed in deeply and then said, "That ain't good."

Then the weights popped up and were drawn to the boat, and Beau had no doubts what he was seeing.

"Is this going to be a problem?" Kingston asked.

"It's been what, twenty-three years?" Beau said. "What evidence could there be? I would think there isn't nothin' but muck in the bag."

"What concerns me is the man on the boat with the Tennessee Volunteers ball cap." Kingston handed the binoculars to Beau. "It's Reese Carlton."

Beau took a long, thorough look and shook his head in confirmation. "Yeah, that ain't good."

"What's not good?" Angie and Grayson stepped to the window. "One of your dirty secrets coming to light?" asked Angie. "You look spooked."

Kingston composed himself before he spoke. "I resent you implying I did anything wrong. I don't even know what's going on down there. We're purely looking out of curiosity. There are police there, so it can't be good." Beau continued to stare through the lenses while not moving a muscle or speaking a word. "What is your problem, Angie?"

Shaking her head, she rolled her eyes and headed back to Noah's bedroom, her laptop in her hand. "I've got work to do and a child to watch."

Once Angie disappeared, Gray asked, "Dad? Trouble?"

"No, Son. A diver must have found something interesting. That's all. But your work buddy is down there. If

26

you don't care to, maybe next time y'all work together, you can ask him what he found...just out of curiosity."

"Maybe I will. I'm heading back to Angie and Noah." Gray left his dad and Beau at the window.

"I need you to do me a favor, Beau." Kingston took a square of paper out of his wallet. "Find out what you can about this woman." He read his friend the note he'd copied from his phone. "Ella Dixon, ARNP. Find out where she lives, her hours of work at the Cookeville Medical Center, who she hangs out with and where, what she drives. You know the routine. And do it ASAP."

"Yes, sir. And what about the bag?"

"There's nothing we can do about that right now except wait and see what our detective friend figures out. I assume we'll be hearing from him, but let's wait and see."

Chapter 5

Finding information about Ella Dixon was more difficult than Beau expected. She had almost no internet presence. Her Facebook settings were so private, all that was visible was one profile picture, but the picture alone made Kingston's interest understandable. She had no Twitter or Instagram accounts nor anything to view from YouTube or TikTok. Considering her age, Beau expected to find a lot. Her work biography explained she graduated from Vanderbilt University where she played on the women's golf team and then worked in the pediatric unit at Cookeville Regional Medical Center as an advanced registered nurse practitioner for six years.

Nothing could be found about any family. Truthfinder.com had a home address on Bradley Drive in Cookeville, and he knew where she worked. Her house was a cute ranch, less than 1,200 square feet, but well-maintained. A one-car attached garage sat at the end of the two-car-width driveway, but it was empty. She wasn't home, so he climbed back into his truck and headed for the hospital. His huge size and memorable facial features made it nearly impossible for him to not be noticed, so he went into the pediatric ward only once to go through the charade of asking about billing information for Noah. From her nametag, he knew the nurse's name was Nancy. While waiting, he saw Ella, who he easily recognized from her surprising Facebook profile picture. She had no ring on her finger.

"Second shift, huh, Nancy?" he asked the nurse as she searched the computer for Noah's information.

"Two p.m. to ten," she answered without looking up. Her blue scrub top had a greasy smear from lunch in the cafeteria. "I have my request in for first shift, but it's second for now….Noah's bills are currently up to date. Is there anything else I can help you with, sir?"

"No, ma'am. I thank you for your help."

"It's so sad about that poor boy. He had such a gentle spirit."

"Yes, ma'am. Thank you again and have a nice night."

Beau left the hospital immediately, grabbed a quick take-out meal, and parked next to the staff parking lot to wait for second shift to end.

At 10:10, Ella exited the building alone and walked to her car, a practical white Kia Sportage from Cumberland Kia. She clearly had no Friday night plans because she drove directly home. No lights shone inside the modest house until she entered, and within an hour, they were all off again. She was in bed for the night. Beau exited his vehicle and picked the lock on the side door of the garage, leaving it unlocked, a plan formulating in his mind. He then returned to stake out the house the rest of the night in his truck.

The next morning, at 5:00 a.m., lights switched on in various rooms, and her garage door opened at 5:35. Ella drove back to the hospital, walked into the building without talking to anyone else, and disappeared for another shift. Beau headed back to Byrdstown to get some rest before reporting to Kingston what little he'd learned.

***

Reese read through the property deed for Kingston Phipps's lot on Lake Hollow. A land surveyor had properly and accurately drawn a survey map which was stamped and sealed. The register of deeds accepted and recorded the documents thirteen months before Dale Hollow Dam began releasing water to form the lake. Ground was broken and the Phipps home was completed on what was one of the prime lots on the lake two months before the first water flowed from the dam.

It took a year to complete the formation of the lake, but considering the weights attached to the body bag, a logical conclusion would be the bodies were deposited in the lake to sink after or during its formation, and the fact they were discovered in front of the Phipps home was more than a coincidence in Reese's mind. But it was the call from Ashvi Patel, the coroner, that made him wonder if he had finally turned up some clues in his twenty-three-year-old murder investigation.

"Hey, Reese, this is Ashvi." Reese had worked with the coroner off and on for twenty years, and they'd even gone out together a few times. Neither was married, except to their careers. Ashvi, the daughter of an immigrant from Nagpur, India, was a cute lady in her late forties. Reese found her long, dark hair and expressive brown eyes attractive, but her smile and energy amazed him, especially because he felt tired all the time.

"Thanks for calling so soon. I hope you're having a good day." Reese stepped out of the coffee shop where he'd eaten a morning bagel. "I assume you're calling about the bodies I had delivered yesterday?" Reese looked left and right as he made his way across the street to his parked car on Main Street.

"Yes, and there are some interesting details. First, the bodies are male," she said. "One is six feet three inches tall. The other is five feet nine. They were murdered. Both had two gunshot wounds to the head. Almost exact angles. The bullets passed downward from the left frontal lobe tip toward the temporal lobe and brainstem from close or intermediate range. Two shots at that angle would be devastating. Both instances reek of an execution."

"You can tell the range from a skull?" Reese sat in his car, his mind whirling.

"Well, obviously with no skin, there is no muzzle imprint, skin lacerations, or powder stippling, but the shots on both victims were one to one-and-a-half inches apart. Do you realize most handgun shootings occur at less than seven yards, yet statistically, only eleven percent of all assailants' bullets hit their targets? Either the shooter was incredibly accurate or very close to his victims. I'd put my money on close range."

"Yeah, I'll have to agree with you. Any guesses about the gun?"

"No guesses needed. They were penetrating wounds. Neither of the bullets exited either skull. Amidst that horrific goop, I found all four bullets. Jacketed hollow points for a .38 Super revolver."

"Super? That's not too common. How can you tell?"

"The bullets have a semi-rimmed casing. Most semi-automatic revolvers have rimless rounds, but the Super has semi-rimmed casing which is wider than the rimless rounds. The Super is semi-automatic."

"So close range, semi-automatic capability would help explain the accuracy of two shots on both victims."

"Exactly. My best guess is the shooter stood within a foot or two away and executed the victims."

"How about the decomposition? Can you tell how long they were in the lake?"

"Now you're asking a difficult question. At eighty feet deep there's a lot of water pressure to slow decomp. At that depth, the water is cold—colder yet in the Tennessee winter months—which would slow decomp also. Plus, both bodies were stuffed into one body bag, and it was airtight and watertight. It kept the bones preserved quite well, but the bodies were completely decomposed, creating that disgusting goop. How long had it been lying there? Fifteen years? Twenty? Twenty-five? I've done all the math computations and research I can, and I can only guess. I'd say over twenty years, but I can't be definitive."

When Reese played basketball and baseball in high school, he often felt "butterflies" in his stomach before a game. He liked the feeling because he knew his focus was good. His game improved. The same knotting in his stomach occurred as he sat in the car, speaking to Ashvi Patel. More than twenty years? The bodies could be two of the missing men from the Willow Grove disappearances. "So my next question, Ashvi, is can the bodies be identified?"

"I can get DNA from the bones and make a determination if there is something to compare it to. I can also get a match from dental records. But twenty-plus years? Is there anything to match with?"

"Well, we had three men disappear from Willow Grove twenty-three years ago before Dale Hollow Lake was created.

There's never been news of any of them. I'll get you evidence to test for those three, but I'll need some time, and tomorrow is Sunday, so you may not get anything before Monday or Tuesday if I'm lucky."

"All right. The bodies aren't going anywhere. I'll be waiting....Hey, Reese, there's something else." Ashvi hesitated. "Once I cleaned away all the decomp at the bottom of the bag and cleaned off all the bones, I had some work to do before I could measure. The bones joining at the hip socket—the pelvis and femur—were shattered. All four legs. But that's not all. The bones at the knee joint—the femur, tibia, and patella—were cracked, broken, or shattered as well in all four legs. Also, there were broken bones at the elbows too, be it the radius, ulna, or humerus. All four arms."

"What does that suggest to you?"

"I don't think I'm going out on a limb here to say whoever murdered those men then put the bodies in a freezer where they froze solid. They probably didn't fit well, so they were packed in there in a fetal-type position, and then when they were removed, frozen, the murderer had to break their arms and legs to get them both to fit in the body bag. Someone powerful and amoral had to do that."

"I hope we're able to identify the two bodies. I think if we do, it'll shed some light about what happened after the murders. Did your lab learn anything about the weights we retrieved from the lake?"

"Just that they're old York dumbbells. Two fifty-pounders and two forty-pounders—the kind a person would take from their home gym. They could have been purchased at any sporting goods store. No way to get prints or other evidence but let me tell you something. Let's say the two bodies were 150 and 200 pounds. Add 180 more pounds of weight to the bag handles and we're talking 530 pounds to drop off a boat. It would be a two-man job, at least, and it would have to be a large boat—at the minimum, a pontoon boat. Anything else and I'd think the boat would capsize trying to drop that load over a side. The point is, there had to be more than one person involved."

"Interesting. That's a lot to think about. Thanks for the call, Ashvi. Hey, I'm retiring soon. We…uh…should go out again."

"I'd like that. I'll look forward to it. Give me a call sometime."

"I will. Thanks again…and have a good day, Ashvi." Reese ended the call and smiled. Less than two weeks before retirement, and possibly, he had his first evidence of the Willow Grove disappearances and the first date he'd had in months.

Chapter 6

Grayson walked into Noah's room on Sunday morning to find Angie standing in front of the huge window overlooking the lake. Her lips moved as she prayed. Sunshine streamed in through the window, and a ceiling fan swirled above. He tried to be silent, but she sensed his presence. Without turning, she said, "Good morning."

"I hope I didn't disturb you."

"Just having a chat with God." She stood on an expensive ivory and blue area rug, her back to her husband still.

"About what? Noah?" Gray looked toward Noah sleeping silently in his bed.

"Yeah, his head hurts. He's having trouble seeing and hearing sometimes. He has those small seizures. I hate how much he's suffering. But I'm praying about us too." Finally, she turned her gaze from the water below.

"What do you mean, Angie?" She looked beautiful to Gray; she always had, but he missed her smile.

"He's going to die. What does that mean for us? This has been the hardest time in our lives, but what is our future?" She turned back to the beautiful view beyond. "I used to dream of living right here in this house when I first met you. Your father promised we would. Remember? It's so peaceful and beautiful, but now I need to leave to get away from him. For good. And if you aren't willing to go with me, I'll go alone, but if that happens, we're done. This is *his* home…his town…his county. I need to leave, so you'll have to choose to go with me…or stay for him."

"There has to be a better solution than to run away. I have a business. You have a career. We have family here…and we still might get this house."

"Him or me, Gray. I'm leaving, and I'm never coming back. He's an evil man. If you stay, it says a lot about you, and I'll know making it on my own is the path for me. I didn't tell you, but your dad threatened me to get us here…to get his way. Is that the type of person you'll choose to stick with?"

34

"How did he threaten you? I'll have a talk with him."

"No…I hope you don't because it doesn't matter. He'll never apologize. Never change. He'll blame me. He'll manipulate you. He'll argue like a lawyer in front of the Grand Jury. It never changes with him, and if you don't see it, you're blind. Noah needs me, so I'm staying to the end. Then, if *you* don't need me, I'll leave without you."

Gray walked across the room and gave Angie a hug. He then leaned in and gave Noah a kiss on the cheek, but he didn't know how to respond, so he left and headed for the kitchen. There, his father sat on a bar stool at the gray, marble island where he drank coffee and chewed on a muffin.

"Sit down, Son, and have something to eat. How's Noah?"

"Sleeping." He opened the refrigerator and removed a can of Coke. He sat and peeled the paper cup from a muffin. "Angie said you threatened her to get her to agree to come here."

The red splotches appeared immediately. He stood, walked to a cupboard, removed a bottle of Jamison Irish Whiskey, and poured a splash into his coffee. Finally, he said, "She's lying to turn you against me. I did no such thing. You know I love you and your family. Look what I've done for you. She hates me. She's jealous of all I have and how much you and Noah care about me. She's always been dishonest when it comes to me, so how can you believe her now? I've been too good to you for you to believe her lies."

Grayson shook his head. "I love you, Dad, and I'm grateful for what you've given me, but yes, I believe you threatened her. Actually, I'm sure of it because it's put her over the edge, and she's planning on leaving. She wants me to go with her."

Kingston glared at his son. "You can't do that. I'm not the person she's convinced you I am. She's a hateful woman. Totally selfish." He slammed his coffee cup on the table and slinked away with anger in his eyes. From Gray's point of view, it looked like pouting.

***

Reese sat at home with his twenty-three-year-old police file. Three Willow Grove properties sold and were leveled only days before the first water release from Dale Hollow Dam. Three married couples signed purchase agreements, but each of the families hurriedly moved without the man of the house, who disappeared. Their wives closed cash sales of more than double what other Willow Grove families accepted—he knew that from the public record of the warranty deeds and mortgages filed at the courthouse—but they did so without the presence of their husbands. All three men disappeared without a trace, but two bodies were fished from Dale Hollow Lake—bodies which possibly belonged to two of the missing men. They probably weren't murdered by Paul Miller though. His gun was a .22 caliber pistol. His Ruger was found in his house by the police after his body was discovered.

If the men from the lake were two of the missing men, he needed DNA or dental records for the coroner to match. That meant he needed to locate the three families after more than two decades, hoping they could help. They wouldn't talk before, but maybe he could get their cooperation, knowing it could bring closure. He had addresses from his initial investigation, so that was where he needed to start.

He started with Truthfinder.com to look for the scattered family members. Barbara Hill, whose missing husband was John Hill, had two girls named Sloan and Grace. Susan Stone, whose missing husband was Stephen Stone, had three children—Luke, Levi, and Hannah. Monica Dale, whose missing husband was Robert Dale, had only one child by the name of Dorella. Because he had prior addresses, ages, and family members' names, he located each woman easily. Using police informational channels, he verified the addresses and found phone numbers. His next move was to contact the women to set up visits. Unexpectedly, Susan Stone and Barbara Hill both agreed to talk to Reese that same day.

He visited Susan Stone first. She had never remarried, and her youngest son, Levi, who was twenty-six, lived with her in Clarksville, Tennessee. When Reese called her and told her he was the detective from two decades past who tried to talk to her, she quickly said she still had nothing to say to him. When he said he may have found her husband's body but needed DNA evidence, she told him he could visit. Closure. Reese knew people needed it. So he went on a Sunday drive. It took nearly three hours.

Susan lived in a modest ranch home near town. At fifty years of age, she looked much older. Her hair was completely gray and unkempt. Overweight, wrinkles lined her round face anyway. She wore stretchy pants and a huge sweatshirt even though the temperature sweltered in the 90s. "Thank you for agreeing to see me, Ms. Stone," said Reese.

"I always assumed Stephen was dead, but I think it'll be nice to know for sure. Come in." She opened the door for him. An air conditioner whirred in the living room. Matted, dingy carpeting in the hallway led past Formica counters in the kitchen and into a living room with a huge, white great Pyrenees sleeping on the floor. "My son lives with me, but he's working today. Can I get you some sweet tea?"

"Thank you, but no. I don't want to take a lot of your time." Reese paused. Finally, he spoke again. "Ms. Stone, I believed twenty-three years ago Kingston Phipps had knowledge of what happened to your husband. I still believe it. The two bodies we discovered were extracted from the lake in front of his property. The bones were preserved over the years, so if we have DNA or dental records from your husband, we can see if they match, and you'll finally know if he was murdered."

"You think the realtor might have murdered him?"

"That's what I'm hoping to find out, ma'am."

Susan sat on the sofa on top of a blanket, so to be polite, Reese sat in the lounge chair next to the dog. It squeaked when he sat down, and the dog opened one eye to look. Then she closed it again. "The realtor said Stephen signed the purchase agreement and then left and would never return. He said Stephen did it for our safety. I took that as a threat, so I signed the papers too and took the check. Mr. Phipps gave us twice what he said was his final offer, so I moved the kids and started over."

"I'm sorry for your loss." Reese paused sympathetically as Susan grabbed a corner of the blanket and dabbed her eyes.

"We left the next morning with everything we could fit in Stephen's truck, and they knocked the house down the next day. I went back to get a few things we couldn't fit, and the house was gone. I cried for weeks."

"Maybe the DNA will match, and you can have closure. And maybe I'll find evidence Kingston Phipps was involved. Does your husband have dental records anywhere I can check?"

"He didn't go much, but he had an abscessed tooth once, so there might've been X-rays....Detective Carlton? Please don't let Mr. Phipps know you talked to me. Please don't involve me at all."

"I won't involve you, Ms. Stone. You have my word. Do you remember the name of the dentist?"

"Clemons? McMillon? I don't remember. But it was on Main Street in Byrdstown by the funeral home."

"I'll check it out. How about DNA? Did you find something that might work?"

"I've kept a box of some of his things. It has a toboggan he used to wear a lot. There are hairs. Is that good enough?"

"Yes, ma'am. It should be." Reese took out a plastic evidence bag, and Susan shuffled to another room and came back with the knit hat. She dropped it in the bag. "Thank you. And when we do the tests, I'll tell you what we find out." Reese stood. More tears welled up in Susan's eyes. He reached out and shook her hand—a gesture that seemed pathetically inadequate. She walked him back to the door. "By the way, how tall was Stephen?"

"Five foot nine...and a half. He aways said the half inch part."

Reese nodded. "Thank you again for your time." He stepped off her porch, got in his car, and drove away. Once he was back on the road, he called and confirmed his arrival in McMinnville next. Barbara Hill, who had remarried to a man named Mark Irons, lived two hours from Clarksville. Barbara's directions sent him to South Riverside Drive near Christian Fellowship Church. At fifty-seven years old, Barbara had aged much better than Susan Stone. Her new husband met Reese at the door and stepped out onto a roomy porch with furniture and an overhead fan. The vinyl-sided, cream two-story had blue shutters and what looked like a brand-new roof. The two men introduced themselves.

"Listen, Detective," said Mark, "Barb doesn't talk about her past, and she made it clear to me, she doesn't want to talk about the events you're here about. It was a long, difficult process getting her husband to be declared dead so she could remarry, and it was hard on her."

"Yes, sir. I'm here hoping to figure out who the men we found in Dale Hollow Lake were. That's all."

"Okay. If you don't care to, then, c'mon in….Barb, Detective Carlton is here." Mark walked Reese into the kitchen and pointed to a dining room chair for him to sit in. "Sit down, please, Detective."

Barbara was already seated in a chair at the other side of the table. Her brown hair was styled nicely. She had neatly applied make-up and an attractive sun dress on. Glasses rested on the top of her head. She had a small tube in her hand that looked like the thing the old time rolls of film were stored in. "Ma'am," said Reese, "thank you for allowing me into your home."

She nodded. "These are memories best left alone, but if I can help you identify John's body, I think I'll be relieved."

"Thank you. As I told you on the phone, we recovered two bodies from Dale Hollow Lake, and the coroner believes they are at least twenty years old. One might be your husband."

"He didn't want to sell. Can't believe he'd do it unless he was threatened concerning me and the girls. We moved away and never went back because I don't think it was safe. I'm only letting you come here because Mark said I should. Closure, you know?"

"I'm sorry for your loss, Mrs. Irons. Hopefully we can identify the bodies and give you the closure you're looking for. I hope I don't have to bother you any further, but I'll tell you, I'm hoping to figure out what happened twenty-three years ago and find justice. Do you have anything belonging to your former husband that might contain his DNA?"

She held up the tube. "John was a great athlete. Loved basketball and softball. People marveled at how high he could jump. Anyway, once when he was playing and went up to dunk the ball, he caught his front teeth on the net, and bless his heart, both of 'em flipped right out of his mouth. He collected the teeth and kept 'em in this tube when the dentist couldn't save 'em. You mentioned DNA or dental records; well, there will be plenty of DNA in these teeth, and if one of the bodies is John, he'll have two false teeth. I think this should do."

Reese reached across the table and accepted the plastic tube from her. "Was John tall?"

"A little over six foot three."

"I thought he might've been." He stood. "Thank you, Mrs. Irons." He followed Mark to the front door. They shook hands, and Reese backed out of the driveway. Forty-five minutes later, he sat in front of his television, opened a can of Mountain Dew and a bag of chips, and smiled. Two down and one to go. The third woman, Monica Dale, hadn't returned his calls all day, and she lived in Tucson, Arizona, but he'd made the most progress he'd ever made on the case, and he settled in, feeling he'd had a good day.

Chapter 7

As soon as the Monday workday began, Reese made his way to McClymond's Family Dentistry on Main Street. Marty McClymond retired years before, but his son, Mark, took over the family business. Dental records from twenty-three years in the past were in storage, but Mark agreed to have one of his employees find them to share.

Reese next began his two-hour drive to Nashville to turn over the DNA samples to the forensic laboratory. When he approached her, Ashvi Patel had a smile on her face. "Good morning, Detective. It's nice to see you…and I have good news for you."

"Good morning, Ashvi. I have good news for you too, but you go first."

"As you wish," she said. She flashed a wide smile and winked. "We have the murder weapon."

"What?" The news shocked him.

"Nine years ago, a man by the name of Jake Gooden, emptied his Colt .38 Super revolver in an attempt to shoot his girlfriend whom he was convinced was cheating on him. All six bullets missed."

"That's some nice shooting."

"He has nothing to brag about, for sure. The bullets were all retrieved, and the rifling 'ballistic fingerprints' are on file. We matched the bullets to the ones from the lake victims, and we *have* the gun."

"Hard to imagine his skills eroded so badly over the years. I'm going to go out on a limb and guess he isn't our executioner."

Ashvi scurried to her desk with the energy she always seemed to possess and grabbed a file folder. She handed it to Reese. "He's not your guy. When he was arrested, he was twenty-four years old. He would've been ten at the time of the shootings if these are the guys you think they are, but regardless, he would have been a child when the men from the lake were murdered. But besides that, he got the gun from a pawn shop, about a year before. However, because we have

41

the gun, we have the make, model, and the serial number, so the ATF was able to track down the original manufacturer. From there, we could identify the federally licensed gun shop where the firearm was originally sent for retail sale twenty-five years ago."

"From where?"

"The Gun Shop in Livingston. The business has changed ownership twice, but when it sold the first time a dozen years ago, the owner was required to send the Shop's 44-73 forms to the ATF. The documents are stored in paper form in boxes in warehouses. Once they dig up the form, we'll know who the original buyer was. Could take a few days, but we'll get a name."

"That's an amazing stroke of luck. Thanks. And I have DNA for you. I still haven't reached Monica Dale, but I interviewed the other two women yesterday, and they gave me items you can test."

Reese gave Dr. Patel both labeled evidence bags. "Susan Stone gave me the hat with hair samples, and Barbara Hill gave me the teeth. The dentist for Stephen Stone is searching for his dental records, but Barbara Hill assures me her husband has two false front teeth. The teeth in the bottle are the originals."

"She saved his teeth?"

"Yep, and it'll be ironic if they help us take a bite out of crime, wouldn't it?"

"Oh, that's bad. I hope you didn't spend your drive trying to come up with it. I might be rethinking that date request."

"I tried to come up with something about 'incisor trading,' but I couldn't make it work. Sorry." Reese's face reddened. "How long will it take to see if they match the bodies?"

"Two to three days, but we'll know soon if these are your guys."

Reese looked at Ashvi and smiled for the third consecutive day—a near record—and he realized two of the smiles were because of the county coroner. "Hey, they're having a retirement party for me. Would you come with me? Week from Wednesday…just ten days away...if I didn't scare you off with my dental humor."

"Let me chew on that offer for a while, and I'll let you know." She started laughing. "Wow, as hard as it is to believe, my awful joke was worse than yours, which I think obligates me to give you another chance. I'm sure I can fit your party into my schedule, Reese."

"Great…Chew? Really? They're front teeth." Another smile. "Well, I'm sure we'll be talking, so I'll finalize plans later. It's evening though because unless I call in sick, I'll be working that day." Reese gazed at her uncomfortably long. Embarrassed, he excused himself so she could get "back to work."

Emotions consumed Reese the entire ride home. Anxiety about retirement. Excitement about the first clues toward solving multiple homicides, but impatience for having to wait two or three days for results. Curiosity about Ashvi's apparent interest in him. Or not. He planned to make his report to his captain, and if nothing else needed his attention, he decided to help Grayson back at his worksite. The thought added another emotion—guilt. Using his friend gnawed at him because Gray seemed to be an upright guy, but there were three murders to solve, and Gray unknowingly kept him informed about his prime suspect.

***

Angie sat in a chair beside Noah's bed. Awake, Noah gazed at his mother as she read from a Bible story book. Sunshine flooded the bed while a hummingbird flitted at the window, casting a vibrating shadow on Noah's blanket.

"…Hannah wanted a boy to love. She was so sad she cried and wouldn't even eat. Elkanah, her husband, asked her why her heart hurt so much. One day, she went to church where she prayed and made a promise to God. She asked God to take away her sadness and give her a baby boy. She made a promise to give him back to God for his whole life."

"How can she give him back?" asked Noah.

"Well, a priest named Eli saw her praying and asked what she was praying about…"

"What's a priest?"

"It's a man who works at the church like the pastor of our church."

"Oh."

Angie laughed softly. "Sweetie, you ask good questions."

Noah smiled and grimaced slightly.

Angie patted his hand. "So Hannah told the priest she would give him her boy to raise to be a servant of God. Eli the priest said he hoped God would give her the child she wanted so badly. God answered her prayer, and Hannah soon had a little baby boy who she named Samuel. When Samuel was still young but had grown into a good little boy, Hannah took him back to the priest. She said to him, 'I prayed for this child, and God gave me what I asked for. So now I'm giving him to you to raise like I promised.' Hannah would visit Samuel and bring him new clothes because he grew big."

"He still had his mommy even though she gave him to God."

"That's right. You're very smart." Angie closed the story book. "Noah, when you were a baby, I told God you belonged to him. I promised to raise you the best I could, but when he wanted you, he could have you. God wants you, sweetie, and he's going to take you to his home where you won't hurt anymore. You won't be sick, and you'll be able to play with other little boys."

"You'll be sad, won't you?"

"Oh, yes. Very, very sad. But I'll be happy too because God loves you and will take good care of you until he lets me see you again."

"When will that be? I'll miss you."

"I know you will, honey, but God will bring me to him too when it's my time. And I'll hug you and kiss you with the biggest hugs and kisses." Noah smiled while Angie held his hand. As soon as he drifted off to sleep, Angie's strength crumbled, and tears flowed from her eyes.

Grayson appeared in the doorway. "Are you okay?"

"No. My heart is breaking. I want his suffering to end, but I don't want to lose him, and it's tearing me apart."

Gray gently placed his hand on her back and stared at the fluttering shadow created by the hummingbird in the window which darted away and returned as if curiously watching the grieving family. "It won't be long, and it'll be over....How're we ever gonna move on from this?"

"We'll move away. That's the first step."

"Maybe we'll do that."

"Maybe? There're no maybes for me. I'm leaving, and I won't come back."

Gray took a deep breath and pinched the bridge of his nose. "I'm going to talk to my dad about this house. He has other homes, and he said we would own this lake house someday. Maybe he'll agree now is a good time to make that happen. Then we'll have this beautiful home, and we can start our life over. Maybe have another baby. Maybe that's what we need to begin to move on."

Angie wiped a straggling tear from her eye and stood from her chair. Her face was inches from Gray's when she said, "You aren't listening to me. It's your father. He controls and manipulates and does underhanded things. I can't be happy or at peace even in this house if he's still around. I have to leave…with or without you, and you're running out of time to decide what you want—me or him." She stomped out of the room, leaving Gray to stare at the hummingbird and to wonder how it could possess so much positive energy when he was running on an empty tank.

Chapter 8

After first shift ended at the hospital on Monday, Ella, Stacy, Sam, and Sam's brother, Scott, met at Southern Hills Country Club in Cookeville at 4:10 to play nine holes. Ella had been introduced to golf her freshman year at college when one of the guys from the men's golf team took her on a date. She took to the sport so spectacularly, that within a year, she became a scholarship golfer on the women's team, which is how she managed to come out of school with a career minus a load of debt.

As she turned into the golf course parking lot, the black truck she'd noticed behind her the entire drive continued past. She noticed a black truck behind her when she left the hospital for home on Friday, and since she saw one following behind her on her trip back to work on Saturday, it was the third time she'd seen it.

Quietly, almost sullenly, Ella put her clubs on her cart, practiced a few putts, and eventually teed off on the first hole, a par four which she parred.

Beau walked into the pro shop after the foursome teed off. He walked up to the check-in counter. "Is there anything I can help you with?" asked the assistant pro.

"I was hoping to get a message to my daughter-in-law, but I don't see her outside. Her name is Sandra Jones. She's golfing with Ella Dixon today sometime around 4:00."

"The pro looked at the tee sheet. "Ella Dixon teed off a few minutes ago, but she's not playing with Sandra Jones." Beau could see the tee-time. It said Stacy Howard and Sam and Scott Garrett.

"Hmmm. That would explain why I didn't see her out there. I must've got my signals crossed. Thanks. I'll try to give her a call." Beau exited, but he left with knowledge about Ella's friend, whom he could look up while the foursome played their nine-hole round.

In the cart to the second tee, Stacy asked, "Is there something wrong?"

"I think I'm being stalked," Ella said. "Three times now, I've noticed the same black truck following me on the road."

"Did you get a license plate number?"

"No. All I can say is it's black, and it's a Toyota, I think. The symbol is a sort of vertical, skinny oval with a curve through it like a smile. It's like an awkward looking T. Anyway, it drove past when I turned into the parking lot, so I might be imagining it."

Stacy, as usual, couldn't have looked more cute. Her blonde ponytail poked through the back of her white Titleist golf hat. Her short white golf skirt was trimmed in pink to match her polo shirt and shoes. Her dark tan and pretty smile had everyone turning heads. On the other hand, Ella didn't care if she turned heads. She wore khaki shorts to her knees and a black and gold Vanderbilt Commodores shirt from her golf team days. She wore a light blue visor, not even concerned she didn't match. She couldn't understand why Sam was interested in her instead of Stacy. Not only was Stacy gorgeous, but she was a good listener who cared about people. "It's probably nothing, but you should keep an eye out for it in the future….Hey, let's get a picture. It's a beautiful day, and you should be having fun."

Ella squeezed in next to her friend and forced a smile for the selfie. Then she landed a perfect drive over the water and birdied the second hole, which impressed the guys who both had double-bogies and were three shots behind her already. Sam and Scott both hit awful tee shots on the par-5 third hole with a sharp dogleg to the left. Stacy's shot was straight but barely onto the fairway. Ella stepped around her cart for her driver, but her foot landed on the raised edge of the cart path. She rolled her right ankle and fell. Laughing, Sam rushed to her side. "Are you okay?"

Embarrassed, she lied about the pain. "I'm okay." She grimaced as Sam and Stacy helped her to her feet, and she limped to the tee box and placed her ball on the tee. She took two deep breaths and swung. There was pain at the top of her swing, but as her weight shifted to her left foot, she managed a solid swing. The club connected with the ball, but the driver's head flew off the shaft, landing twenty yards ahead. The ball settled safely in the fairway, still by far the best drive of the foursome.

Stacy let out a giggle and chased the club head down to save her friend from the walk. "So on one leg and with half a club, she still outdrove you wimps." She laughed so much Ella had to smile. Stacy took the bag of ice from the cart cooler and tossed Ella a Gatorade. She placed the ice on Ella's swelling ankle while Ella opened her drink, spilling the red liquid all over her shorts.

Stacy started laughing again. "Well, since bad things happen in threes, you should be safe the rest of the round." She kept giggling, but Ella never said anything—didn't even attempt to wipe the liquid away. Stacy looked up and said, "What's wrong?"

"I'm sorry. I have a bit of history with bad things happening together, except with me, it's in fours, and when it happens, the last two are especially bad."

"Maybe you're being stalked too. That would be four."

"But it's already different because none of the three or four things today are particularly bad…well, maybe the ankle sprain."

Determined, Ella limped around the course the rest of the round, drove with her three-wood or four-iron off the tee, tried to ignore the embarrassment of the red stain covering her khaki shorts, and after a par on the par-3 ninth hole, ended with a thirty-eight. She was so gloomy throughout the round it wasn't much fun, but she never gave up, and Stacy left her to her thoughts. The girls declined the invitation to have something to eat in the clubhouse with the guys afterward.

Stacy walked with Ella to her car. "How's your ankle? Do you want me to drive you home?"

"No, thanks. I made it around the course. It's tender, but I can make it home."

"Okay." Stacy started away but then turned back. "What do you mean bad things happen in fours, and the last two are *really* bad?"

"That's how it works with me; the third thing is extra bad. The fourth thing is even worse."

"You sound worried. What are you talking about?"

Ella pushed her clubs into her trunk and lowered her tailgate. She unlocked her front door and groaned as she sat in the driver's seat. She turned her head to look at Stacy who waited patiently for an answer. Finally, Ella spoke. "This isn't one of those times. It's just your comment—and the thought of being stalked—that has me spooked. But for me, the third thing is always death. Someone I care about dies. The fourth one is death too, but it's worse because I'm responsible." She rolled her window down and eased her door shut. Looking out the window at her best friend, she said. "I don't think there's anything to worry about today."

They said their goodbyes, and Ella cautiously drove out onto the main road, wincing at the pain. When she looked into her rearview mirror, a black truck turned onto the road two cars behind her.

***

Reese spent the late afternoon with Grayson, working on the house since his investigation had temporarily stalled. Monica Dale still hadn't answered or returned any of his calls, so he had nothing else to investigate for the time being. Gray worked on ceramic tile on the kitchen floor while Reese put up trim along the floorboards in the living room.

Country music played lightly in the background as both men made trips out to the garage and back with cut pieces of materials. No one talked for quite some time. Finally, Gray broke the ice. "I noticed you in front of the lake house, pulling a bag out of the water."

"Yes."

"Was that a body bag?"

"Uh huh."

"With a body?"

"Two."

"Have you identified them?"

"No."

"Any suspicions?"

"Yep."

"Murdered and dumped in the lake?"

"Yeah."

"Well, listen to you wax eloquently about your investigation. I've dragged six words and a grunt out of you. Is there anything to add, or are you going to just chat in monosyllables?"

"It's an open investigation, and you're not a suspect. How's that?"

"Thanks. I was about to lawyer up." Gray placed a few tiles in place and measured for a piece he needed to fit under the cabinets. "My dad seemed mighty interested."

Reese had to bite his tongue. He could imagine Kingston ringing his hands up in that extravagant house, his blood pressure rising. "Well, dead bodies were recovered from the lake in front of his house. It's something of interest, don't you think?"

"Sure, but my dad specifically mentioned you were on the boat, and Beau said, and I quote, 'Yeah, that ain't good.' What ain't good about it, Reese?"

"I don't know. What do you think?" Reese pounded in a few nails, waiting for Gray to answer. Then he measured and went to the garage to saw another piece of trim. He pounded some more nails.

Finally, Gray spoke as if the internal debate to say what was on his mind was finally over. "Angie thinks my dad is a corrupt criminal narcissist. She asked him what wasn't good, and she told him he looked spooked. He said it can't be good the police were there, and then, of course, he attacked Angie. But the troubling thing was he wanted me to ask you what you found. I'm trying to figure out if it's simply curiosity or if he was actually spooked and worried about you."

"Maybe you should ask him. You're the heir to his fortune."

"I've tried to stay out of his business. As a kid, I didn't care. As a young adult with college and Mom, it was the farthest thing from my mind. But he wants me to be part of it, and Angie wants nothing to do with him. I've managed to skirt the issue for a lifetime, but with Angie pressuring to leave, things are changing."

"So what do you think? Is Angie right about him?"

"Probably."

"You're not sure?"

"I love my dad…but I don't really like him, you know? My mom has nothing good to say about him. I assumed it was because of a messy divorce, but Angie feels the same way, and I see what she's talking about. I meet people who hear my last name, and I can see the judgement. I can feel it. No one says anything to me, so I can only wonder what he's done to alienate so many people. He honestly believes people admire and respect him. What do you think about him?"

Reese set down his hammer, sat on the floor with his legs crossed, and looked at the ceiling as if trying to lure the words from above. Finally, he spoke. "I'm no expert on his personality, but I believe he's broken a lot of laws and managed to get away with all of it."

"So when he sees you on a boat in front of his house, fishing two dead bodies from the lake and says it isn't good you're there, you think it's because he had something to do with the bodies?"

"I haven't even identified the bodies yet, so I can't answer the question."

"Maybe he thinks you're going to accuse him of something he didn't do. Being valued and revered by others is high on his priority list."

"Well, that's a personality thing I know nothing about, but if this is a crime he's tied to, I'll be coming for him even though he's your dad. That's my job."

Gray had all the tiles spread in place and set firmly on the thin-set mortar and backed away to observe his handiwork. Once he satisfied himself there was no lippage between tiles, he said. "I'm going to let that set for a while before I start grouting." He took a drink of water and then washed his hands in the bathroom. When he returned, Reese drove his

51

last nail and stood. "Good work, Reese. You all done for the day?"

"Yep. Figured I'd get a burger and head home."

"Is this case gonna put your retirement plans on hold?"

"Nope. I've got nine days. If I don't have a solution, I'll pass my information on to the next guy to complete."

"Won't that bother you?"

Reese stuffed his hammer into his tool belt, finished his bottle of water, and tossed it into a garbage can with scraps from the job. "Probably, but it's been bothering me for twenty-three years, and I've learned to live with it. I gotta run. Have a good night, Gray." As Reese climbed into his car, leaving Gray alone, he couldn't help but wish he'd kept his mouth shut. "Twenty-three years. I'm an idiot. He'll figure out I've suspected his father the whole time."

Chapter 9

A hospice nurse watched Noah Tuesday morning while Angie drove to her tax office and back to check messages and mail. Several minutes before eleven a.m., she drove up Kingston's long, private driveway and put her car in park, but before she could turn off the engine, Beau opened the passenger door and sat in the front seat. He had Angie's luggage in one hand and a legal-sized envelope in the other.

"What's this?" Angie asked. "The boss man sending me home? He's got my son, so I'm not leaving."

"You're partly right. We're going to your house, but it's to do some more packing. You ain't comin' back."

"He's sending me away? What...on a vacation while my son suffers alone? I'm not going anywhere."

"Yes, you are." Beau slid his gun from a shoulder holster and pointed it at her. "Turn the car around, and drive me to your house." Angie stared at the gun, speechless. "Oh, and I need your phone please." He held his hand steadily out as he aimed the gun at her head. She took her phone from her purse and handed it to him. He turned it off and put it in his suit-coat pocket. He hesitated as if considering what to say, but finally, he spoke. "Let me ease your mind. Your son will be taken care of. There's a plan in place. Kingston will take care of him."

They drove in silence the twenty minutes it took to traverse slightly more than ten miles into the city of Byrdstown, and then Angie turned into her own driveway. The car idled in park for a moment before she looked at Beau. "Are you going to shoot me once we get inside? I'm not afraid to die." There were tears forming in her eyes.

"That's nice, but nope. You're gonna pack, and then we're gonna take a drive. But if you do anything stupid, your mother and father will be shot. Yeah, I know where they live. And that'll hurt you worse than you can imagine, knowing it was your fault. Park in the garage. You need to go inside and finish packing."

Angie pushed the automatic door opener and eased the car inside the garage. She put her foot on the brake and pushed the button to turn off the vehicle, a silver Honda HR-V. Slowly, she opened her door and climbed out, Beau encouraging her to move into the house at gunpoint. She stopped once they entered the living room. Beau moved into the kitchen and took a Coke from the refrigerator, flipped the can tab, and took a drink.

"Pack for a permanent move. I'll sit here and wait. And don't even think about running off. I have a colleague at...let's see..." He took a notepad from his suit jacket pocket. "...14 NW Benjamin Circle, Cleveland, TN. Your parents will be dead before you exit the neighborhood."

"Kingston hates me that much? Enough to kill my parents?"

"Does he hate you any more than you hate him?"

"I'm not threatening his family."

"You aren't? Seems like I heard you say you were taking his son and leaving Byrdstown for good. Sounded like a threat to me. Go pack...and then we have a letter to write." Beau took another long swallow from the soft drink and belched.

With more anger than fear, Angie started packing, but not carefully. What did she care about the contents? She knew she'd either be dead, or she would return to her son. Either way, it didn't matter much what she threw into another suitcase. She took a few moments to pray, however. She prayed for her son, for her parents' safety, for Gray, and for courage. When she went to the hall closet for a jacket, Beau was going through her wallet. "What are you doing?"

"Oh, I need a credit card. Just trying to decide which one you use the most. I see two and a debit card." Beau held them all up for her to see. "Well?"

"It doesn't matter. I use all three." Angie stepped close enough to see and said, "The middle one. The Master Card. What are you buying for me?" She glared at Beau.

"You're a feisty one, for sure. Almost admirable. A plane ticket. I was thinking Honolulu. United has a flight from Nashville to Dallas to Los Angeles to Honolulu. Takes fifteen hours, and it's only $547 dollars one way. Departs at five today, and you'll be arriving at six a.m., considering the time change, giving you plenty of time to get a car and a hotel before heading out to the beach. I'll book it for you." He held up Angie's phone. "Tell me your passcode, please."

"Twelve, twenty-six. Even if you get me on that plane, I'll come right back. My son needs me."

"If you come right back, your son will still die, but so will your parents."

"Your boss is a monster. What will Gray think if I abandon our son?"

"You're also going to ask for a divorce. The way Kingston sees it, his son will be upset with you, and when you're gone, he'll manipulate Grayson to become a bigger part of the business. He thinks you're a bad influence. It's crazy, I know, but he don't like you." Beau took his last swallow and tossed his Coke can in the waste basket under the sink.

"Doesn't."

"What?"

"He doesn't like me."

"Exactly. Now finish up packing while I make your reservations. Then we have a letter to write."

Consumed with dread, Angie left Beau alone on a bar stool at the kitchen island to make her plane reservations. She listened as he spoke on the phone and realized it was true. He was going to ship her to the farthest point away in the United States and tear her family from her. She had to do something. She opened the nightstand on Gray's side of the bed and grabbed the box he stored his gun in at the back of the drawer. She didn't know how to load it or use it, and it scared her too much to consider trying, so she returned it to the drawer and considered a different option. The softball bat! She got down on her knees and lifted the bed skirt. Her eyes fell on the knob end of the bat, and she quietly lifted it and dragged it out. It was stored there for a situation like she currently found herself in.

Next, she had to figure out how to hide it, so she could use it. She grabbed her king-sized pillow and tested to see if she could hide the bat behind it if she let it dangle from her hand. It worked. She could hear Beau still talking on the phone with the airline, giving her credit card number. She quickly slipped her shoes off and moved down the hallway as silently as she could.

She froze as Beau finished the call and looked her way. "The ticket is purchased. We'll drive to the airport after you write Grayson a letter. I have a pen and paper here."

He turned his head to the kitchen counter to retrieve the large envelope he'd brought with him. When he turned away from her, Angie attacked. She dropped her pillow and swung the bat with all her might at Beau's head. He reacted in the nick of time, raising his right arm to block the blow. Angie shattered carpel bones in his wrist, and Beau screamed out in pain. He dropped his arm from in front of his face and grabbed it with his left hand, giving Angie time to try again. She took another vicious swing, but Beau raised his arm again, his right hand drooping, unusable. The bat connected with his forearm, snapping his radius in two.

Two tries for his head and two misses, but she wound up for a third swing. Beau ducked under the bat, and it sailed over his head, leaving Angie off balance. He pivoted on his stool and swung mightily with his left arm. Backhanded, he connected the back of his fist to Angie's jaw. Her head snapped back violently, and her body went airborne. She landed with a crash on the back of her head on the ceramic tile floor and lay there unconscious. Beau kicked the bat out of her hands and stood over her angrily while holding his shattered right arm with his left hand.

There was no movement on the floor, not even the rising and falling of Angie's chest. It didn't look like she was breathing. Beau bent down and tried to find a pulse, but he felt nothing. Angie was dead.

***

Beau knew he was in trouble. Things hadn't gone as planned. He meant to leave Angie at the airport and manipulate a divorce. Her death changed everything, and he went into damage control mode. Besides some blood in her mouth from a smashed lip and lacerated gums, there was no blood to clean up. He gathered her luggage and purse and put the bags in the back seat of her car. He tossed the pillow back on her bed. With his lone good arm, he picked her up and put her in the trunk. He took the softball bat and put it in the bedroom closet where he found other softball gear—cleats, hats, softball glove, and pants.

He couldn't write a note in Angie's handwriting, so he needed to use a computer to type one out and print it. All of those things were problematic. First, his right arm and wrist were killing him. Second, he couldn't find paper for the printer. Third, he couldn't use the computer in Grayson's office without a pin to open the screen. He didn't have a printer at his own home, so he had to drive Angie's car to the Pickett County Library and sign in to get a log-in from the librarian.

He then had to return to Angie's place, leave the note, and search for any evidence of his presence in the house. He wiped down the counter, bar stool, softball bat, and the faucet water controls. He took out the SIM card and smashed Angie's phone, cleaning up the mess and putting the pieces in a Ziplock bag. He put the note in the envelope and placed it on the counter, locked the door, and drove to his own house, his arm hurting so badly sweat poured from his body. But his problems weren't over.

His truck was at Kingston's home, so he could put Angie's car in his garage, but he had no opener and had to park, unlock his house, and open the garage door from inside. He drove the car in, shut the door, and opened the trunk hatch. He moved some meat from his freezer to make room for the body. Then, with one arm, he lifted Angie's body from her vehicle and stuffed it inside. He still had to figure out what to do about the car and the luggage. He could move the car to the airport, but he had no way to get back home from there, and he had to clean the car out to make sure there was no forensic evidence. And all of that was in addition to the fact he needed medical attention. He needed to call Kingston and get some help.

Kingston arrived within fifteen minutes of Beau's call, and then Beau gave his uncomfortable portrayal of the events in the afternoon. "I hate that woman. I tried to give her a break. This is on her," said Kingston.

"She was trying to survive. I'd've done the same thing." Beau grimaced. The pain was excruciating.

"Well, she obviously isn't going to get on a plane to Honolulu, so we have to manufacture her disappearance on the way to the airport. Drive her car off a cliff, maybe?"

Beau shook his head. "They'll find the body right away and figure out she died before the crash. Will her body even bleed? She probably has a broken neck. Will that make sense when she's found?"

"Then she has to disappear some other way. Abduction?"

Beau thought a minute. "We could drive her car to a gas station on the way to Nashville and use her card to pump gas. That would suggest she was on her way to the airport. Then we could leave the car sitting there. Cops might figure she was kidnapped."

"But if there are video cameras, all they have to do is check the footage, and you'll be identified. There has to be another way."

"How about a rest stop? It makes sense she might stop to use the restroom. Maybe we could stage an abduction there."

"That could work. There's a rest area past Cookeville if I remember correctly. Somewhere near the Center Hill Lake area."

"Buffalo Valley. I've stopped there before." Beau worked on a sling for his battered arm, using a towel he draped from his neck. "Will you tie this for me? My right arm in unusable." Kingston helped Beau place his arm in the towel, and then he tied a knot at his neck. Beau groaned as he stood to leave. "Let's go as soon as possible. We need to finish this, and I need a doctor."

58

Beau went inside his house and put on a knit hat and gloves. He took a vacuum and went over the entire two front seats and floor as well as the trunk. He then wiped down the steering wheel, Angie's keys, and anything else he may have touched to leave fingerprints. Finally, to Kingston who didn't lift a finger, he said, "I think I'm ready." Beau reversed the process of opening and closing his garage door and pulling the car out into the driveway. Then he followed Kingston to I-40 and the Buffalo Valley rest stop near mile marker 267.

Beau ripped open Angie's luggage and threw some of it haphazardly around the back seat of the SUV. He removed Angie's laptop and some jewelry. He took her money from her purse and removed all the cards he'd touched at Angie's house. Nothing else seemed particularly valuable. He left the car unlocked and climbed into the passenger seat of Kingston's yellow truck. At the first exit where they turned to head back east, they dumped the laptop, jewelry, and Angie's keys and smashed phone into a trash bin outside a Shell Gas Station. Beau took off his hat and gloves as sweat dripped from his nose.

Kingston drove to Cumberland Medical Center's Emergency Room and dropped Beau off. "I don't know what you're going to tell them that happened to you, but I hope it doesn't put me in a bad position."

Beau took a double take at his boss. "I got your back. Thanks for the lift." Beau climbed out of the truck and walked toward the Emergency Room without looking back. To himself, he said, "He's been like a brother to me, but everything Angie said about that man is true."

Chapter 10

Gray entered his father's home Tuesday evening after he finished work. The only cars in the driveway were Beau's and the hospice nurse's. He headed directly to Noah's room to find Nurse Connie sitting in a chair, reading *The Eyes of the Dragon* by Stephen King. "Did you know King wrote the book for his then thirteen-year-old daughter because she wouldn't read his horror books?"

"The book isn't scary?"

"No, it's more like a fairy tale, except not for little kids. Where's Angie?"

"I haven't seen her all day. She went to her work and hasn't returned."

"Where's my dad?"

"I don't know. He said he had an emergency and had to run out."

Gray left the room and walked around the house, but only he, Connie, and Noah were present, so he returned. "Did Beau go with my dad?"

"I haven't seen him since this morning. He must've left."

"His truck's in the driveway."

"Maybe he left with Mr. Phipps."

Gray called Angie's phone, but it went straight to voicemail. "Where are you, Angie? I'm at the house with Noah. Call me back."

"Where's Mommy?" said Noah. "My head hurts." He started crying.

Gray moved to the bed with the nurse. "Is there anything we can do to help him?"

"I want Mommy," said Noah. He squinted at Gray, and then tears filled his eyes.

"He's getting his medicine. I've given him everything prescribed to make him comfortable," said Connie. "I'd say finding his mother is the one other thing you can do."

For the next two hours, Noah drifted in and out of sleep, and each time he woke and didn't see his mother, he cried some more. Gray spent the two hours at his bedside but tried calling Angie at least a dozen times. Finally, his dad arrived home and entered the room with a bottle of Scotch and a half-drunken glass in his hands.

He told Connie to go ahead and take a break, leaving him in Noah's room alone with Gray. "How's Noah?"

"Upset. He wants Angie, and I can't reach her. Apparently, she's been gone all day. I'm worried."

"Maybe she just needed to get away. I'll bet she's exhausted."

"She would never leave and not explain." Gray looked at his phone, but there was no call or message from his wife. "Will you sit in here while I shower? I need to clean up." His dad nodded and took another drink before pouring some more into his glass.

When Gray entered the bedroom, he knew immediately something was wrong, and it took only a short investigation to confirm it. Angie's duffle bag she brought her things in was missing. Her clothes weren't in the closet or any dresser drawers. Her toiletries were gone, but not the make-up bag under the bathroom sink. Her Bible was on the nightstand. If she left, she would have taken it. And then he noticed a strap under the bed. It belonged to the computer bag for Angie's laptop, and she would've taken that also if she left for any time at all.

Gray marched back into Noah's room. "Her things are gone. Everything." He chose not to mention the Bible and make-up and computer bags. "It's like she left us."

"That's ridiculous," said Kingston. "She must've gone home to do laundry or something."

"And not take my clothes or Noah's? I don't think so."

"Well, maybe you should go to your house to see if she's there. Maybe she needed some time alone to rest. Connie's been here all day, so maybe she took advantage and took a break."

"Why isn't she answering her phone? Or why didn't she tell me about it before she packed all her things? Something's fishy." Gray tried calling again, but it went to voicemail immediately. "Her phone must be turned off, and that doesn't make sense either because of Noah. I'm heading to the house."

"That's a good idea. Connie can watch Noah while you're gone."

Anxiously, Gray drove the ten miles home and entered the house. His eyes fell on the envelope on the kitchen island. He opened it, read it, and immediately called Reese Carlton.

As soon as Reese answered the phone, Gray spit out, "Angie's missing, and I need your help."

"Explain."

"She wasn't at my dad's when I got there, and she's not answering her phone. Her things are packed and gone, and when I went to our house, there's a note. I'm not a detective like you, but none of it adds up."

"You're at the house now?"

"Yes."

"Okay, I'm on my way. Look around to see if there's anything unusual, but don't touch anything. I'll be right there." Reese hung up, holstered his gun, and left immediately.

Gray made a tour of his home. More clothes were missing. The drawer where he stored his gun was partially opened. His gun box sat at the front of the drawer, but the gun was inside. He took it out and loaded it. He went to his closet, took a belt from a hanger, and put it on, including strapping on his holster. He continued his tour of the house, noting some irregularities, and then his doorbell rang.

Reese stood on his porch as Gray opened the door and invited him in.

"Thanks for coming. This is wrong. I can feel it."

"Okay. I know the feeling. Tell me what's bothering you."

"I got to my dad's after work, and Angie wasn't there. I've tried calling her, and it goes straight to voicemail. When I went into our room, her things were packed and gone."

"Like she left for good?"

"Yeah, but her Bible and her computer bag and her make-up bag were still in the room. She would've taken them if she planned to leave. I rushed here next, and there are things that don't compute here either."

"Okay," said Reese, "let's hear them."

"There's a note. Let me read it to you: 'Grayson, I'm leaving for Hawaii. I know it don't make sense to you but I can't watch our son dir and I can't be part of your family anymore. I'll never find peace and joy in the presence of your fahter. I hope you can find the happiness with your father that would always elude me. Take care of Noah. Angie.'"

"She wouldn't leave Noah," said Reese.

"Of course not, but she also didn't write this note....Look. It says 'It don't make sense.' She'd never in a million years make that grammar error in a note...and that's in addition to the missing commas and the two spelling errors. But also, we don't have any paper in our printer. We've been out for a while. She would've had to handwrite it on a notepad or a legal pad, not on copy paper. Maybe she typed it out at my dad's house, but why not leave it there where I'd be more likely to find it? And Reese, she would *not* have referred to me as Grayson. She never calls me Grayson."

"So someone else typed and printed the note," said Reese. "Did you find any other oddities in the house?"

"A few. She has clothes missing, but not her swimsuits and sandals. She'd take them to Hawaii, wouldn't she? There are no pictures missing. No way she wouldn't take some of Noah, at least. Her pillow was lying on the mattress, but it was tucked in under the bedspread when we packed for my dad's house. My gun case was at the front of the drawer instead of the back where I keep it. And the softball bat we keep under the bed was in the closet. So someone was here. Maybe Angie, but there's no way to know for sure."

"The house looks neat and orderly to me. Is anything missing?"

"Not that I can tell. Not that I've noticed." Gray opened the cupboard door and tossed the note at the waste basket in frustration. But he followed the shot and took the wastebasket from under the sink. "Reese, someone else was here for sure. There's a Coke can in the wastebasket. Angie doesn't drink

Coke...ever. I do, but I took out the trash the day we left for my dad's house. This is new."

"Hold on. Don't touch the can. There could be fingerprints. Maybe on the envelope and note too. I'll get someone here to dust for prints, and I'll put an APB out for Angie's car. I'm going to agree something's not right, so foul play is my starting point. Check and see if she's used her credit card recently. If she's heading to Hawaii, she'd have to purchase a ticket to get there. See if she has. Any other transactions may give me a clue where to start looking."

While Reese called the department to send Carl Donaldson from forensics to the house, Gray logged into his VISA credit card account. There was no recent activity, but when he checked on the Master Card, there was a hit. A ticket for $547 from Nashville to Honolulu on United Airlines had been purchased at 11:27 a.m., but nothing else had been charged that day. He called the airport, but without the boarding information or login details, they refused to say if Angie had boarded the plane. All they would do was confirm she had purchased a ticket. The service agent mentioned a warrant would be needed to access the plane's manifest. It would be a task for Reese to accomplish.

Eventually, the department forensics officer, Carl Donaldson, arrived. He took Gray's fingerprints and found an obvious print on a make-up mirror for Angie. He took prints from the Coke can, the envelope on the kitchen island, and the note to Gray. The countertop, barstools, and sink handles had been wiped clean. The refrigerator door handle had so many prints, there was no way to separate them. The gun box had prints, but the softball bat didn't have a single friction ridge. It had obviously been handled and wiped clean.

When Donaldson left, Reese and Gray sat in the living room. "We'll identify unusual prints and check our database to see if we have matches. I'll get a warrant and check with the airport to see if Angie got on the plane. Hopefully, we'll find her car right away too."

"I have a bad feeling." Gray sat with his head forward, elbows on his knees, and hands folded.

"I'll do what I can to help. I'm in the middle of a case, but it's kind of in a holding pattern right now, so I can give this my attention." Reese stood. "I'll call the Department of Transportation about the manifest, and possibly we'll know tomorrow if she's on her way to Hawaii. I'll have one of my men canvas the neighborhood to see if anyone saw Angie here today. Is there anything else I can do for you?"

"No…thanks. I need to get back to my son. Thanks for helping…but Reese? I'm worried."

"I know you are. I'm sorry." He placed his hand on one of Gray's hunched shoulders.

Both men rose sullenly and walked to the door together. Reese drove away while Gray locked up. On his drive home, Reese tried calling Monica Dale again, but the call went immediately to voicemail. He didn't bother leaving a message.

***

Soaking wet from perspiration, Beau entered the Emergency Room. The pain was excruciating, and his arm and wrist were wrecked. He needed help. After giving insurance information, he sat down to wait. Five hours later, his name was called. He walked behind a nurse to a "room" behind a curtain. She asked him the same questions he was asked upon his arrival, and his response to the question of what happened to him mimicked his original response. "I'd rather not say."

They put him in a wheelchair and an orderly wheeled him to X-ray where pictures were taken, and then he returned to his room. The doctor showed up twenty minutes later with the X-ray images in his hand. He looked like a kid to Beau. "How are we doing?"

"I don't know how you are, Doc, but I'm in a bit of pain." He felt like throwing up.

"I'm guessing your pain is about a ten out of ten."

"Eleven."

"Yeah…I imagine. I'm Doctor Bill Gatfield." He extended his left hand for Beau to shake. "When did this happen?"

"Seven or eight hours ago."

"How did it happen?"

"I'd rather not say."

"Why is that?"

"I'd rather not say....Can I maybe be given something for my eleven pain?" A nurse arrived to hook an IV to his left arm as he spoke. "Great timing."

"Morphine sound good?" Doctor Gatfield asked. He had a dimple in his cheek when he smiled, making him look even younger.

"Sounds great."

After the nurse finished, the doctor cleared his throat and held up the first of three images. "So let's start with your arm. The ulna is snapped in two and the radius is cracked. You hit something with a lot of force. You need surgery. And it'll be an open reduction. We'll have to cut the arm open to set the bone with plates and screws. But that's the easy one." He showed the second image. "Three carpel bones in your wrist are a mess. I refrain from using the word 'shattered,' but I think it's a word you can understand. This includes an additional break to the ulna where it attaches to your wrist. To reduce those..." He saw the look of confusion on Beau's face. "...set those, it'll take more plates and screws and pins. The pins are removable after the bones heal." He cleared his throat and took out his third X-ray. "The fifth metacarpal...the pinky...is broken. Plates, screws and pins are necessary there as well."

The morphine made Beau feel better, but the diagnosis didn't.

The doctor continued. "How's your left hand?"

Beau looked at it like it was a foreign object.

"You'll be using it for everything for a while. You'll be in a cast from the tips of your fingers to your elbow. And it'll be months before you're healed." He hesitated. "The arm and pinky, once set, should heal perfectly. The wrist is more of a mystery. How old are you?"

"Sixty-three."

"You look to be in good shape, and clearly your pain tolerance is incredible. You'll have to do therapy if you have any expectations of getting your wrist back to at least close to normal."

"I can do that."

"Good. We're going to get you a room. A real room. We'll try to make you comfortable, and then we'll have you in surgery in the late morning. We'll put you in a cast, and you can be out of here in half a day."

"You're doing the surgery?" Beau looked at the man again, wondering if Mr. and Mrs. Gatfield knew their high school son pretended to be a surgeon.

"Yes."

"Will you have adult supervision? What are you, sixteen? Seventeen?"

"Ha, ha. I'm thirty. I've done hundreds of surgeries. I'll take good care of you." He laughed again. "Rest well, and I'll see you later."

Once the doctor left, Beau called Kingston, waking him from sleep. "Why are you calling at this hour?"

"Yeah, I'm great. Thanks for asking."

"You didn't tell them how you were injured did you?" Kingston's lack of compassion shouldn't have been surprising.

"I'm not a moron. I'm scheduled for surgery later today...late this morning. I can't get home without you." The irritation was obvious in his voice.

"Jeeze. You woke *me* up, not the other way around. You'd think I was inconveniencing *you*."

"I'm going to bed, Kingston. They're here now to take me to my room. Sorry for the inconvenience."

Chapter 11

The Wednesday workday started out with Reese working the phones. He contacted the Tennessee Department of Transportation in Nashville, who would have received the passenger manifest for Angie's flight to Honolulu. After identifying himself as a police officer, he waited for TDOT to call the police station. Once they were satisfied he was working on a missing person's case, they verified Angie had not boarded the flight she scheduled on Tuesday.

He called Gray with the news. "That means finding her car is our next important step," said Reese. "I'll keep you notified."

"Yes, please do. Noah's upset...and obviously, so am I. Please find her."

Next, he called about the fingerprints taken at Angie and Gray's house. The forensic technician, Carl Donaldson, gave his report. "The prints we pulled from the Coke can weren't Grayson's or Angie's, but the person they belong to isn't in the database. However, those same prints were on both the envelope and the note. Grayson's prints were on both also, as well as a third set on the note, but Angie's weren't on either. Unless she wore gloves, she didn't touch them. The gun box had prints for both Angie and Grayson, but not the unsub's. I hope that helps you."

"Thanks. It confirms what Gray said about the letter. He was certain she hadn't written it. And it confirms a stranger entered their home. Thanks, Carl."

"You're welcome. Have a good day, Reese."

His next call went to Officer Shady Rogers. Shady was soon to get the promotion to lead detective once Reese retired in a week. He was the son of Reese's former police chief, Steve Rogers, but his first name was so inappropriate for a cop that everyone in the office called him Shaggy instead. Shaggy Rogers was Scooby Doo's human buddy, and since Shady was a detective with scruffy facial hair, which always looked in need of shaving, the name seemed a better fit. Shady had a doctor's waiver for some odd medical condition allowing his awful beard. "Have you learned anything, Rogers?"

"The neighbor across the street saw Angie's car turn into her garage sometime around eleven or a little after. She thinks there were two people in the car but couldn't say for sure. She heard the garage door open again maybe an hour later but didn't see the car leave. The neighbor next door thought he saw Angie's car around lunchtime. When pressed for the time, he said half past twelve or so. That's the best I could get from him. No one else saw or heard anything."

"At least it confirms where Angie was when she made her plane reservation. Thanks, Rogers. I'll let you know if I need anything else."

Next, he checked the department about the APB on Angie's vehicle, but nothing had been reported.

Reese parked and entered Southern Dreams Bakery on Skyline Drive near the high school and ordered two donuts and a water to go. He returned to his car and mulled over his next steps. Thinking of none, he called Ashvi Patel at the coroner's office.

"Good morning, Reese." Her sweet voice spoke English with near perfect diction. "I planned to call you this morning. The DNA tests are back. You don't have to bother with Stephen Stone's dental records. The two deceased men are Stephen Stone and John Hill." A donut bite stuck temporarily in Reese's throat, sending him into a coughing fit. "Are you okay?" She started to laugh.

Reese took a swallow of water, which helped some, but he still coughed while he laughed back. Finally, he could speak. "Thanks for your compassion."

"I was going to make a cop joke about you choking on a donut, but I figured that might be offensive, and since it sounded like you were dying, I didn't want those to be my last words to you."

"Well, since it *was* a donut, I can't be offended, can I?" He wiped his eyes with his sleeve, grateful he hadn't choked to death but also happy to be smiling again. "It's just it's been two decades, and I finally have some evidence. Two men were murdered, and the last person to see both of them, more than likely, was the person who got the men to sign purchase agreements for the sale of their houses. And the one person who benefitted from that was Kingston Phipps. Maybe the wives will talk to me now."

"That's great, Reese. I still haven't heard back from the ATF, so we don't know the first owner of the gun, but it shouldn't be much longer before we know."

"Please call me as soon as you know, okay? Thanks for the good news too."

"It's my pleasure. Have a good day....Oh, and maybe lay off the donuts. They seem dangerous."

Reese hung up with a sense of accomplishment. But then another thought entered his mind. Since he knew the two gunshot victims' names, he also knew who made the call to him twenty-three years earlier. It was Monica Dale's husband who was shot in the chest, so it was her child who called the police station. Monica only had one child, so Dorella Dale had to be the person who made the call. He tried Monica once again, but the call went straight to voicemail. It was time to make a trip to Tucson, Arizona. He had questions for Monica; most specifically, where was her daughter?

***

Grumbling to himself, Kingston parked in the hospital visitor lot a little before two o'clock. As he exited his vehicle, several heads turned to look at him and his truck, so he puffed out his chest, believing everyone thought he was impressive and important. Out of his peripheral vision, he saw Ella Dixon limping toward the Cancer Center entrance to start her afternoon shift, a walking boot on her right ankle. He resisted the urge to follow her, and instead, walked through the parking lot, past the cancer center, and in through the main entrance. He was directed to the north patient rooms on the fifth floor to find Beau in room 520.

Beau sat in a visitor chair with a cast exposing only three fingertips and the tip of his thumb. It went to his elbow and the cast rested in a sling. He stood as soon as Kingston entered the room. "I see you're ready to go," said Kingston.

"I've been out of recovery for more than an hour. I'm ready to go home."

"Pain?"

"I'm on a nerve blocker for now, so I feel fine. And I have a prescription for pain meds. Let's get out of here." Beau buzzed the nurse. She poked her head in and then left, returning with an orderly who pushed Beau to the elevator and the main exit in a wheelchair.

The two men walked together to Kingston's truck. Beau leaned his head back on the headrest and fell asleep immediately. Kingston left the parking lot, maneuvered onto TN-111 north, and drove in silence for nearly fifty minutes.

Finally, Beau stirred. When he opened his eyes, Kingston said, "We've got a mess on our hands. Noah cries every moment he's awake, and Grayson has Reese Carlton investigating Angie's disappearance in hopes of bringing her back."

"That ain't gonna happen."

"Duh. So you have to get back on your horse and finish our plan."

"*Your* plan, Kingston. *Yours.* There's nothing I can do for you right now. You'll have to get your own hands dirty because I'm not available."

"What? It's only a broken arm, and it's in a cast. You're fine."

"I'm not fine. My arm is broken in three places and my wrist in about a dozen. A finger is broken too. Plates, screws, and pins are holding me together. My wrist might never heal properly. I need some time to heal."

"What am I supposed to do, Beau? You've put me in a bad spot."

"I've given you my notes. If you want something done today, you'll have to do it yourself."

"This is your fault."

"Sir, your daughter-in-law was brave. I'll give her credit. She fought, and she put me out of commission. You'll have to step in. It's *not* my fault." Beau looked ahead as he inhaled deeply to keep his composure. "Stop at Garrett's Drug Center if you don't mind. I have a script to fill."

Kingston rolled his eyes, but he stopped. Irritated, he got Beau home. "I'll need you at the house tomorrow if all goes to plan. Get some rest."

"Call me. Thanks for the ride, Kingston. I need some rest." Beau climbed out of the truck and went inside his house without looking back, and Kingston drove away.

***

When Kingston returned home, he went directly to the liquor cabinet. He grabbed a glass and plopped in a chair to fume. After drinking nearly half a bottle of Weller Bourbon, he felt better. His problems hadn't gone away, but the buzz made them easier to accept.

Grayson burst into the room to talk. "Where have you been?"

"Beau broke his arm and had to have surgery. I brought him home from Cookeville."

"Why's his truck in your driveway?"

Kingston hesitated, considering a lie, but instead simply said, "I don't know, but I imagine he'll come by tomorrow to get it." Kingston downed the last of his glass. "How're you holdin' up?"

He pinched the bridge of his nose and rubbed his temple, unable to keep his hands still. "Not well, to be honest. Noah's confused and upset. When you add that to the pain and discomfort he's going through, my heart is breaking for him. He wants his mom, and I couldn't be more worried about her."

"Have you tried contacting family or friends or work associates? If she didn't get on the plane like you told me earlier, maybe she's with someone now, and she'll be back."

"I've made a ton of calls. No one has heard from her except at the office yesterday morning, and she didn't give any indication she was leaving. It's a dead end right now. Reese said we need to find her car." Gray took out his phone. "I'll call him and see if there's any news."

Reese answered his phone while driving. "Do you have any news about Angie? Like, has her car been found?"

"I've got a detective working on it, Gray."

"A detective? Not you?"

"I'm on my way to Arizona to interview the wife of one of the Willow Grove victims."

"Wait…the town that Dale Hollow Lake flooded? Everyone knows about the missing men. Why do you call them victims?"

"It's an active case, so I can't tell you why. But it's important to me. It's something I've been working on a long, long time."

"Does it have anything to do with the bodies you found in the lake?"

"I can't tell you about that."

"And that's why my dad and Beau said it wasn't good you were there on the lake. My dad bought up all those properties, and you think he had something to do with the so-called 'victims.' You've been trying to find evidence against my dad all this time. Am I right?"

Reese took a deep breath. "I'm trying to find out what happened to those three men."

"And pinning crimes on my dad is more important than finding my missing wife. I thought you were a friend." Reese didn't respond, and during the pause, Gray asked another accusatory question. "You've been working for me to keep track of my dad, haven't you?"

"I've been working for and with you because my job is stressful, and it's the best thing I've found to do to take my mind off it and off my lonely life."

Reese's hollow words didn't satisfy Gray. "I don't believe you, and I suppose there's nothing you can tell me about Angie's case?"

"I've got Detective Rogers trying to locate Angie. He's a good man, but Gray, I've made some calls today. I can tell you Angie was home when the plane reservation was made.

According to neighborhood witnesses, she arrived at the house sometime around eleven and left about an hour later. She returned about a half hour later, but no one saw anything but the car or heard anything except the garage door. Also, the prints on the Coke can weren't yours or Angie's and Angie never touched the note or envelope unless she wore gloves. That's all the information my forensics guy could help me with. Whoever touched the can is not in the database."

"How about the gun box?"

"The only prints were yours and Angie's."

"Angie touched it? She wanted nothing to do with that gun. Why would she touch it?"

"Maybe she thought she was in danger? I don't know. We can ask when we find her."

"But you can't find her from Arizona."

"I don't have any other leads right now, but I have this other case to work on. I should be back in Tennessee tomorrow. Rogers will let you know if the car is found."

"Screw you, Reese. I was counting on you." Gray ended the call and turned to his dad. "Did you do something bad Reese is going to find out?"

"It's nothing you need to worry about. What you need to worry about is preparing yourself to take over my empire."

"Your empire? You think you're some kind of king? Ha…that's ironic, isn't it? Kingston…king. I'll tell you what I'm worried about, Dad. Angie. Let me have the house you promised you'd give Angie and me. One of the last things she said to me was how she once had her heart set on owning this house like you promised. Let me have it, and maybe she'll come back and be happy."

Kingston's head spun from the alcohol. From what he heard of the phone conversation, Reese was back to tracking down the murder victims' wives. Could he have identified the bodies that were found in the lake? What else might he have found out? "Son, I'll gladly turn this house over to you…and Angie…but I want you to agree to work one year for me to learn what I'm doing. You can be my right-hand man."

"Beau's your right-hand man, Dad."

"Beau's always known he'd have to step back as soon as you got involved. He'll help you get acclimated."

"You're selling me the house for a year of labor?"

"I've got two other homes, and other property to build on, but I've only got one son. I need you, so yes. The house is yours if you'll work one year with me."

"I think Angie will agree to that. She's been stressed and upset about Noah. When we find her, she'll change her mind."

"Give her some time, and we'll figure all this out. In the meantime, we need to help Noah through his final days. I hate hearing him cry like he is."

"I agree. We need to do whatever we can to get him through this. He needs his mom, though."

Kingston put his bottle away with a smile and noted the clock. He had things to do since Beau wasn't available, but he and his son were finally on the same page. And his drunken state gave him courage. He called his real estate office and explained he needed the paperwork drawn up to transfer the ownership of his home to his son. Next, he paid Nurse Connie to go home. He told her to take some time off, and he'd pay her handsomely to stay away. When Noah passed on, he would give her a call. And then he climbed into his truck and headed back to Cookeville. He had other business to take care of by the end of the night.

Chapter 12

On the way through Livingston, Kingston stopped at Southern Woods Outdoors and purchased a taser. He explained to the owner he'd received some threatening messages, and he hoped the gun would be protection. The owner convinced him to purchase the TASER X2, which would remove the need to reload in case of a missed shot or a bad connection. The double-shot technology and the dual lasers to eliminate aiming guesswork would be the perfect defense system. Kingston paid the money in cash and returned to his truck to finish the drive.

His next stop was at Bradley Drive. As night fell, the property was shadowy, and lights popped on in neighborhood houses. Kingston parked in the street, looked carefully around, and then walked to the door at the side of the garage, hoping it was still unlocked as Beau had left it. It was. He entered the garage and pulled the rope hanging from the garage door motor, disengaging the automated opener. He then returned to his truck, drove down the street, and waited.

At 10:18, Ella Dixon turned into the driveway in her Kia. She slowed, slowed some more, and then stopped in front of her garage door which didn't open when she pushed the opener button multiple times in her car. Finally, she turned off her car, took out her keys, and limped to her front porch in her hospital scrubs and walking boot to enter through her front door. She stepped into her house, turned on a light, and closed her door. It was then that Kingston, with his headlights off, drove his truck down the street and parked next to Ella's white Sportage, shutting off his engine. No lights illuminated the driveway, so he stood in the dark next to the garage door, holding his newly loaded taser and a roll of duct tape.

He could hear Ella in the garage talking to herself, but finally, she lifted the garage door by hand. Once her arms extended over her head and the door was raised, Kingston stepped from the side of the building, aimed the lasers at Ella's stomach, and pulled the trigger. A pair of barbed, needle-like darts attached to thin copper wires fired from the taser from a small nitrogen canister. Both darts hit their target, and Ella dropped to the cement floor in an electrified convulsion.

Kingston swooped in as Ella's body shook and slapped a piece of tape over her mouth while she writhed in pain. He rolled her over as the convulsions stopped, yanked her hands behind her back, and quickly taped her wrists together. He did the same thing with her ankle and boot. Then he closed the garage door, turned off the garage light, and left her on the cement while he went inside and grabbed some clothes from hangers and drawers. He stuffed them into some plastic grocery bags he found in a waste basket.

When he returned, he used his phone's flashlight to look down at Ella's body, squirming on the floor, attempting to break the tape on her wrists. "You might as well stop, Ella, because if you manage to get your hands free, I'm going to tase you again, and I assume that doesn't feel good. I learned something today. My taser sent a shock of 50,000 volts through your body. That's more than six times the voltage allowed for an electric fence. You might be better off not going through that again. Right now, you're likely suffering from a reduction in some aspects of your brain functioning, but it's only temporary. If I have to shoot you again while you're still recovering, though, your brain might not bounce back so fast. I'd hate to do that to you because I need your help. My grandson needs your help. So I'm going to cut the tape at your ankles to allow you to walk, and you're going to get in my truck and ride with me to my home. Any questions?"

Her eyes shot daggers, but her mouth was taped, so there was no response.

"Good. Let me help you." He cut the tape with a pocketknife. Ella rolled over into a sitting position while Kingston stood over her, looking down with a smirk. She kicked him hard in the right knee, and he fell to the floor in pain. "Ow!" He grabbed her boot and twisted until she moaned out in pain. "Next time, I'll tase you again. I'm not kidding." He stood with great effort, putting all his weight on his non-injured leg. "This is what's going to happen. I'm going to raise the garage door again. If you try to run, you won't get far with that boot and your hands behind your back, and I'll tase you again and drag you back. Your other option is to let me walk you to my truck and help you inside. And then we have an hour drive to my home where you're going to tend to my grandson. Do you understand?"

She nodded her head in the affirmative.

"Good." Kingston shut off his flashlight feature and raised the garage door. When he pivoted to help Ella up, she kicked him again in the same knee. He crumpled to the floor in pain. Ella scrambled to stand, but before she could create any distance between the two, Kingston raised the taser and shot her in the back. Ella fell onto the driveway in agonizing pain. While her body shook, she could barely breathe.

Ella lay on the cement for several minutes, trying to compose herself and figure out what to do. Kingston groaned as he stood. With a pained, exaggerated limp, he made it to his truck and reloaded his taser. "I might tase you a third time just because I'm angry," he said. "You try something foolish like that again and I'll hit you with both shots." He held Ella's arm, yanked her to her feet, and directed her to the truck, and then he helped her climb in, her hands still secured behind her back. He then lowered the garage door, got in the vehicle, and drove out of the neighborhood without turning on his headlights. The taser remained in his right hand the whole time. Each time he stepped on the gas or brakes, he moaned and aimed the gun at Ella as if considering whether to shoot her again.

Ella rested and recovered as she sat still in Kingston's truck. Her seatbelt wasn't attached. She took that as a good break. Her door wasn't locked either and the door handle was a simple handle that pulled away from the door to open it. A half hour into the drive, at a stoplight, Kingston took the tape from her mouth. She glared at him but didn't speak right away. Finally, she said, "Why are you doing this?"

"I have a grandson who's dying from brain cancer. His mother is missing, but I'm certain he'll take right to you. You're going to watch him until he dies."

"You look familiar."

"You've seen me at the hospital probably. My grandson is Noah Phipps."

Recognition flashed in her eyes. "Why did you take him from the hospital if you weren't able to take care of him?"

"We had a hospice nurse and his mother. I've dismissed the nurse, and he misses his mom. You're going to fill in."

"And I have no say in the matter?" He didn't respond, keeping his eyes on the road as he continued toward his home. "You're going to hold me prisoner, aren't you?"

"That's right."

"I'll escape."

"Not if you care about Stacy Howard. I know where she lives, where she works at the hospital. Heck, I know where she golfs." He laughed. Beau may have been at home nursing a broken bone or two and not doing his job, but his information had come in handy. Kingston subconsciously gave himself a pat on the back. He had no regrets or concerns. He felt powerful.

Ella swallowed uncomfortably. She turned to face Kingston directly, her back to the passenger door. "If I do what you ask, you'll stay away from her?" The smile on his face turned to a grimace, and he didn't reply. "What's going to happen to me when little Noah passes away?"

Even in the dark, Kingston's face showed pain from his injury. Finally, he said, "I'll figure it out." As he slowed to a stop at another stoplight, he grimaced and let go of the taser to reach out and massage his knee. It was then Ella kicked his knee again. She kicked once, twice, three times while he screamed out in pain and while she also kicked the taser to the floor. She pushed her back against the passenger door, feeling for the door handle. Kingston angrily massaged his knee. Ella pulled the handle, the door swung open, and she fell backward with a thud on the pavement, knocking the air from her lungs.

She forced herself to her feet, sucking in air, and began to run the best she could with the boot, bad ankle, and hands taped behind her back. The truck idled in the darkness on the side of the road with no lights to be seen other than the headlights. Kingston flipped them off, swung his door open, and began to chase Ella, who fought to breathe and to run with some pace. An uneven field with long scrub grass made her flight difficult. Shadowy trees outlined the sky in the distance, and Ella struggled to run toward them.

Kingston limped as badly as Ella, but he could breathe and use his arms and make out her path through the long grass, so he gained on her even though he was grossly out of shape. Adrenaline and the alcohol he consumed helped him to ignore the pain to some degree, and finally, when he was within fifteen feet, he took another shot from the taser. One barb hit her, but the other didn't, and she kept running, stumbling several times over rocks and undulations in the field. She made it to the trees and hid behind a trunk in the dark. By nearly dislocating her shoulders, she slid her hands under her butt and around her feet, so they were in front of her. Using her teeth, she ripped off the tape, but it made noise, and as she stood to run some more, Kingston tased her for the third time, and that time, she fell unconscious.

Though in his sixties, he still possessed strength, and with his adrenaline flowing, he carried Ella back to the truck where he taped her mouth, hands, and feet once again. When she awakened, her grogginess kept her aggression at bay.

Kingston parked in his garage at twenty minutes after midnight, exhausted and anxious because the next step would be to get Grayson to buy into a kidnapping. Kingston believed once he saw Ella, he'd understand why his father did what he did. He would find out in the morning.

He struggled, carrying Ella through his dark house, trying to not awaken Grayson or Noah. He took her to his master bathroom where he took a long, thick chain and padlocked it to one of the large sink pipes, groaning from the pain in his knee. He then wrapped the chain tightly around Ella's left ankle, locking it in place. He cut the tape around her ankles and wrists. "It won't be comfortable, but you'll be sleeping here tonight. There's a toilet, a sink, and a shower you can get to. I'll get you a blanket and a pillow. In the morning, I want you to cut your hair to shoulder length, put some curls in it, and put on some make-up. I don't want to hear a peep from you. If I do, I'll hurt you. Do you understand?"

Ella nodded her head.

"Good. You can take the tape off your mouth too. And I'll get you some ice for your ankle. If you cooperate, you'll be okay."

He limped away and returned ten minutes later. Ella huddled in a corner, leaning against the bathtub. He set down the bags of clothes he took from her house. In his other arm, he carried a thick blanket and pillow. He hobbled out of the bathroom momentarily and returned with a large bag of ice and Angie's make-up bag. "I'll bring you some scissors in the morning. There's make-up and a curling iron. Fix your hair and your face in the morning, and then I'll take you to Noah."

"You're an evil man."

"I told you I didn't want to hear a word from you. I meant it."

She glared at him but didn't say anything, and once he left, she washed up, taking time to investigate her taser injuries. She washed them thoroughly and applied the ice pack to the wounds. She found some ibuprofen and swallowed four tablets. She also found some aloe to rub over the punctures and the irritated skin on her wrists and face. Finally, she took off her walking boot, elevated her foot to the edge of the tub, draped a towel over her swollen ankle, and laid the ice pack on top. She wrapped herself in her blanket, put her head on the pillow, and drifted off to sleep.

Chapter 13

While in his bathrobe on Thursday morning, Kingston woke Ella when he entered the bathroom. She felt stiff and sore, but the ice, elevation, and ibuprofen had helped her ankle feel better. "Clean up, cut and curl your hair, and put on some make-up. Make yourself look pretty. I'll get you some breakfast, and then I'm taking you to Noah."

Anxious, Ella did her best. When he returned, his white dress shirt was buttoned to his neck with a tie perfectly tied, and he had a plate with a bagel and cream cheese and some juice to drink. Ella hadn't showered because she couldn't take her pants and underwear off with the chain locked to her ankle, but she had washed, dabbed more aloe on the punctures, and shampooed her hair.

"Cut your hair next," Kingston demanded.

"There are no scissors." She looked at Kingston in the mirror, trying to look cooperative. "Plus, I need a couple of rubber bands so I can put it in a ponytail."

Kingston shut the bathroom door and limped off to retrieve the needed items. He stopped for a shot of whiskey to steel his nerves. He called Beau, who agreed to get an Uber ride to the office to pick up some papers and come to the lake house. Then he returned with the items, grimacing each time he put weight on his right leg. He held the scissors but handed her the rubber bands. Ella gathered her hair behind her head and put in a rubber band above the nape of her neck. Then, about two inches below her shoulder blades, she tied in a second band.

"My hair is wet," she explained, "so I need to cut it three or four inches below my shoulders; otherwise, it'll be too short. And since you want it curled, it might even need to be five or six inches below. How far below the second rubber band is that?"

"I'd say three inches."

"Okay. If you want me to cut it, I need the scissors."

He handed them to her and stepped back out of her reach. Ella went through the physical gymnastics of trying to hold the ponytail straight while straining to reach the hair behind her back with the scissors. She knew she could lift it up above her head to cut it, but that wasn't her plan. "I can't reach, and I can't see. I need you to cut it."

Kingston hesitated but stepped forward, reaching out his hand for the scissors. Ella spun, gripping the tool like a knife. She wanted to spear his eye or temple or ear, but aiming wasn't possible. She lunged and Kingston dodged. The scissors found a landing point between his left shoulder blade and chest and tore through his shirt and flesh. He cried out in pain and punched Ella below her chest in her solar plexus. She doubled over, out of breath. Then as she hunched over on her knees, Kingston roundhouse punched her in her left kidney, and she fell to the floor, unable to breathe. As she gasped for breath, Kingston yanked the scissors out of his bleeding shoulder, tugged her ponytail tightly, and snipped off everything three inches below the rubber band in one violent bloodstained snip.

"Curl your hair. Put on make-up. And if you ever try something like that again, I'll hurt you worse than you can imagine. And maybe I'll do the same thing to Stacy Howard." He started to leave and then turned back while Ella sucked in air on the floor, and like a bratty child, he took her bagel and juice with him.

Tears rolled down Ella's cheeks as she did her best to put curls into her brown hair. Once she made herself stop crying, she applied make-up to her cheeks, eyelids, and long eyelashes and applied a light coating of lipstick to her full lips.

When Kingston returned, he had on a fresh shirt. He inserted his arms into the sleeves of his suitcoat, wincing as he yanked the jacket over his damaged and bandaged shoulder. "You're going to meet my son next, and then it should be clear why I chose you to watch over Noah." He motioned with his hand. "Sit on the side of the bathtub."

Once Ella sat still, Kingston unlocked the padlock holding the chain to the sink pipe, but he left the chain attached to her left ankle. He directed her to walk into the long hallway extending upstairs the length of the house.

Grayson dressed in the bedroom he and Angie moved into. Ella could hear him moving around in the room behind the closed door. She stood, the chain tightly around her ankle, and waited. Soon, the door opened, and Gray stepped into the hallway. He started left but saw the two people in his peripheral vision, so he stopped and turned toward them.

"Angie?" He moved quickly down the hall to hug her, but she recoiled and backed away from him. As she stepped back, the chain rattled. Gray slowed and looked to his father who held one end of the chain in his hand. His eyes followed the length of the restraint, and he saw it was padlocked to her lower leg. He looked at her again. "What is this, Dad?"

"She looks exactly like Angie, doesn't she?" Kingston had an unsettling smirk on his face.

Gray stared at Ella. The gears in his mind worked slowly through what he saw. "You're not Angie." He looked at his father. "Why is she chained up?"

"Noah needs his mother," said Kingston.

"So you what? Kidnapped someone? You can't do that, Dad. Let her go." Down the hall, Noah started crying. He'd awakened, and his mother wasn't present.

"Ella," said Kingston, "you're on. He'll think you're his mom. I brought you here because you look like her. Play the part...or else."

Ella went into doctor mode. Without comment, she followed the sound of Noah's crying and entered the bedroom.

"Or else what? Dad? You've got to be kidding me." Gray followed Ella into the room, the chain dragging behind her across the wood flooring, Kingston trailing and holding the other end.

Ella stood next to Noah and grabbed his hand. "Mommy!" Noah stopped crying immediately. "Where have you been?"

Ella turned and glared at Kingston, but then she responded to Noah. "I had an accident and hurt my ankle, but I'm here now. How are you feeling?"

"I missed you. I'm better now, Mommy."

"How does your head feel?"

"Better now. I'm hungry."

"Then I'll get you something to eat. You're a sweet little boy."

"I'm sweet because you're sweet. And because it makes God happy."

"Yes, it does. Would you like some pudding?"

"Lemon. Do you have lemon?"

"I'll check, sweetie."

Ella stood, but before she could move, Kingston bent down with a grunt and padlocked the chain to the bed frame. "I'll get the pudding. You'll be staying here with my grandson."

Horrified, Grayson followed his father out of the room. "What are you doing? You can't kidnap someone and chain her to the bed. This is crazy. You have to let her go."

"No. We'll talk about this later. She's here for your son, and Noah thinks she's his mother. She'll make his last days better. Isn't that what's best?" Kingston hobbled down the stairs and into the kitchen, taking a lemon pudding from the pantry and tossing it to Grayson. "I've got work to do." He moved past Gray, taking several limping steps down the hallway parallel to the living room and into his den, shutting the door. Gray heard a click as his father locked himself inside.

Gray stood in the immaculate kitchen which opened into the huge living room with a wall of windows giving a gorgeous view of the lake. What a house. But it had become a crime scene. Before he could make sense of his father's evil deed, the doorbell rang, and then Beau stepped in, carrying a folder in his left hand.

"What happened to you?"

"I broke my arm…and wrist and finger. Where's your dad?"

"In his den. Do you know he kidnapped a woman to watch over Noah? Did you have anything to do with that?"

Beau raised his right arm, dragging the sling awkwardly up his neck, but he didn't say anything. Just rolled his eyes and walked to the den where he knocked on the door. "It's Beau with the paperwork."

Kingston opened his door, leaned out, and then directed Gray to come inside the den also. Kingston grabbed the folder from Beau, took a seat behind his gaudy desk, and motioned for Gray to sit down. Beau stood like a statue in front of the full wall of bookshelves and books. Kingston flipped through the papers and took out a pen from a holder next to his copy machine. "These are the documents from my title company that'll transfer ownership of my home to you. It's a quick claim title." He signed his name on one of the pages. "I'll sign this sheet stating I'm giving you the house, and you'll sign this one stating you're taking claim of it." He handed the sheet to Gray to sign. "These three papers say I'm giving you the contents and you're paying closing costs and property taxes."

Once Gray signed, he continued. "This is our personal contract. I'm making you my equal business partner. You're agreeing to be my partner, learning my business operations for a minimum of one year starting today. In my absence, you are empowered to make business decisions, decisions I'll be training you to make. That's for the real estate, mortgage, title, and construction companies, restaurants, lake rentals, etc.— the whole gamut. Is that acceptable to you?"

"What about the woman upstairs?"

"Gray, she's here. She's staying until Noah's gone. I'm paying the hospice nurse to disappear until Noah passes away. The woman upstairs will act the part of Noah's mom. She's not part of this typed agreement, but if you want the house, the kidnapping is part of the deal." Kingston glared into his son's eyes because Gray seemed on the fence about his decision. "So are the terms acceptable to you?"

"What about my business?"

"Keep it…sell it…hire someone to work for you. Whatever you want. But for the next year, I expect you to be by my side, learning everything I do. This is what Angie would want. You know that."

"I don't know that, but when we find her, I think the house might be enough to sway her not to leave…to come back home. I'll sign the contract." He took a pen and scribbled his name where he was instructed.

"We have a deal then." Kingston smugly stuffed the documents back in the folder and handed it to Beau. His shoulder and knee hurt, but he'd gotten his way. "Her name is Ella Dixon. Beau will be here to make sure she doesn't escape and to make sure you keep your mouth shut. You got what you wanted, and I got what I wanted. That's today's first lesson. Accept your victory. The girl is of no consequence."

"You're wrong, Dad. She matters…probably to a lot of people."

"I'll pay her well. Money solves most problems. That's the second lesson for today. Everything will be fine."

Chapter 14

It was barely ten a.m., and already it was over one hundred degrees in Tucson. Reese drove his rental car through a middle-class neighborhood where most homes had pools and not much besides rocks; scorched, brown dirt; and cacti in their yards. But the homes were well-maintained, and Monica Dale's driveway was empty. He could see her pool and glass-enclosed patio through the front window.

Reese knocked on her screen door and waited patiently on the porch. He knocked a second time as the hunter-green front door opened and a tall, attractive lady in her mid-fifties stared out at him. "Monica Dale?"

"Not anymore. Who's asking?"

"My name is Reese Carlton. I'm a detective for the Pickett County Sheriff's Department. You've been ignoring my calls."

"So you think I wanted you to visit me in person? I ignored them because I didn't want to speak with the police."

She intimidated Reese. Her arms were tanned and muscular, and she looked like she spent a lot of time in the gym. "Why?" She wasn't what Reese expected—strong both in physique and personality.

"Because what you're bringing up is something I've been trying my whole life to forget and keep quiet about. I've moved on."

"But I have information you might be interested in hearing."

"You don't."

"I do. We found the bodies of your neighbors, John Hill and Stephen Stone. They were murdered and dumped into Dale Hollow Lake."

"Of course they were murdered. Just like my former husband. You're not telling me anything I didn't already assume."

"May I come in…please? It's too hot to breathe out here." Reese smiled sympathetically at Monica. She had on a cotton blouse, shorts, and sandals and had likely been sitting on a chair in her enclosed patio facing the swimming pool when he knocked. The house was decorated and tidy. "I only have a few questions, and then I'll leave; I promise." Reluctantly, she opened the door. The stifling heat broiled anything outdoors, and Monica had enough sense to appreciate Reese's lack of comfort. Inside, the air conditioning felt cold, but Reese finally had his audience after twenty-three years. "Thank you."

"Come in. You might as well take a seat. My husband is out of town on a business trip. May I get you a glass of water?"

"No, thank you." Reese looked at her curiously. "I didn't know you had remarried."

She poured herself her own glass and sat down at the table. "It's not easy, but people move on."

Reese nodded and then took out his phone and scrolled to the camera app. "You saw a man murder your husband; is that correct?"

"How do you know that?"

"I'll get to that in a minute." He held the phone out for Monica. "Is this the man who shot him?" The picture was of Paul Miller, over two decades earlier.

Monica squinted at it, and then nodded her head yes. "He was the scrawny, weaselly realtor who harassed us to sell our house. Several tried but mostly him. Bobby repeatedly told all of them no. The weasel pointed his revolver at my daughter and threatened to shoot her, so Bobby hit him…hurt him, but not bad enough. He shot Bobby in the chest right in front of us. I heard a few days later the man committed suicide. I can't say I cared too much." Monica looked down at her hands folded in her lap.

"I don't think it was suicide. I think Miller was murdered."

Monica's head popped up, surprised, but her voice was calm. "Again, can't say I care."

"The real estate documents have Bobby's signature. Why is that?"

"He signed to protect Dorella. I can only assume Bobby figured if he hurt the man, he could get his gun and call the police and then the signature wouldn't be binding. My husband was the kind of man who took things into his own hands. Dorella and I learned that from him, may he rest in peace. I signed the purchase agreement after he was murdered to save myself and my daughter."

"We found Miller's gun when we found the body. It doesn't match for the two men we found in the lake."

"Maybe he used different guns. Maybe it was someone else who killed John and Steve. We moved on like we were told to do. Once we got our money, we forged a different life. We had nothing to worry about from the murderer because he was dead like he deserved. We've kept quiet, and we've been left alone."

"Your daughter called me."

"What? When?" Reese saw the concern in her eyes.

"After the shooting. She didn't give a name, but she described what happened. Basically the same story you just told me. All three of the Willow Grove families had kids. Girls. None of you let me talk to them, but when we found the bodies in the lake, we could see they were executed, and we recovered the bullets. They didn't match Miller's gun. Both men were shot in the head, so once we identified the bodies, I knew by process of elimination the call came from *your* daughter who said your husband was shot in the chest. I'd like to speak to her. Do you know how I can find her?"

"Don't you think it would be traumatic for nine-year-olds to witness murders? Events like murders are things children may never get over. You should leave her alone. She was especially close to her father. They fished, boated, hunted, and even grew our vegetables together. I already told you Miller murdered her father...my husband. That one is solved for you."

"Well, I'm determined to find who's behind the murders—including Paul Miller's—and I'd like to prove it before I retire. If she doesn't want to talk, I won't push her. I promise. You've confirmed what I needed to know, but two witnesses are better than one. Will you tell me her name now?"

Monica got out of her chair and paced across the kitchen. Finally, she spoke. "Miller killed my husband, and he's dead. If someone killed him because of what he did, it's what he deserved. Suicide or murder makes no difference to me. Leave it alone, Detective, and leave Dorella out of it."

"Dorella Dale? Is she married now?"

"I got remarried when Dorella was twelve. My husband adopted her, and we legally changed her last name. She's unmarried and still lives in Cookeville. She works in the cancer ward at the hospital. Our name is Dixon now. She goes by Ella. I'm confident she won't have anything to add."

Reese scribbled down the name and other pertinent information as they both sat in complete silence. "Thank you, Mrs. Dixon. Maybe she won't have anything to say, but I appreciate the chance to ask." Once back in Tennessee, his next stop would be the Cookeville hospital to find Ella Dixon. "I have one more question for you. Do you think Paul Miller was sent by Kingston Phipps to kill your husband?"

"Phipps is the real estate owner, right?"

Reese nodded.

"I don't know. Phipps is the one who benefitted the most, I guess. Miller seemed pretty shook up, so I don't know that he *planned* to shoot anyone. At the closing, the huge man with a crooked nose who also harassed us said Bobby's murderer committed suicide and wouldn't be a problem for me, but I should still keep my mouth closed if I knew what was best for my family. I believed him. We took the cash money and left for Cookeville. Until today, I never spoke of any of this."

"I apologize for making you relive it all, but I think I'm narrowing in on the man who's guilty of orchestrating all three murders—all *four* murders. You've helped, so I thank you. Mrs. Dixon, I'm sorry for your loss, and I promise to tread lightly with your daughter. Thank you for your time." Reese stood, shook Monica Dale-Dixon's hand, and exited her home. He had a flight scheduled for one o'clock that afternoon.

***

"Mama, I'm cold?" Noah shivered as he spoke, so Ella tucked his blankets around him.

"Noah, let me check some readings on you, okay? I won't hurt you." Ella took out his chart with his last recorded vital signs from the hospital. As she worked, she recorded the statistics. His blood pressure had decreased along with his oxygen saturation. His heart rate was higher, and his temperature had elevated slightly. He fell asleep as she tested him.

Beau quietly entered the room and observed. When he spoke, he startled Ella. "Your face looks concerned. How's he doing?"

She held in her yelp, but her heart pounded. She glared at Beau. "Why do I feel like I've seen you before?"

"Maybe at the hospital. I don't know. I'm fairly memorable."

"Maybe." Ella felt it was something else but didn't say so. "From the change in his vital signs, I'd say he has three days at the most. Studies have shown in the last three days of terminal cancer victims, there are marked differences, all of which he's exhibiting."

"Apparently, I'll be your babysitter for as long as he hangs on." Beau sat in a chair and arranged his arm in a comfortable position. "I like what you've done with your hair. You look exactly like Angie. I've done some reading about doppelgangers. It's German for 'double goer.' In German folklore, it's usually a spirit double—a sort of invisible replica. The traditional view is doppelgangers are sinister or evil entities. Does that describe you? Supposedly, seeing a look alike is considered an omen of misfortune or bad luck. Often it means death will follow."

"Is that a threat?"

Beau smiled. "Kingston suggested he could purchase your silence, but I think it's more likely he'll see you as a loose end. I don't make those kinds of decisions."

Ella tilted her head, thinking. "I haven't seen my look alike, but you have. Maybe you should be the concerned one."

Beau laughed. "You're the one chained to a bed."

"You're the one with a broken arm. And from the looks of that cast and the pins I can see, it's more than a simple break."

Beau's happy mood subdued. "What did you do to Kingston?"

"I'm confident I wrecked his knee, and I stabbed him."

Beau laughed again. "I think I like you. I'll put in a good word for you when this is over. Have you had breakfast?"

While Ella explained Kingston took her bagel and juice from her, Grayson entered the room. "Then she needs something to eat." Gray had Noah's pudding in his hand, but his son slept quietly. "Go ahead, Beau. I need to talk to her." When Beau didn't move, Gray said, "Listen. I sold my soul to the devil for a year, but that means I'm the right-hand man now. I'm your boss now. She'll be fine while you get her something to eat."

Beau stood without argument and left the room.

"Are you going to let me go?" Ella asked immediately.

"It's not so simple."

"It is to me."

"Yeah, but Noah thinks you're his mom. He's going to die soon..."

"Very soon."

"I figured." Gray pinched the bridge of his nose. "He cried for two days when his mother wasn't here. He stopped as soon as he saw you. I don't want him to suffer more than he already is."

"I've been kidnapped. That's a crime. If you don't let me go, you're an accessory."

"Yeah. I've considered that, but if I let you go, Noah suffers...*and* my dad gets arrested. As awful as he is, he's my dad."

"That means you're never letting me go. Is murder next?"

"No. I have to figure something out, but in the meantime, I can make sure no one hurts you."

"You can? Your father already tased me three times. He re-injured my ankle too, and he's punched me two times already today. You aren't doing very well."

Anger flashed in Gray's eyes. "I don't have the key to the padlocks, so even if I chose to get you away from my dad, I can't."

"What is your name?"

"Grayson. Call me Gray."

"That's ironic because you think you're in some sort of gray area with me, but it's not. It's black and white. Right and wrong. Either you free me or you're an accessory. You're a kidnapper. Maybe a murderer."

"My dad will pay you a lot of money to keep quiet about this."

"You think? If that was his plan, don't you think he'd have approached me to hire me to babysit Noah. The man's a psychopath. He's cold-hearted and calculating. He plotted out this kidnapping and used his aggression in a planned-out way to get what he wanted. He doesn't care he's hurting me. He's deranged."

"Angie—my wife—said he's a narcissist."

"You ever study psychology? The traits overlap. Psychopaths can't sense the feelings of other people or see the world from a perspective apart from their own. A sense of conscience or guilt won't stop them from behaving immorally because they don't have that sense. They think they're superior and like manipulating and controlling people— hurting people. But at the same time, they need to feel respected and admired and the center of attention. Does any of that sound familiar?"

"It all does."

"Where's Angie?"

"I don't know."

"Why would she leave her son?"

94

"She wouldn't."

"Yet she did."

Gray had nothing to say. He paused…looked at Ella.

She broke the silence. "Find the key. Get me out."

"Not going to happen," said Beau as he entered the room. "Here's a sandwich. Some yogurt, chocolate, and water. A spoon for you and Noah. I'll be right here if you need anything else. Grayson—I mean, Boss—you must have work to do with Daddy." He handed the items in a bag to Ella and smugly sat in a chair where he crossed his legs and grinned at Gray.

Noah awakened and said, "Mommy, I'm hungry." Ella yanked off the top of the lemon pudding and gave him a spoonful. He swallowed and looked at Gray and smiled.

"There has to be a solution that doesn't include any more violence or put people in prison. I'll work on it." He started out of the room and then turned back to Noah. "I'll be back soon, Noah. I love you."

"I love you too, Daddy."

Chapter 15

At a little past noon, Gray got a phone call from Shaggy Rogers. The number showed as coming from the Pickett County Sheriff's Department, so Gray answered on the second ring.

"Hello."

"Is this Grayson Phipps?"

"Yes, do you have information about my wife?"

"Yes, this is Detective Rogers. Your wife's car has been found at a rest area off I-40."

"Her car. But not her."

"I'm sorry, but no, there's no sign of her. Would you like to meet me there? We have a team on site going through the car."

Gray agreed and jotted down the directions—the Buffalo Valley rest stop on I-40 west at mile marker 267. He ran to his car and sped out of the driveway. He traversed the seventy miles in a little over an hour. When he arrived, Carl Donaldson and an officer with a dog gathered beside his wife's car with a scruffy-looking plain-clothed policeman whose police lights swirled unnervingly.

Gray jumped out of his truck and walked directly to Shaggy Rogers. "I'm Gray Phipps," he announced. "What happened?"

Shaggy shook his hand. "I'm sorry we don't have good news about your wife. I need you to take a look and tell me what you think…but don't touch anything."

"Well, it's her car. Her travel bag and clothes…and her purse, I assume. With everything scattered back there, it looks like someone went through her things."

"Is anything missing? All there is in the car are clothes and the purse."

"I don't see her computer."

"There's no computer. No valuables we could recognize. Money and cards gone from her wallet."

"Why is the car parked way down here? The restrooms are a long walk from here." Gray looked around for no logical reason for any sign of Angie.

"That's a good question. Detective Carlton told me she was supposed to fly out of Nashville. This is on the way, so maybe she stopped to use the restroom or get a snack or stretch or something, but why park here? But that's irrelevant anyway." Shaggy scratched his scruffy beard.

"Why's that?" Gray didn't like the grim tone of the detective's voice.

"Well, our tracking dog could easily get a scent from the car and clothes. Far as we can tell, she never exited the vehicle."

"That's impossible. She's not here."

"It isn't if she didn't drive the car here. But there are other clues. There are no keys. No prints on the steering wheel, door handles, seat belts, rear-view mirror, gear shift, visors, mirrors, windows, control buttons, garage door opener…except for two odd places. The car was nearly wiped clean. There weren't even any hairs on the seats. Vacuumed out is my guess."

"So the car was planted here?"

"That's what the evidence says."

"What are the two odd places you found prints?"

"How tall is your wife?"

"Five-eight."

"Is the seat where she'd normally have it?" Shaggy walked to the driver's side door and Gray followed. Using a gloved hand, he opened the door. "Get in. What do you think?"

Gray eased himself into the seat and stretched his legs out. He looked into the rear-view mirror. "It's too far back and too low. Someone else drove here."

"Well, we got a print from both the button that directs the seat back and the lever that lowers it. The only two prints we found inside the vehicle. A large person drove the car, and the driver forgot he had to move the seat to fit." Shaggy let those words sink in a moment. "I'll impound the car and go over it more closely. There are prints on the exterior, for instance. Since it was wiped down so thoroughly, they're probably your wife's or yours, but we need to check more carefully."

"Is there anything I can do?"

"Well, if someone stole her cards, you might check to see if they've been used. You better put a stop on them." Shaggy took a long look at Gray. "It looks like something else is bothering you."

"She didn't get on the plane. She didn't drive here. It looks like someone else drove the car here to hide it or at least make it look like she tried to get to the airport and was abducted. Wouldn't you think that means she's still back in our town? That she never left at all?"

"That's a logical assumption, but she could have caught an Uber ride or took a bus or borrowed a car or left with a friend. I mean, it looks like foul play, but maybe *she's* the one who staged it."

"I hope that's not what you believe. She's been missing for two days, and I'm worried about her. She wouldn't leave our son. Not on purpose. And she didn't write the note saying she was leaving. She's been taken."

"By amateurs. Or someone distracted enough to make mistakes," said Shaggy.

"I'll make some more phone calls to see if anyone's seen her and to check on the credit cards. Let me know when I can pick up the car, and keep me informed, okay?"

"I will, and Detective Carlton will be back this evening. I called him, and he was heading for the airport already."

Gray shook his hand. "Thank you." He returned to his car and headed back home.

***

Reese landed in Nashville at 3:30, and with his carry on, he exited the airport within fifteen minutes. He arrived in Cookeville after 5:00 and drove directly to Bradley Drive, where he learned Ella lived. The small ranch house was in no way extraordinary, but it was a cozy-looking place. A Kia Sportage sat in the driveway. He drove up behind it and used the license plate to look up the owner. Dorella Dixon. He exited his vehicle, walked to the front door, and knocked.

No answer. No movement. He tried again.

"The car's been sittin' there since last night. She always parks in the garage, so it's kinda odd." The neighbor across the street sat on his porch sipping sweet tea.

Reese turned to the neighbor. "Did you see anyone give her a ride?"

"No, sir. But I ain't been out here all day. I figured she was in the house. Quiet girl. Never hear a peep from over there 'cept when she mows her lawn."

"You hear anything last night?"

"Nope. But like I said, it's odd she parked in the driveway. Never saw her do that before."

Reese knocked one more time and then headed for the back of the house in case she was outside, but she wasn't. He tried the side door to the garage, which was unlocked, but he didn't enter except to see the garage had no other vehicle inside.

"Thank you, sir. I'll try to find her at her work," said Reese as he climbed back into his car. He backed out of the driveway and headed for the hospital.

He parked in the visitor parking lot off N. Cedar Avenue, entered through the Cancer Center entrance, and located Ella's name on the directory on the wall. He took the stairs to the pediatric ward and walked to the counter where Nurse Nancy spoke on the phone. He waited politely until she finished and asked, "How may I help you?"

"My name is Detective Reese Carlton from the Pickett County Sheriff's Department." He showed his badge. "I'm hoping to talk to Dr. Ella Dixon."

"She isn't here. She didn't show up to work today."

"Did she call in?"

"No one's heard anything from her. Not even Stacy, her best friend."

"Is Stacy here? Is it possible I could talk to her?"

"There she is right there," said Nancy. She pointed to the prettiest nurse he could remember ever seeing.

Reese approached her and displayed his badge. "I'm Detective Reese Carlton from the Pickett County Sheriff's Department. May I speak with you a moment."

"I'm busy here, but I can talk for a minute." Her gorgeous smile disappeared, a typical reaction to a questioning police officer.

"I'm trying to locate Ella Dixon. I wanted to ask her some questions about a case I'm investigating. She wasn't at her house, so I came here to talk to her."

Stacy bit her bottom lip and looked at Reese with her worried, pretty, blue eyes before she replied. "She worked here last night with me even on an ankle she sprained badly on Monday. She's tough. It's not like her to miss work."

"Nurse Nancy said you're her best friend. Have you tried to contact her?"

"A bunch of times. It's also not like her to not respond."

"Her car is at her house, parked in the driveway, but she isn't there. Is there anyone else she might be with?"

Stacy thought a moment. "I mean, yeah, I guess, but no one I can think of. She doesn't socialize much, and her mom is the only family I know of, and she lives out of state."

"Yeah, Arizona. Well, when you hear from her, would you have her give me a call?" Reese gave her his card with his cell number.

Stacy held it, read it, and then nodded. "Should I call the local police? You've made me even more worried now."

"It's been less than twenty-four hours since you've seen her, so that would be premature." Stacy seemed relieved to hear that. "Thanks for your time, Stacy. Oh, and if you think of anywhere she might be, will you let me know?"

Reese exited the hospital. Another dead end. He drove back to Byrdstown, wondering what to do next.

Chapter 16

"Beau, take a break," Gray said as he entered the room Friday morning. He'd figured nothing out, but he tossed and turned the entire night trying to determine a course of action.

Beau raised his eyebrows but left without a word.

Ella stood at the window overlooking the lake below. Gray stepped beside her and admired the view as well. It amazed him how much Ella looked like Angie, and it made him more anxious about her disappearance.

"Where are we?" asked Ella.

"We're about ten miles west of Byrdstown. The house was built on Safe Harbor Eagle Cove. That's Dale Hollow Lake."

"I thought it might be. We were headed this way before your dad tased me unconscious."

"I'm sorry."

"Do you have the keys to let me go?"

"No."

"Then you're not sorry enough."

Gray shuffled his feet...continued to stare at the lake. "How's Noah?"

"He's sweet...and hanging on for some reason."

"Because of you."

"If you're trying to make me feel like I should be here, it won't work. His mother should be here, not a kidnapped stranger."

"I'll help you...somehow." His hand reached for the holstered gun at his side. One option he'd considered was to kidnap Ella back from his dad and Beau at gunpoint.

Ella returned her gaze to the lake. "I used to live on a lake. At least that's what my dad called it. It was the Obey River Valley, but the property would flood regularly. I've dreamed of living on a real lake ever since we moved when I was nine."

"Why did you move?"

"You ever hear of Willow Grove?" Gray nodded his head. "Everyone moved. We were all forced to. It's down

101

there somewhere. My father's land. William Dale was my great-great grandfather. He was a government surveyor who came to this area to survey the boundary line between Tennessee and Kentucky. He was invited into the home of his soon-to-be wife, Rachel Irons. The Irons family was one of the five families who came down through the Cumberland Gap from New York before the Revolutionary War. They bought land from a Cherokee chief who sold it to them because they treated the natives with respect and traded with them fairly.

"Later, my great-great grandparents started Willow Grove. William Dale bought an additional nearly five hundred acres from a land developer. The government didn't honor the purchase, so he was forced to buy it again. The town grew and flourished. We had one of the nicest elementary schools in the state. And then the state decided to put in a dam, and we were all forced to leave."

Gray was a boy of eleven years old when the Dale Hollow Dam was built, but he knew his dad bought up all the land, including all the properties in Willow Grove. A sense of dread flooded his emotions. "Do you know my father's name?"

"No. You're Grayson Phipps, the father of Noah Phipps. The big goon is Beau. That's all I know."

"Have you heard of the stories of the missing men from Willow Grove?"

"Why do you ask that?"

"Two bodies were discovered at the bottom of the lake a week ago. Several years ago, I hired Pickett County's police detective to work with me part time at my construction business. When I asked him about the bodies, he called them 'victims' from Willow Grove, but he wouldn't tell me anything else. It was so important to him he flew to Arizona to talk to one of the widows instead of leading the investigation to find my wife."

"My father was one of the victims, and my mother lives in Arizona."

"What happened?"

"He was murdered."

"Are you sure?"

"I witnessed it. And so did my mother."

"Reese—my friend, the detective—is trying to find the murderers."

"I know who killed my father. Some guy named Miller. But he's dead." She stared out at the water. "The police ruled it a suicide."

Reese let out a sigh of relief. It wasn't his dad…unless his dad arranged for it to happen. It was hard to put it past him. "I'm sorry about your father."

"You know, we dreamed about a house on a lake. My dad would've given up his land if the realtor had promised him a lot like this. Lakefront. Great views. A dock and a fishing boat. Instead, we were run off and told to go away."

"I'm going to get you out of here. I'll make it up to you too…somehow."

"Give me your gun."

"What? Do you even know how to use a gun?"

"Of course. All the kids at Willow Grove knew how. We practically lived in a wilderness. If you aren't going to get me out, I'll get myself out. Your gun would come in handy."

"You're brave, but I can't have you shooting people. Then I'd be an accessory to murder *and* kidnapping. There's got to be a better way."

"He'll kill me, you know."

"Who, Beau?"

"Maybe…but surely your psychopath dad will. Noah will die soon. You're running out of time to figure something out."

Noah stirred, and Ella took a deep breath. She limped to his bed, dragging the chain behind her. She looked so much like Angie that Gray felt a tug at his heart. He had to help her, but he couldn't decide what to do.

***

103

"Officer Carlton, this is Stacy Howard. We talked at the hospital yesterday."

Reese had been in the middle of punching in Gray's number to let him know the prints extracted from Angie's car didn't match Angie's but also didn't match anyone in the database. Since he didn't look forward to springing the news on his friend, he took the call from the unknown number. "Yes, have you heard from Ella?"

"No, but I visited her house this morning, and she's still not there." She hesitated. "There's something you should know." Reese got out his notepad in case it was important.

"On Monday, we golfed. Ella told me she thought she was being stalked. She said she'd seen the same truck several times following her."

"Did she describe the truck?"

"She said it was a black Toyota pickup truck. She wasn't too concerned, and she didn't say anything about it on Wednesday, so I forgot all about it. But the longer she's missing, the more I wonder if I should've taken it more seriously."

"Did she see the driver?

"She didn't mention that."

"Hmmm. I'm going to notify the Cookeville Police Department. Something could be wrong. Do you happen to have a recent picture of her?"

"Sure. I'll send one to you."

"Thanks, and I'll follow up on this. I called her mother this morning, but she didn't answer, and she hasn't responded to my voice messages. Again, if you hear from her, have her call me, okay?"

"I will. Thanks for your help."

Reese ended the conversation, and seconds later, the text notification sounded. He glanced at the picture. It was of Stacy Howard and the nearly-as-perfect Angie Phipps, wearing a light-blue golf hat and a Vanderbilt golf shirt. He immediately texted Stacy. *This is a picture of Ella?*

Yep, took it Monday while golfing.

Okay, thank you.

Reese then called Gray. "Hey, I wanted to let you know forensics has confirmed the prints found in the car weren't Angie's, but they don't match anyone in the database."

"So there's no progress, in other words."

"I'm sorry, but that's correct." Reese paused, but Gray didn't say anything. "Uh, a weird thing happened today. I need to send you a picture. Hold on." Reese went to the text from Stacy and forwarded it to Gray. "Did you get the text I just sent?"

"Give me a minute." There was a pause. Finally, Gray said, "Is this recent? Are you telling me my wife's out golfing somewhere, while Noah dies alone?"

"Is that Angie? It was taken Monday. Is she living a double life or something?"

"What do you mean?"

"You know that case I'm working on? The one I went to Arizona for? Well, this is a picture of Ella Dixon, the daughter of the lady I went to visit. That's her best friend, Stacy, who works with Ella at the hospital in Cookeville."

"Yeah, I recognize the blonde girl. She helped with Noah occasionally."

"Right, and Stacy said her friend Ella's been missing since Wednesday night. The last time anyone saw Angie was Tuesday, and she's missing too. Stacy said Ella mentioned she'd seen the same truck following her several times. She voiced concern some stalker had done something to her. So tell me, is that a picture of Angie?"

"Well, it looks like her, but it can't be her. She's a tax accountant, not a doctor or nurse or whatever."

"She's a nurse practitioner. Don't you think this is an odd coincidence?"

"Yeah, I suppose. But does it help you find Angie? Because that's all that matters."

"Apparently, I'm looking for them both now. I'll let you know if I learn anything." He ended the call and drove to the title company to do the only thing he could think to do at the moment—check to see which Phipps realtor signed the settlement statements for the realty transactions for the three families whose husbands disappeared.

He gave the dates of the sales, Pickett County Real Estate as the realty company that made the purchases, and the names of the three selling families. He was told it would take some time, but they'd call once they recovered the settlement statements.

While eating Taco Bell in his car for lunch, Ashvi called from the coroner's office in Nashville. "Hey, good lookin'. How're y'all doin'?" she said when he answered. "Do I sound like a southerner?"

"You sound so mid-western, no one would know you're from Tennessee, let alone India. What's up?"

"ATF called the office today. I have a name for you for the original gun owner of that .38 Super."

"Hit me with it. I need some good news."

"It was first sold and registered to a Beau—B-e-a-u—Struthers, twenty-five years ago. Address in Byrdstown. He has no priors; I already checked."

"That's great. Will you fax me any paperwork they sent you? I'll look him up and have a chat with him if possible." Reese wadded up a taco wrapper and deposited it in the take-out bag. "Still on for the retirement party?"

"I am. Looking forward to it. I need to get out of this place…speaking of which, I'm crazy busy. I need to let you go. Just thought I should get you the news right away. I'll send you the fax as soon as I get a moment to myself."

"I appreciate it. Thanks. I have to get back to work as well."

After they said their goodbyes, Reese's phone tone rang again. It was Milly from the title company. "Okay, so we dug up the settlement statements. All three were signed by the same realtor, but unfortunately, all we have are initials. That's all that's required of the sales agent to show their approval of the sales."

"Well, initials are better than nothing. With some digging, I can probably match them up to a name. What are they?"

"B.S. All three are signed B.S."

"Hmmm, that's interesting. I just came across the name Beau Struthers, but I'm sure it's a coincidence."

"Uh, no, not really. I've been working here for twenty years. Beau Struthers is someone who I know personally. He's a huge man with a crooked nose and a big chip out of his front tooth. Trimmed beard and mustache. He's polite and rarely talks, but he's quite an imposing, intimidating guy. He's worked for Pickett County Real Estate for Kingston Phipps since I've been here. It's quite likely he's B.S."

"It's a small town, so yeah, I know who you're talking about. I didn't know his name, but B. S. could easily be the same person. Can I get copies of the signatures?"

"Sure. I'll copy the signature pages, and you can stop by and get them."

"Thanks, Milly. I appreciate the help."

"You're welcome. Glad I could be of service."

Reese sat back in his seat for a moment to think, and then turned the swivel mount for his laptop and did a data search for Beau Struthers. Ashvi was correct in that he had no record, not even a ticket, but when he accessed the Department of Motor Vehicles, he struck gold. He was able to access Beau's driver's license with a stoic, unsmiling face and bent nose, and he learned his address. Also, it listed his vehicles. He had two motorcycles, a Harley-Davidson and a BMW. He had a truck registered in his name too—a black Toyota Tundra.

All the information might give him enough ammo to get a judge to issue a warrant to have him questioned and fingerprinted.

Chapter 17

Gray sat on his bed, waiting to be connected to someone in HR at the hospital. Finally, a voice sounded. "Hello, this is Sherri. How can I help you?"

"Uh...hi...uh, I'm calling in for my daughter. Her name's Ella Dixon. Anyway, she's had a family emergency. It was...unexpected. Anyway, she won't be at work for a few days. I didn't want the absences to be unexcused...you know?" Gray began sweating. Lying wasn't his area of expertise. "Anyway, uh, she'll be gone for about a week. She's been tied up and unable to call, so I'm helping her out. Would you get the information to her supervisors?"

"What kind of emergency?"

"It's personal. I can't...won't say...because, you know, it's personal."

"Is it medical?"

"Uh, I have to go. She just wanted you to know."

Gray hung up and nearly had a panic attack. He stood, walked down the hall, and entered Noah's room. Everyone except Beau slept. In his left hand, Beau balanced a book with a sticker from Pickett Country Library on the front cover—*Jurassic Park* by Michael Crichton. "Getting some entertainment?"

Beau shrugged his shoulders. "I kind of like how terrifying dinosaurs are. I remember how two T-rexes fought over some poor dude and ripped his body in half. Can't find that scene in the book though."

"Maybe it's only in one of the movies."

"Maybe. I've always related to dinosaurs."

"It might be because of their tiny brains." Gray grinned to let Beau know he was joking. "Mind if I have a few minutes with the family?" He gestured toward Ella and Noah.

"Sure. I could use a break." Beau inserted a bookmark and dropped the hard-covered novel on his chair before he left.

The sun shined high over the lake, light reflecting beautifully on the water. Gray cleared his throat to wake Ella.

When her eyes flickered open, he asked, "Are you doing okay?"

"I'm chained to a bed in someone else's house. No, I'm not."

"It's my house now."

"Do you have the keys to unlock me?"

"No, but we need to talk." Gray sat down beside Ella, who had rolled over and sat against an arm of the couch. "First, I called the hospital. I told them I was your father, and you had a family emergency and would be out of work for a while." Gray fidgeted on the couch and rubbed his face. "It won't work because my detective friend, Reese, is searching for you. He's been to the hospital, and he's visited your mother. He'll get wind of my call and call your mom, I suspect. But it buys me some time to get you out of here. Second, I got a call from Reese today. He sent me this picture." Gray opened the text and tapped on it to display the selfie of Ella and Stacy.

Ella's eyes opened wide at the image, but she didn't say anything.

"He said this is your friend."

"Your dad said he'd hurt her if I didn't cooperate."

"Really? This is all so wrong."

"Then let me go."

"I will...when Noah dies."

"You're no better than the rest of them."

Gray held his face in his hands. "Reese is looking for you to talk about some murder victims in Willow Grove over twenty years ago. I don't know what you have to do with them, but it's some case he's obsessed with. He won't give up." A flicker of concern showed in Ella's eyes. Or maybe it was hope. Gray couldn't tell.

"If letting me go isn't the reason you're here, what's bothering you?"

"He sent me the picture because you look like Angie, and he knows Angie. He wondered if she's living a double life. I could've easily told him my dad kidnapped you." He paused, looking guilty. "But I didn't." He stared at the ceiling for a moment. Then he stared at his sleeping son. Finally, he spoke. "I hate myself."

"I'm not too fond of you either."

"Noah needs you. And I made a deal with my dad—who, by the way, I don't want to be responsible for putting him into prison. I'll figure it out."

"Give me your gun." Gray stared again at Noah. "I won't do anything until Noah dies, but once he does, your dad—or Beau—will kill me. I think you know that. If you can't get me out before that, at least you can help me to stop them from murdering me."

Gray put his hand on the holster, thinking. "I have another gun. I'll get it for you."

"I don't think there's much time."

"I think you're right." He took his eyes off Noah. "I don't know how many more bad things can happen all at once."

"Two more."

"What?"

"Bad things happen in fours to me. The ankle sprain started it all. The kidnapping is number two. There are two to come, and they're worse."

Gray stared at Ella, bewildered, but then Beau returned. He bit off the end of a popsicle, lifted his book from the chair, and sat back in the seat.

Noah stirred, so Ella and Gray walked to his bed without continuing the conversation. Noah looked at the two. "Hi, Mommy. Hi, Daddy." He yawned and then grimaced.

Gray put his hand on Noah's head. "Hurting?"

Though it wasn't true, he shook his head no and forced a smile. "I'm thirsty."

Ella had been taking his pulse, but she stopped to hold a cup and straw in front of the dying child. Gray steered the straw into his mouth. He took a tiny, slow sip and grimaced again. Ella looked at the clock on the bedstand and then adjusted his pain medication. Before she finished, he fell back asleep. "Soon, Gray," she said quietly so Beau wouldn't hear. "His time is running out, and so is mine."

Gray inhaled deeply, kissed Noah on the forehead, and walked past Beau without acknowledging him. Things were moving too fast, and he still hated himself.

***

After Gray returned from his and Angie's house with a second loaded gun, he sat on the dock, staring over the lake, watching the sun set and trying to figure out what to do next. His cell phone rang. He saw the call came from Reese. "Hey, I hope you have good news for me. I could use some."

"Unfortunately, I don't. And I apologize for calling, but I need to talk to a man named Beau Struthers. I assume you know him, and I'm hoping you could give me his phone number."

"He works for my dad. I have his number. Do you mind me asking what it's about?"

"I have some questions for him. I need him to come into the station."

Gray forwarded the number from his phone contacts and went back to staring across the lake, wondering how his life could get any worse.

Chapter 18

The next morning, Beau stood in Kingston's office, his arm back in a sling for support. Nothing rattled him, so when he told Kingston Detective Carlton had asked him to come to the station for questioning, he didn't seem fazed at all.

Kingston, on the other hand, looked anxious as he continuously clicked his pen. "What do you think he's going to ask you? After the discovery in the lake, I figured *I'd* hear from him. I'm not sure why he wants to talk to you."

"He's fishing...hoping I'll say something stupid. I won't say anything stupid."

"You won't say anything. I'll send Mike Adams over with you so you have an attorney present. He'll make sure you don't say anything at all." Beau could tell Kingston's massive ego was hurt, knowing he wasn't the one Reese wanted to talk to, especially since he repeated himself. "He talked to *me* before. I don't understand why he's questioning *you* now."

"Stop worrying. If he had any evidence of crimes, he'd be making arrests, not asking questions, but I have to go. It'll be all right."

Beau made the short drive into town and entered the police department late in the morning with Attorney Adams. The police officer who greeted them escorted them to an interview room where there was a bottle of water and a sheet of paper and a pen. The page had Beau's name and then some blank lines for his birthdate and address and a line to sign his name. Adams said, "Don't even touch them." Beau sat calmly, not moving until Reese and Shady Rogers entered and sat down across from him. Beau ignored Reese but nodded politely at the other officer.

"My name is Detective Reese Carlton. This is Detective Rogers. We're videotaping this interview, but I want you to know you're not under arrest. Also, you're not obligated to answer any questions other than your name, date of birth, and your address. It appears you're exercising your right to have an attorney present. But remember, if you say anything incriminating, it can be used against you. Is there anyone who knows you're here…because if not, you have the right to notify someone."

"Why *am* I here?"

"Do you understand your rights?"

"Yes."

"Please state your name, date of birth, and address."

"Beau Struthers. February 28, 1960. 111 Willow Drive., Byrdstown, Tennessee." Beau noticed Reese looked at the paper to see if he'd written anything, but he didn't say anything about it being left blank. The paper and pen were in the same place they were when Beau sat down.

"What did you do to your arm?"

"It's broken. I don't know why you asked me here, but I'm pretty sure it ain't about my broken arm."

Reese extended a piece of paper to Beau, and he held it steadily in a position where Beau couldn't read it. Beau sat still. Adams reached for the paper and set it in front of Beau. The paper named him as the original owner of a .38 Super revolver, purchased from The Gun Shop in Livingston County twenty-five years earlier. Beau read it, acting almost disinterested. "Are you the owner of that gun?"

"No."

"Beau," said Adams, "I advise you to not make any comments."

"But you *did* once own it?"

"No comment."

"How long did you own it?"

"No comment."

"Were you aware two bodies were recovered from Dale Hollow Lake last Friday?"

"No comment."

Reese picked up the paper Ashvi faxed over from the ATF and put it back in a folder with some other papers. "Okay, then let's move on. Are you a boater?"

"No."

"Again, Beau," said Adams, "it's best to not talk. Why is my client here?"

"We're following some leads on an active investigation. That's all I can say," said Reese. "Mr. Struthers, do you know what a clove hitch is?"

Beau scrunched his face in confusion, and shook his head no.

"Do you know what a figure eight knot is?"

"No comment. I don't understand what these questions have to do with me."

Reese extended three other papers to Beau, who didn't budge, so he spread them out on the table in front of him. "These are the settlement statements for three home purchases at Willow Grove twenty-three years ago. Are those your initials?"

"It looks like it. Yes, I believe so."

"So you were the one who signed the papers for the title company on behalf of Pickett County Real Estate?"

Beau inhaled, but his attorney interrupted. "Beau…"

"No comment."

"Do you recall the families whose names are listed as the sellers on these documents?"

"No comment."

"Did you know Paul Miller?"

"Yes, we worked together."

"Do you think he committed suicide?"

Beau looked at his attorney who shook his head. "No comment."

"Okay, let's move on to something else entirely. "What do you know about Angie Phipps's disappearance?"

"Only that she packed and left and don't live with Grayson anymore."

"Grayson Phipps doesn't think she left on her own."

"Is that a question?" asked Mike Adams.

"It seems odd she left her dying son," Reese replied.

Beau looked at Adams. "Am I supposed to say something?"

"How about no comment?"

Beau shrugged. "No comment."

114

"Here's a question," said Reese. "Do you drive a black Toyota Tundra?"

"You already know the answer to that," said Adams.

"I do. Have you driven that truck into Cookeville recently, Mr. Struthers?" Reese crossed his arms and leaned back in his chair, glaring at Beau.

"I think the answer to that is no comment."

"All right..." Reese leaned forward, putting his elbows on his knees, his chin only slightly above the tabletop. "Do you know Ella Dixon?"

Beau squinted in confusion and looked at Adams, who tilted his head and raised his eyebrows. "No comment," said Beau.

Reese grabbed the water bottle in front of Beau and twisted off the cap. "Oh, I'm sorry. Would you like some water? You've done a lot of talking; you must be parched."

Beau made a polite grin. "No thanks."

Reese took three swallows from the bottle and set it back on the table. Finally, he said, "I don't think I have any other questions. Detective Rogers? Do you have any?"

"No, sir." Shaggy had been holding his hat in his hand, but he put it on his head.

"All right then," said Reese. "That's all the questions I have for you. You're welcome to leave. We thank you for coming in on a Saturday. If we have any other questions, we'll let you know."

"Okay," said Beau.

"Have a good day, gentlemen," said Adams.

Shaggy stood and opened the door for the two men and directed them down the hall toward the exit. When he returned, he commented. "That didn't go well at all. Did you learn anything?"

"Mostly," said Reese, "I wanted him to know I'm working and putting some things together. He was cool as a cucumber, but he'll tell Kingston Phipps what I asked, and I'm confident I'll hit a nerve with him. I want him nervous."

"What's next?"

"I need some help. I need fingerprints for Struthers and Phipps. As far as I can tell, Struthers never touched a thing in here, so I can't get prints from the interrogation. I have a gut feeling Struthers or Phipps has something to do with Angie Phipps's disappearance. I'm certain they have something to do with the murders twenty-three years ago, including that of Paul Miller. And this weird coincidence of Ella Dixon disappearing too and looking exactly like Angie Phipps feels wrong also. But I'm running out of time, and something in this case needs to break soon."

***

Kingston sat at his desk in the lake house, worrying as Beau told him about the interrogation.

"He asked a lot of random questions, most of which seemed unrelated, but some of which were a bit unnerving."

"Like what?" Kingston stood and began pacing.

"He asked how I hurt my arm, but maybe he was making small talk. After that, he asked about my old .38 I owned when you bought up the Willow Grove properties. There was a document from the ATF, showing I owned the gun. How would he know anything about it?"

"The man's working hard. Must have something to do with the bodies he recovered, but who knows?" Kingston had to sit back down. The pacing killed his knee.

"He mentioned the bodies from the lake, and then he asked me some odd questions about boating. I'm not sure why."

"Well, the bodies would have had to be dumped in the lake after the land was flooded. A boat would be needed for that." Kingston gulped down a drink. Were things getting out of his control again? He'd have to do something about that.

"I'm not sure what he was getting at. Then he took out the settlement statements to three Willow Grove sales—Hill, Stone, and Dale. I was the realtor at the closings."

"That proves nothing, Beau. Only that I bought the houses, and you got a commission."

"It ties me specifically to the three missing men, so it's not nothing."

"What else did he ask you about?"

"Paul Miller, Angie, and Ella Dixon."

"Anything accusatory?"

"Well, he asked what I drive and if I'd been in Cookeville recently, but that's the only thing he said that sounded like he was suspicious. How did he come up with Ella's name?"

"That's extremely odd. What could possibly tie you to her?" Kingston rubbed his temples and looked out over the lake as if the sunlight glinting off the soft waves might give him a revelation. "Clearly, he's digging and hoping something turns up. He didn't learn anything from you, did he?"

"No. He knows the gun was mine. He knows I signed those documents twenty-three years ago. He knows what I drive, but he knew all of that before I came in. He didn't learn anything else from me."

"Beau, I think it's time to get some other people involved. We need to call in some favors to keep Carlton from learning too much—from *doing* too much. We have to get out ahead of this. He knows about too many things, and he's coming for me."

"You aren't the only one who has something to lose. He's coming for me too," said Beau. "I have an idea, though. I'll let you know if I work something out."

They ended the conversation, and Beau headed back to Noah's room. Kingston groaned from worry and pain. He stepped into his bathroom, removed his suitcoat, undid his tie, and unbuttoned his shirt. His forehead sweated but he felt chilled. He eased off the bandage on his shoulder and gasped. It was red and swollen, and pus seeped from the wound. He took a thermometer from the vanity drawer and tested his temperature—100.2. He finished his drink, which helped deaden the pain in his knee, but then he smashed the glass on the floor in anger. Ella Dixon would pay for what she'd done to him, but first, he needed to have her look at his injuries.

He re-dressed, poured another full glass of bourbon, and gulped it down. His head buzzed as he headed off to see Ella.

***

Kingston limped into the room. "Beau, I need some time with Ella."

Beau slipped his bookmark into his book and settled his arm into his sling before heading back to Kingston's office.

"I need you to look at my shoulder." He smelled of booze. His bloodshot eyes and red, splotchy face demonstrated his drunkenness as well.

He glared at her with intensity in his eyes, so Ella didn't argue. "Let me see it."

Kingston unbuttoned his shirt. Red swelling surrounded the purulent wound. A soft scab had been ripped open during the day. Ella reached the back of her hand toward his forehead, so he flinched back. "I was checking for a temperature."

"I just checked. It's 100.2."

"You have an infection."

"How do I get rid of it?"

"See a doctor in an after-hours clinic or the hospital. You need antibiotics and stitches."

"You're a doctor. I'm seeing you."

"I can't exactly write you a prescription in my particular circumstance. And I can't put in stitches either."

"So what can I do now?"

"Soak it in a warm, saltwater solution. About two teaspoons of salt with a quart of water. Put some antibiotic ointment like Polysporin on it. Drink plenty of cold fluids and take Tylenol for the fever and some ibuprofen like Advil for the pain. Put a clean bandage on it to keep it closed. But without an antibiotic, a thorough cleaning, and stitches, the infection won't go away."

"This is your fault." Kingston glared at Ella.

"You can tell yourself that, but I wouldn't have stabbed you if you didn't kidnap me. I never did anything to you."

"I do whatever it takes to make sure I get what I want."

"Stabbing you was what I had to do to try to get away. What's the difference?"

"The difference is I don't care what you want. I operate in my own best interests, and getting stabbed isn't in my own best interests, so you'll pay for it. It's how I always do things."

"Who are you exactly?"

"I'm Kingston Phipps—owner of Pickett County Real Estate. I'm the man the state of Tennessee chose to develop Dale Hollow Lake because they knew I could get it done. They got their dam and their energy, and I got my millions."

"I've heard the words 'Willow Grove' more than once since I've been here. You were behind the sale of those homes?"

"Every one of them."

"How did you manage that?"

"Money talks."

"What if it didn't? What if someone didn't want to sell?"

"Then I used other methods."

"Such as?"

"Threats. Intimidation. Blackmail. Harassment. Most of the people took the money and disappeared."

"And the ones who refused? Did you ever turn to violence?"

"When it was necessary."

"Have you ever killed anyone before?"

"I usually have Beau do the dirty work for me."

Ella glared at Kingston, but she kept her thoughts to herself. She made her way to the picture window overlooking the lake. "All for this? Was it worth it?"

"This is merely a thing. I have lots of things. It's Gray's thing now, and I'll get another one. After all, I own land all around the lake. What's worth it is the respect I have. The power I have. The ability to make people do what I want them to do."

"What happened to Angie?"

Kingston didn't answer. He put on his shirt and smiled. Finally, he said, "Enjoy your days as a mother. It's unlikely you'll have a child of your own." Then he limped out of the room to look for salt, a warm, wet towel, and some items from his medicine cabinet. And another drink.

Beau returned as if on cue and sat back in the chair to finish his book. "He's a lovely man, don't you think?" He laughed. "He pays well, and he's been like the brother I lost, but he's a bit personality deficient."

"He's a psychopath."

"And a narcissist. You ladies all peg him exactly right."

Ella continued her gaze over the lake. "I hope not. I really do."

Chapter 19

Gray's phone rang. He stepped out onto the deck outside his bedroom which overlooked the lake to answer Reese's call. "Any news?"

"Not what you want to hear, but I questioned Beau. He lawyered up, and I didn't learn anything from him, but I asked some questions that should cause some alarm."

"About your murder obsession or about my wife?"

"To be honest...both. And I need to ask a huge favor."

"No promises but spit it out."

"I need fingerprints of both your dad and Beau."

"No."

"I want you to give this some thought—please. Is it possible Beau had something to do with Angie's disappearance? Think about the clues. And if Beau is involved, most likely, so is your father. I know that's not easy to hear, but fingerprints were left in Angie's car and at your house. At the least, we'll eliminate them as suspects. Or we could be finding answers. I understand you don't want to do it, but I hope you'll consider it."

"I'll consider it, but only because some things don't add up, and I'd like to have some answers. Eliminating those two will help ease my mind, but if either is involved, I don't know what I'll do."

"If you get me the prints, I hope you'll trust me I'm determined to find answers. I don't want you doing anything."

"I've been doing nothing. I don't like the feeling. I feel helpless and restless...angry and sad. And as much as I don't like any of those feelings, feeling helpless is the worst...and being indecisive sucks too. I feel so out of control of my life right now."

"You have a son to take care of. That you know. I'll take care of the detective work."

"Except you need me to do something that might hurt my father."

"What if your father did something to Angie? Have you thought about that?"

"She warned me. She believed in her soul he was an awful person, but as much evidence as I've seen in my lifetime, I refused to believe it. I'm still having a hard time even considering it."

"Will you at least let me know what you decide? Wednesday's my retirement day. That's four days from now. If you don't help me, I'm likely to do something I shouldn't. I'm highly motivated to find the answers."

Once the call ended, Gray made his way to Noah's room. Beau sat in his chair, half dozing. The bookmark stuck up at the last page of the book. He looked up when Gray entered. "How was the book?" Gray nodded at the paperback sitting on the nightstand.

"I liked the book ending better than the movie. The island was napalmed, which is what should've happened. Why take a chance for Jurassic Park two? But I guess that's why the movie left the dinosaurs on the island."

"Mind if I read it?"

"Not at all, but it's due back at the library in a week."

"Do you mind if I spend some time with Ella?"

"I'm headin' home for the night tonight anyway, so maybe I'll leave early." Beau stood from his chair, nodded at Ella, and left the room.

Gray went into the bathroom and grabbed a hand towel. He carried it across the room and grabbed the novel carefully by the pages, being sure not to touch the cover. He laid it on the towel and lightly wrapped it, figuring Beau's fingerprints were all over the library book's plastic covering and the bookmark. He removed a large zip-lock bag from his pocket and slid the book inside. Without saying a word, he walked to stand in front of the huge window. The sun was setting to the west. Ella dragged her chain up next to him and stood by his side.

"It's beautiful," she said. "I wouldn't ever get tired of looking at it. I hope my days aren't numbered."

Gray took the extra gun from his waistband and handed it to Ella. "You sure you know how to use it?"

"I'm confident I could shoot you right now."

"See why giving you a gun was such a dilemma? If you do, at least you'll have put me out of my misery. I'm pretty confident the end result would be you'll die too, so I'm hoping you'll show restraint." He smiled.

"I won't shoot you…today, at least. Maybe some other time." She smiled too. "What's the book in the towel for?"

"I don't want to touch it, but also the towel hides what's in the bag. Reese wants fingerprints from my dad and Beau. I finally decided I'd just give him Beau's. Feels better."

"Beau had nothing to do with my kidnapping, so this has to be about something else."

"Believe it or not, it's Angie's case that has unidentified fingerprints. But it might have something to do with the murders from twenty years ago too. Not sure."

"You think Beau might have done something to Angie?"

"I hate to think it, but she didn't leave on her own. That's about the only thing I'm sure of in the past few days." He looked at Ella. "I feel on the one hand, this is a waste of time and a huge betrayal, but on the other hand, I have a lifetime of experiences telling me nothing is beyond the realm of possibility with my father and Beau."

"Hmmm. We've talked a few times—Beau and I. He has a lot of respect for your wife."

"Angie wasn't intimidated by my father, and she spoke the truth to him while no one else seems to be able to do that. Even my mother simply ran away and divorced him rather than confront him. Angie was a fighter. Beau respects a fighter because that's what he knows. But I never got the impression he had such respect for her."

"I have that impression, but maybe it's something new." Ella stared out the window at the sunset and sighed. "Noah will die soon. If there's something you need to say to him, you'd better say it soon."

"Will he make it through the night?"

"I think so."

"Then I have something to do first. I have to meet Reese. I won't tell him about you—maybe ever—but definitely not until we say goodbye to Noah. I'm sorry, but I'll come back tonight." He started to leave, stopped, and looked at Ella again. "Will you tell him you love him? Tell him you'll see him with Jesus someday? That's what Angie would say."

"I can do that." She walked away from the window, dragging the chain into the bathroom, and hid her gun. Then she returned and watched the sun set alone, wondering if Noah's death foreshadowed her own.

***

Gray got in his truck and backed out of the driveway as he called Reese on his cellphone.

"Hello," Reese said. "Before you ask, I don't have any news about Angie."

"It's not that. I have Beau's fingerprints. Where can I meet you?"

"Meet me at the construction site. I'm near there, just finishing dinner. Plus, it's discreet. I can do that for you."

"All right. I'm on my way. Should be less than ten minutes."

Gray and Reese arrived together and parked in the dirt driveway of the new-build Gray needed to finish. They both stepped out of their vehicles and shook hands. "How's Noah?"

"He'll pass soon. Maybe today."

"How are you?"

"Awful."

"I'm sorry."

"I know." Gray looked out into the trees standing in the lot. "I'm sorry I got angry with you. You can have the business. My dad gave me the lake house. He promised it to me and Angie. She would be happier there. But I had to agree to spend a year with him, learning how to run his businesses. I can't do that and this job too. It's yours if you want it."

"Thank you. I'll consider it. I'm also considering moving away. Thirty years here seems like enough."

"I can understand that. Angie wanted to leave too. I think she was right."

"You should head back home to Noah."

"Yeah." Gray opened his truck door and took the zip-lock bag from the passenger seat. "Beau's been reading this book. His fingerprints should be on the front and back cover and the bookmark. I hope they don't match, but if they do, will you tell me?"

"I'll think about it. I don't want you to do something stupid."

"I deserve to know."

"You do. I'll think about it." Reese shook Gray's hand and leaned in for a buddy hug. He patted Gray on the back. "Thank you."

Gray nodded slightly and stepped around his truck to get back into the driver's seat. He backed out of the driveway and drove away.

***

Gray returned to the room, looking reluctant. Ella had Noah's chart out and had finished recording a new set of vital signs. Both his blood pressure and oxygen saturation levels had decreased again. His temperature continued to be elevated as well. She looked at Gray. "I'm sorry. He's tough, but I don't think he'll make it through the night. It's time to say your goodbyes."

Gray sat down on the edge of the bed and gently shook Noah's shoulder. His eyes flickered open, and again, amidst pain and fatigue, he smiled. "Hi, Daddy."

"Hey, buddy. Mommy says it's time to say goodbye." Tears welled in his eyes.

"Are you going away?"

"No, sweetie, you are."

"To be with Jesus?"

"That's right. He's calling for you, I think. He must want the best boy on Earth to be with him soon."

Ella grabbed his hand. "You'll run and jump and laugh."

"Tell me about Jesus."

125

Tears formed in Ella's eyes also. "He loves you so much, he wants to spend time with you in Heaven. He'll take care of you until I can come to be with you."

"That's what David the king told his little boy too."

"You know so much," said Ella. "You're not only sweet, you're also smart. Maybe you'll play with David's little boy."

"I love you, Mommy." Noah squeezed her hand.

"Hey, what about me?" said Gray.

"I love you this much." He held his finger and thumb about two inches apart and grinned.

"Is that all? I love you this much." Gray spaced his hands about a foot apart.

Noah smiled. "I love you this much." He released Ella's hand and with much strain, held his arms all the way apart. He then looked at Ella. "Mommy, I love you as big as this room."

"Oh, really? Well, I love you as big as this house."

"I love you as big as an ocean."

"Ha. I love you as big as the Earth. Try to top that one."

"I love you as big as outer space, Mommy. I love you bigger."

Tears streamed down Ella's face. She leaned in and kissed Noah on the forehead. "You go to sleep now, Noah. You definitely love us the most. We will miss you."

Gray gave Noah a kiss too and turned away so his son wouldn't see the tears running down his cheeks.

Noah almost immediately drifted off to sleep, a smile on his cute but thin face.

Gray plopped in the chair Beau used when he sat in the room with Ella. He cupped his hands over his eyes and sniffled. He settled his breathing. Ella watched him without saying a word, wiping her tears away with the back of her hand. "I need to go get my dad, so he can see Noah one last time."

When he exited, Ella went into the bathroom and retrieved the gun Gray had given her. She slid it into the waistband at the small of her back and stood in the bathroom doorway. A few minutes later, Gray returned alone. "He's passed out on the coach. Drunk. Again."

"Did you get his keys?" Ella looked hopeful.

"I checked. I couldn't find them. Pockets, desk drawers, key rack. I don't know where they are." Gray could see the skepticism in her eyes. "I looked."

Ella nodded. "Stay in here tonight. You should be here if he passes." She sat in her chair. "This isn't going to end well. I know. The third bad thing will happen when Noah dies. The fourth thing will be worse. It always is." She didn't say anything else, leaving Gray wondering what she was talking about.

Chapter 20

Noah slept through the night and through the whole morning except to get a swallow of water one time. At 11:33 on Sunday morning, he breathed his last breath. Gray broke down in tears once again. He buried his face in little Noah's chest, trying to mask his weeping. When he finally lifted his head, tears dripped onto the bed. "Angie should've been here. I've lost everything."

"I'm sorry for your loss, Gray." Tears filled Ella's eyes, as well. "He was a sweetheart, but he's not suffering anymore."

"My heart is broken, and I don't even have Angie to share the pain with."

"I can't even imagine how you feel, but I think my heart's broken too. And I'm dreading what's going to happen next."

"I think Angie had it right. She wanted to get away from here and start our own life without my father involved. It's looking like a good plan."

"You're certain that's not what she did?"

"I believe it's what she *would have* done—she didn't even want this house anymore—but her disappearance before Noah died makes no sense, and there's plenty of evidence she didn't plan to leave when she did. Something happened to her." He looked away so Ella wouldn't see the tears rolling down his cheeks. When he composed himself some, he asked, "How can I live here without her? Without our son? I don't think I want the house either." He wiped his eyes with the sleeve of his shirt and then walked into the bathroom to blow his nose. He looked into the mirror and didn't like what he saw. "What do I do next? Call an ambulance?"

"Beau told me there was a hospice nurse. Call her and have her return. It's Sunday, but there should be an answering service at whatever funeral home you've chosen. She'll call, and they'll come for Noah."

Dejected, Gray grabbed his phone and located the contact number for Nurse Connie. It went to voicemail, so he left a message telling her the news and explaining she needed to return and then contact the funeral home. Ella took off her walking boot and examined her ankle. It was still swollen, but the bruising had turned more of a yellow color than the previous black and blue. She walked gingerly to one of the bags of clothes Kingston had packed for her and tried on a tennis shoe. It was uncomfortable, but it felt better than her boot. She took out a pair of jeans and a shirt.

Since all either of them had eaten was a bagel, Gray left the room and cooked an early lunch of bacon and scrambled eggs with juice for himself and Ella, and he returned with the plates. "I'm not the greatest cook, but I can make eggs. You're probably hungry."

They sat in silence, eating. When they finished and Gray grabbed her fork, plate, and juice glass, Ella said, "What's next? For me, I mean."

"What I'm hoping for is a big check. A few days ago he said he'd pay you well—that money solves most problems. I hope he meant it. Could you walk away from this and not go to the police?"

"Your dad won't let me walk away."

Gray's cellphone rang before he could respond. Ella slid off into the bathroom and closed the door as much as possible with the chain in the way. She put on the long-sleeved cotton shirt which hung well past her waistline. She checked the safety and tucked the gun into her waistband and prayed she wouldn't end up dead.

Gray's call was from the hospice nurse, so he explained the situation and told her to return to the lake house. While he spoke, he noticed his father leaning in the doorway, looking awful. When the call ended, he broke the news about Noah.

"Why didn't you wake me so I could say goodbye?" Ella put her ear to the door to listen.

"I tried to. You were passed out drunk."

Kingston limped to Noah's bed. He placed his hand gently on Noah's shoulder and stared at him for a long moment. "The funeral home is coming for him?"

"No. Ella said the protocol was to call the hospice nurse, and then she'll call the funeral home to send someone for Noah."

"She can't be here when they come."

"Then let her go."

"I can't do that."

"You have to. You brought her here for Noah. Now Noah's gone. Let her go."

"She stabbed me. She ruined my knee. She has to pay for that."

"You kidnapped her. You tased her three times. You twisted her ankle. You beat her. You deserved what you got. Did you even consider maybe you could've paid her to watch Noah? So pay her to leave. You said that's lesson one. You *told* me you'd pay her well. You said money solves most problems."

"No." Kingston's face turned red from anger, but he calmed himself and spoke in an even tone. "I'm going to move her, and you'll make funeral arrangements. We'll talk about her again, but for now, we're going to move her and keep her quiet and out of the way. You're an accessory to this kidnapping, so we have to think through what to do with her. For now, I won't hurt her."

He left the room momentarily and returned with keys and the taser. He unlocked the padlock securing the chain to the bed and told Ella to open the door and come out slowly with her hands up. "I'll take her downstairs to the furnace room." To Ella, he said, "Bring a blanket, a pillow, a light jacket—whatever you need to be comfortable for a few hours."

Ella first put on a hooded sweatshirt, further hiding the gun at her back, and then grabbed a blanket and pillow like Kingston suggested. Kingston grabbed the end of the chain and aimed the taser at Ella. "Walk." He directed her down the hallway and stairs to the bottom floor. Then he guided her to a door into a room with a cement floor, a work bench, a commercial sink, a furnace, hot water heater, and sump pump. "Wrap it around you?"

"What?"

"The chain. Wrap it around your body."

"Seriously?"

"I could shoot you with my taser and do it myself, but my shoulder and knee hurt. Do it."

Ella picked up the chain and had to turn her body in 360-degree increments to get it wrapped around her arms. She spun slowly until she was no more than five feet from Kingston. "Now what?"

Kingston shot her in the leg, and she dropped like a stone on her back onto the cement floor, spasming. He looped his free end through the chain wound around Ella's body. He pulled it tightly and wrapped the end around the leg of a workbench, locking it securely. There was a roll of duct tape on the bench, so he slapped a piece firmly over her mouth. He put her head on her pillow, tossed the blanket haphazardly over her body, and looked at Ella, who glared at him. "I said I wouldn't hurt you. I lied." He limped away without looking back.

***

By noon, Reese had his results. Beau Struthers's fingerprints were on the supposed letter and envelope from Angie, on the Coke can, and on the seat adjuster buttons in Angie's car. Beau was in Angie's house and had wiped prints clean, but he was sloppy. He'd driven Angie's car to the rest stop, but he'd made a mistake there as well. Someone must have picked him up, so he had an accomplice. So where was Angie? And what other deductions could he make from what he'd learned? The first was Angie didn't pack to leave Kingston's lake house because she wouldn't have left some of the items Gray found in the house. Someone packed for her. The second was the neighbor lady was right when she said she thought she saw two people in Angie's car. Someone—most likely Beau—forced her to go to her house to make it look like she was leaving town. Third, Angie knew she was in trouble and considered using Gray's gun but decided against it. Which led to the fourth assumption. Angie chose something else to protect herself. A softball bat. It was wiped clean of prints, so Beau must have touched it too. Reese knew he was reaching to assume Angie had used it to break Beau's arm, but it fit the timeline and explained Beau's silence about the injury. From the look of the cast and the pins he could see, something had done some serious damage, and a softball bat could do the trick.

While he spent time deep in thought, his phone rang. It was Stacy from the hospital. "Hello."

"Mr. Carlton?"

"Yes."

"This is Stacy, Ella's friend. I wanted to tell you I haven't heard anything from Ella—not even a text. But today I was told Ella's father called the hospital to say there was a family emergency and Ella wouldn't be in to work for a week. Tied up with some personal problem. Do you know how to reach her mother?"

"I'll give her a call. She wasn't too keen on me talking to Ella, and she's never answered any of my calls before, but if Ella's having some sort of family emergency when the police are considering her to be a missing person, I'd think she'd call me back for that. Thanks for the information, Stacy."

Reese ended the call and immediately tried Monica Dale-Dixon, but she didn't answer, so Reese left a message telling what he'd learned from Stacy and asking for confirmation or denial of the claim.

Back in thought, Reese figured he had enough evidence to get an arrest warrant for Beau in the missing Angie Phipps case. He figured the news Beau's gun was used to kill Stephen Stone and John Hill would be damning as well and would play into the D.A. pressing charges. If that didn't go well, he figured he had enough to get a judge to issue a search warrant for Beau's house, where maybe more evidence could be found. He'd have to wait until Monday morning, but that would give him three days to solve his case. Cases. Maybe three cases. And maybe they were all tied together somehow.

Chapter 21

Kingston hobbled upstairs and poured a drink. He made three phone calls dealing with the annoyance of Reese Carlton, and then he called Beau with the news and asked him to come to the house as soon as possible. "The situation with Ella is under control," he explained. "It's the Reese Carlton situation we need to get a better handle on." As he settled onto his desk chair for a second drink, the doorbell rang. Connie stood on the front porch, her purse in her hand. Kingston grunted at her and told her she knew the way to Noah's room. "I'll get you a check for the three days you were away and for today…and a bonus for keeping quiet about not being here." He turned his back to her and groaned in pain as he started away.

"My lips are sealed. I'm sorry for your loss," she said. Kingston's only response was a closed door as she stood alone at the entryway. She made her way to Noah's room. Only Gray was present, standing in front of the huge window, looking at the lake below. She stepped quietly to Noah and confirmed the obvious. He was no longer among the living. "I'm sorry, Mr. Phipps. Mrs. Phipps must be devastated. Is she here?"

"I'm not sure where she is right now, Connie." He kept his gaze on the water while he wiped another tear from his eye. "I think you're supposed to call the funeral home. It's Crestlawn. Do you have a number?"

She confirmed she did and made the call, leaving a message. Fifteen minutes later, she took a return call and gave the address. Less than an hour later, they arrived and loaded Noah into the hearse as Beau parked in the driveway. The hearse driver explained Gray needed to follow them to the home to help them make arrangements for the funeral. "Your wife should come too."

"I don't know where she is right now," said Gray.

"That makes it more important for you to be there when we deliver his body. Your wife can come when she's available."

Beau went directly to Gray and engulfed him in a one-armed bear hug. "I'm sorry, Gray. He was a good kid. We'll all miss him."

"He's not suffering now. Apparently, suffering is reserved for me. Thanks, Beau."

Beau sucked in a deep breath and let it out slowly. He didn't make eye contact…just nodded his head several times and walked away, eyes directed on the cement at his feet.

Gray got in his truck and drove off behind the hearse. Beau entered the house as Kingston handed Connie her check. Connie left without an escort to the door. "You okay?" Beau asked.

"Gray will marry again and have more kids. Eventually, he'll accept Angie left him, and he'll move on and have a healthy boy to give his heart to. He's a better person than I am, but that doesn't mean I'm about to change." Kingston poured another drink and offered one to Beau. When Beau shook his head no, Kingston spoke again. "I made some calls today…called in some favors. I want to know if you're doing anything on your end to keep Carlton's nose out of my business."

"As a matter of fact, yes. It's best if I keep it to myself for now, but I called in a favor too. Things should be handled in a day or two at the most."

"Okay. That's what I hoped I'd hear." Kingston reached into his suit pocket and grabbed his truck keys. "Take my truck for a few days. Seems Carlton has his eye on yours."

Beau caught the keys with his left hand when Kingston tossed them over. He took his keys out of his pocket and tossed them to his boss, who reached out and missed them. They banged off his desk and jingled when they slid off and hit the floor. Without another word, Beau left Kingston alone with his filled glass and his drunken, depraved, selfish thoughts.

***

Once the shock passed, Ella lay on her back, angry, for quite some time. Eventually, she took note of her circumstances. Chained in close proximity to the workbench, she had no room to move, but the loops around her body weren't tremendously tight, so she could move her arms. On the bottom shelf of the workbench, among other tools, she saw a medium-sized screwdriver she decided to try to procure. She worked her right arm painstakingly out of bondage and gripped the tool in her hand. Working her arm back inside the chain loops, she managed to slide the screwdriver into the kangaroo pocket of her hoodie.

As she lay there on her back, she could hear voices, footsteps, and doors opening and closing. In time, it all became silent, and that made her nervous. If she ended up alone with Kingston, there would be trouble.

Once Kingston had the house to himself, he finished one last drink and reloaded his taser so it had two shots again. He put the gun in his suit pocket and headed for the furnace room, courageous from the alcohol. His left shoulder ached constantly and each step on his right leg sent a painful message to his brain. He hated Ella for hurting him, so he looked forward to hurting her back.

When he opened the door, Ella's head rolled to the right, and she made eye contact. She was in nearly the same position as he'd left her except the blanket covered only a small portion of her body. Ella took deep breaths and tried to calm her nerves. He ripped the tape from her mouth, leaving a red mark across her face, but Ella said nothing. "Sit up," Kingston said.

Using only her abs, she managed to sit upright.

"I didn't realize how enjoyable this would be. And here I always had Beau or someone I paid do the dirty work. I didn't know it would bring me such pleasure. I'm going to torture you, and then I'll most likely kill you."

Ella didn't say a word. She didn't move. She tried to think of a plan, but everything depended upon her getting the use of her arms. All she could think to do was flatter the man and hope his threats were empty.

"I enjoy being powerful. I enjoy making you fear me. I enjoy knowing you're helpless and I'm stronger than you."

Finally, Ella spoke. "I don't fear you, but I *do* recognize you're stronger than I am. I respect your power…your wealth. I can see how people respect you, and I can see how you brought me here because you cared about Noah and Gray."

Kingston turned his head and looked at Ella curiously. "Are you for real? Didn't you hear me say I'll most likely kill you?"

"I'm sorry I hurt you. That was before I figured out what you were doing. That was before I knew who you are."

Kingston was drunk. Drunk from alcohol but also a warped sense of self-worth, and his mind was trying to wrap itself around Ella's words.

"There's something I don't understand," said Ella.

"What's that?"

"I don't understand why Gray is so hesitant to work for you. I think I'd jump at the chance, personally. The hospital is stressful. But being in charge of a business…having people answer to me—that would be a dream."

"Gray's mom poisoned his mind against me. I'm not saying he doesn't have family loyalty…I mean, he kept his mouth shut about your kidnapping, but he thinks I'm too egotistical. He thinks I need to always get my way. That I'm manipulative. He doesn't respect me like he should, so he's tried to make it on his own. All I've ever wanted was for him to be like me."

"Why don't you unchain me from this workbench and take me back upstairs to the bedroom—lock me back up there—and maybe I can talk some sense into your son—sense that his wife obviously didn't have. Give me a couple of days with him, and I'll have him happy to be your apprentice by the time of the funeral, and then, together, you can decide what to do with me."

Kingston fought the effects of his bourbon. He fought the effects of his narcissistic pride. But finally, he staggered over and unlocked the chain from the workbench and dropped the key into his pants pocket. Slowly, Ella started turning in 360-degree circles, and the chain unwound. None of her moves were hasty or aggressive. She settled her hands into her sweatshirt pockets and stood completely still, trying to look relieved, humble, and contrite. She gripped the handle of the screwdriver and waited for Kingston to direct her forward.

Again, Kingston aimed his taser at her. "To Noah's room?" Ella asked.

Kingston nodded his head yes, but the movement made him lose his balance briefly. Ella yanked her hand from the sweatshirt and impaled the screwdriver into Kingston's infected shoulder. He cried out in pain and dropped the taser. He reached for the handle, focusing his attention on the gushing wound. Ella took one step toward him and jumped, bending her knees. As she came down, she kicked her feet. Using her weight combined with the strength of her legs, she smashed into Kingston's kneecap. His injured right leg buckled backward, shattered. He dropped like a rock to the ground, screaming out in agony.

Ella climbed off the floor and bent over to pick up the taser. She shot him with it, sending him into convulsions that rolled his eyes up into his head. While he shook in agony, she grabbed the padlock key from his front pocket and unlocked the chain around her left ankle.

The kick to Kingston's knee made her ankle throb, but she ignored the pain and laid the chain out on the floor. She pushed one end under his body, wrapped the chain around his torso and arms, and pulled it tightly, locking it with the first padlock. Kingston recovered enough to begin to struggle, so Ella calmly picked up the taser and shot him again. While he was still convulsing, she started rolling him over the chain, occasionally grabbing the free end and tightening it around him. She continued the process until its entirety enveloped him. His body lay on the floor at the base of the block wall. She then locked the other padlock.

She helped him sit up, his back against the wall while sitting on a thin, flat eight-by-ten rug. The screwdriver, though he'd rolled over it several times, was still embedded in his shoulder. Fear and pain showed in Kingston's eyes. He swore at her. "Beau will kill you. You can't run far enough away. Your life is over."

Though adrenaline shot through Ella's veins, she calmed herself. "I remember you."

"What are you talking about?"

"You weren't so fat and ugly. Probably not an alcoholic in those days. Twenty-three years ago, you looked more like Gray, but I remember you coming to my home and trying to convince my parents to sell our house. When they stood firm, you started sending Paul Miller to threaten us."

"Who are you?"

Ella laughed. "You didn't realize you kidnapped Dorella Dale, did you? My dad was Robert Dale. My mom was Monica." Recognition showed in Kingston's eyes. "You know, all we wanted was our own lake house. If you would've offered us a plot of land after the lake formed, my dad would've sold to you."

"And what? Built another shack on a parcel of land where I built a million-dollar home, where the lot alone was worth more than your house?"

"So you sent Paul Miller to kill him? I was nine years old when I had to witness him murder my father."

"He wasn't supposed to do that."

"Of course not. He was only supposed to threaten us, hoping my dad would sign, and then you would've had him killed. Beau, most likely, because you're too pathetic."

"I paid your mother well for the plot."

"You think? What did Gray say you said? 'Money solves most problems'? Well, it didn't for my mother and me. We lost my dad, and that money barely gave us enough to start over."

"Your beef is with Miller, not me. And he's dead. He committed suicide."

"Again, is that what you think? My father always preached to my mom and me that if we wanted something done right, we needed to do it ourselves. We learned to take things into our own hands. Miller didn't commit suicide. My mother strung him up and killed him. I watched while pointing the gun at him that was used to murder my father."

Kingston's eyes opened wide in fear as Ella took Grayson's gun from the back of her jeans. "Bad things always happen in fours to me. And the fourth is always the worst because it's death. It's death at my own hands. The sprained ankle started it all. Then a kidnapping. Then I watched your sweet grandson die. And now, I'm going to watch you die."

Ella clicked off the safety, stepped within a few feet of Kingston, and emptied six shots into his chest. As Kingston tipped over sideways and fell on the floor, blood began pooling on the rug. She picked up the key from the floor, unlocked the chain, and uncoiled it from around Kingston's body. She grabbed a rag to use so she wouldn't leave fingerprints and went to the kitchen on the lower level where she found some rubber gloves, Dawn dishwashing liquid, and a soft dishwashing brush. Ella filled the furnace-room sink with water and dishwashing liquid and then carefully washed every link clean with the brush. She did the same with the locks, the key, and the screwdriver before draining the water and thoroughly washing the sink. She stuffed the chain, locks, and key under the workbench, and finally, she used the rag to wipe the gun and taser clean.

Still wearing rubber gloves, Ella grabbed the blanket and pillow, walked up the stairs, located the room she deduced Gray slept in, and put the gun, the screwdriver, and the taser in a dresser drawer under a pile of folded shirts. She entered Noah's room, replaced the pillow on the bed, grabbed a washcloth and filled the sink with hot water and Lysol. She proceeded to wipe down everything she could imagine she touched in the bathroom and Noah's bedroom as well as Kingston's bathroom. After she emptied and cleaned the sink, she put on the pair of jeans she had set aside and refilled the grocery bags with her clothes, all of Angie's make-up and the toiletries she had been using, her pillowcase, and her walking boot and carried them and the blanket out of the room. Then she hobbled across the kitchen and out the front door, free, stuffing her rubber gloves into a clothing bag. She looked into the sky for the setting sun and turned the opposite way, heading east across the driveway. It was there she saw Beau's black Toyota Tundra sitting unoccupied on the pavement. Behind it was a trail. There was no way she'd risk Gray or Beau discovering her on the road, so she ducked her head under a low-hanging branch, catching it on her hoodie top, and snapping it off to lie in the dirt on the trail. Without looking back, she limped away from the lake house.

Chapter 22

Ella entered the trail and headed east. That's all she knew. What she didn't know was she had entered the Highland Rim of the Eastern Temperate Forest. Between her and the city of Byrdstown were ten miles of trees, rocks, and streams if she managed not to get lost. The only decent road she might cross would be Tennessee Route 325, but not if she tried to keep the lake within view. If she trekked north of Route 325, she might cross a couple of small roads that were barely used. The only other peopled area she might stumble upon was Cordell Hull Birthplace State Park. But not knowing anything except she was ten miles west of the city of Byrdstown, she started her hike.

She had a few hours before the sun set completely, but the forest was already dark, and she knew if she could somehow manage a pace of one mile every thirty minutes, it would take her five hours. If she got lost, it would take longer. It would be dark long before she could make it to Byrdstown, and her ankle ached from the kick to Kingston's knee. She carried no water, but she figured she could drink from a stream along the way. It was a warm August day, so she removed her hoodie, folded her blanket, and carried them along with the bags, assuming she'd have to sleep in the forest that night.

After an hour of walking, her arms were exhausted. She went off the trail and found a leafy area to bury her clothes and other items she'd removed from the house. After a moment of considering putting the walking boot on, she decided against it. It would slow her down, so she buried it with the bags.

As the evening ticked away, her ankle began aching, making her regret her decision to leave the boot behind. She folded the blanket in a manner that she could wrap it around her lower body and then used her hoodie over the top of the blanket to tie the sleeves tightly and hold the blanket in place. Then she found a decent stick to use to help her walk and take some of the pressure off her ankle. Eventually, at a

141

stream, she cupped her hands to catch some water and take a drink. It was getting dark, and the trail she used disappeared. She could no longer see the sun, so she began to doubt she was still heading east.

It was time to stop before she got lost. She figured in the morning she could find the sun rising in the east and get back on target for Byrdstown. To her left, she saw a rock outcropping that could give her shelter, but being on the ground worried her. It looked as though she could climb the rock several feet to a flat spot overhead she could sleep on. She leaned her walking stick against a tree and put her left foot on a rock. She stepped up, putting her weight forward as she leaned against the wall. She settled her right foot, the injured one, on the rock and stepped up to the next foothold jutting out, but her right foot stood on the hanging blanket, and she couldn't step all the way up. The blanket pulled her, and she fell backward. Instinctively, she tried to land on both feet, but her injured foot landed on a slanted stone, and she turned her sprained ankle.

She didn't hear a bone break, but it felt like it. She lay on the ground, fighting tears. The pain was excruciating. She rolled into a sitting position and rolled up her pantleg. The swelling was immediate, and Ella was certain she'd torn a ligament. She tried to stand, but the pain kept her on the ground. She needed ice, but the best option she had was the stream, so on her hands and knees, she crawled back to the water. She took off her shoe and sock and placed her foot in the water. In the near darkness, she had to decide how to proceed. The best thing she could do was ice and elevate her foot, so she needed to try to find a place where she could lie down with her foot above her heart yet in the water still. After a few minutes of navigating the waterbed on her hands and knees, she gave up. She found a level area, put on her sweatshirt, pulled the hood over her head, and wrapped the blanket around her body twice. She lay down with her foot in the water.

After an hour of listening to horrifying forest sounds, somehow, she managed to fall asleep.

***

When Gray returned after an exhausting evening at the funeral home, he needed rest. Beau's truck sat in the driveway, but when he looked in the garage, he could see his father's truck was missing. That made him nervous. His father hadn't left the house in days. He hurried inside and headed down the hallway toward the room Noah had occupied. Ella wasn't there and neither were her things. He ran to his father's office. He was missing too. After a quick trip around the top floor, there was no sign of Beau either. So down the stairs he went. No one occupied the living room or lower-level kitchen. Knowing Ella had been taken to the furnace room, that's where he looked next.

Lights blazed, and his eyes immediately fell on his dad, fallen over on the floor, partly leaning against the wall, blood thick on a rug, his leg broken in a gruesome, awkward angle, his eyes open, staring in horror. His dad had been shot numerous times and possibly stabbed. He was already cold in death when Gray touched his father's cheek with the back of his hand. He closed his eyelids, feeling guilty about his thoughts. "This is the way you deserved to go, Dad." He sat on the cement, his back to the wall and tried to think of a happy memory, but he couldn't. He'd lost his wife, his son, and his father. Was there anything else bad that could happen? He spoke out loud. "Yeah, there is."

He looked, and there was no sign of the murder weapon. He slid open the glass doors and ran down the steps built into the mountainside down to the water, wondering if Beau was dumping another body in the lake like Reese suspected from twenty-three years earlier. But the boat bounced in the light waves at the dock and appeared unused. The only explanation about the missing truck was Beau or Ella had it. Maybe Beau had Ella in it and was taking her to her execution.

He began thinking logically. His father's dead body lay in the house, certainly murdered by the woman he'd kept hostage in his own home. What would he tell the police? His father wasn't murdered by him but rather, by the woman he'd kidnapped and kept against her will? A woman who'd left no sign of her presence in the house? A woman who he *gave* his gun to? Besides, after murdering his father, there's no way she'd admit to anything, including the kidnapping, so who would be the number one suspect? He would be. He had motive, opportunity, and the means. He'd inherit millions, and what a convenient way to get his wife to come home—no father-in-law, a beautiful house on the lake, and millions of dollars. And he was certain Ella had used his own gun to kill his father. That would be further evidence he'd be seen as the murderer.

He needed to find Ella. If she went to the police, Gray was going to prison. And if she didn't go to the police, her life was in danger because Beau wouldn't rest until he found her and made her suffer. He made another walk through the house. No Beau. No Ella. No *sign* of Ella. He went back outside and circled the house, looking for who knew what. But when he made it to the side of the driveway next to Beau's truck, he saw the broken branch lying in the path into the woods. It was getting dusky, so he shined his phone flashlight onto the path and could see faint traces of footsteps. Ella may have left on foot.

He headed back into the house for a sweatshirt, a ball cap, and hiking boots he kept at his father's house. He took some food, a water canteen, and numerous other items he thought he might need, including a flashlight and a pocketknife. He stuffed the articles into a backpack he also stored at the house and slid it over his shoulders. Then he locked the house doors and headed into the forest to try to catch up to Ella before she got to the police or Beau found her.

Gray thought back to his conversation with Ella about their location. He'd told her the house was ten miles west of Byrdstown. If she planned to trek back to civilization, Byrdstown was way closer than Cookeville, where she worked and lived, and way easier to navigate because the sun sets in the west and rises in the east. It would be easy to make it through the trees keeping the sun behind her as it went down and in front of her when it came back up. There was no telling how much lead time she had, but she escaped on a gimpy ankle, so if Gray hurried, he figured it was possible to catch her. Chances were, she'd have to finish her hike in the morning, so Gray had some time. In a forest, it would be unlikely to find her, especially at night, but Gray happened to be an excellent hunter, and hunting sometimes included tracking. He stepped over the broken branch, recognized how the leaves had been disrupted on the path, and focused on what he assumed was Ella's escape route.

Chapter 23

According to an app on his phone, Gray covered a mile in thirty-three minutes. It was a slow pace, but it was dusk, and the trees made it dark in the woods even though there was some light in the sky. He navigated using his flashlight and keeping his eyes barely in front of his feet. Occasionally, he saw deer hoof marks indicating the "trail" was naturally made. Besides rustled leaves, he'd seen no other sign of Ella. About five minutes later, he noticed the first oddity. Ella had turned off the trail and headed into the woods...but then it looked like she'd returned. To save time, it made the most sense to ignore the detour, but curiosity got the best of him.

He laid his backpack in the trail and settled his flashlight against it, shining its light into the sky, so he could easily find it when he returned. He then used his phone's flashlight to guide him on his detour. She'd made it back to the trail to the same spot she entered, so common sense told him he wouldn't have to go far to see what she did. Maybe it was just to go to the bathroom. About thirty yards from the trail, the disruption through the vegetation stopped, but he could see she'd dragged some leaves together in a pile. He pushed them aside and found two bags of her clothes and her walking boot. Gray picked them up and walked another twenty yards deeper into the woods where he found a downed tree lying over some soft ground. With his bare hands, he dug a hole and buried the clothing.

He kept the walking boot because he had a bad feeling Ella's ankle wouldn't hold up well in the forest. He spread leaves over the dirt and then used his pocketknife to cut off a branch of a pine tree. He used the pine bough to rake over the leaves as he made his way back to the shining light. When he finished, Ella's detour was indiscernible. He turned off his phone flashlight, put the boot in his backpack, and put his arms back in the straps. It took him twenty minutes, and when he started back on the trail, the sky was completely dark.

Gray followed the trail another mile when he noticed another difference. Ella had begun using a stick to help her walk. Forty-five minutes later, the trail appeared to stop, but Gray could see the deer had veered toward a stream, probably drinking from it and crossing to the other side. He scanned the ground, trying to figure out what Ella had done. Mountain rocks jutted from the ground to the left, making a wall about seven feet high. He scanned it thoroughly, including stepping up a few feet to see if she had climbed to the top. When he didn't see her, he made his way to the stream to the right. His light illuminated a trail on the other side where the deer had crossed.

Gray turned on the flashlight app on his phone and nearly doubled the illumination because to his right, it looked like something had dragged along the ground, but it stopped down the stream, so he made his way back. The dragging marks continued upstream, and that is where he found Ella asleep, wrapped in a blanket, a hoodie covering her head and face. Her foot lay in the water, swollen and bruised. He shut off the flashlight app and sat down two or three steps away. He whispered her name. "Ella?" She didn't stir. "Ella, it's Gray. I can see you're hurt. Let me help you." He repeated himself two more times, the second time, more loudly.

She sat up and scooted back several feet, moaning lightly as she dragged her foot from the water. Gray shined the light on his face. "I'm not here to hurt you. I'm here to help you. I have a plan that will benefit us both."

"How did you find me?"

He couldn't see Ella, hearing only a disembodied voice that sounded tired and weak. "I did a lot of hunting and spent a lot of time in this forest when I was young. It was better than being home. Anyway, you were following a deer trail, so it wasn't too difficult."

"Why are you here?"

Gray understood she didn't trust him, considering the circumstances, but he needed her help, and she needed his. "We have a major dilemma, but I have a plan to fix it."

"Have you been in your house?"

"Yep."

"He was going to kill me. If he wasn't such a narcissist, he would have. He tased me again just for the fun of it—bound me with the chain, locked it up, tased me, and left. When he came back, it was either him or me." Gray didn't shine the light in her face, but he could hear anger and possibly fear in her voice.

"I believe you. Come back to the house with me, and we'll fix this."

"I don't trust you." She moved farther away.

"I could leave you here to try to get out of the forest on your own. If you make it, Beau will hunt you down and kill you."

"How do I know you won't kill me?"

Gray felt sadness nearly overwhelm him. "My wife is gone. My son is gone. My father is gone. I had no control of any of those things, but I have control of my future, and it doesn't include violence unless I'm forced to protect you from Beau. Or the police. I'm not going to kill you. My father didn't mean it when he said he'd pay you well. Now I have the resources to do it, but we need to do some things together first."

Ella hesitated, sighed, hesitated some more. "Do you have your gun?"

"Yes."

"Give it to me. I don't want you shooting me while I sleep."

"Are you going to shoot me?"

"I didn't last time you gave me a gun. If you want me to trust you, you'll have to trust me."

"You *did* shoot someone with my other gun."

"It was either him or me. Do I need to worry about you? If not, give me your gun." Gray took it out of his holster and handed it to her. Putting the gun in her hand, she gestured with it. "Now empty your bag and your pockets."

Gray did as she said. Out spilled her walking boot, a camping pillow and a light blanket, a pocketknife, granola bars and peanuts, his canteen, water treatment tablets, Benadryl, bug spray, and a rope. He handed over his knife, the rope, and a granola bar. "In case you're hungry."

"I am. Thank you. I could use a drink too."

Gray took two swallows from the canteen and reached out, handing it over to her. "Keep it."

Her voice softened. "Why did you bring a rope?"

"It seemed best to be prepared. It was lying next to my hiking boots and canteen I've used hiking the trails around here, so I grabbed it."

"Anything else you might use as a weapon?"

"Well, I could use your walking boot to kick you." Gray put the remaining items back in his bag.

"Give me that too. I'm going to need it…in the morning. I'm going to try to sleep again. You can sleep over there." Ella pointed to the rocks on the other side of the trail.

"You know I could hit you with a rock or a tree branch or something if I wanted to hurt you."

"Do you?"

"No, we need to solve our problems together."

"Then go get some rest, and I'll let you know what I think in the morning."

"Here's my flashlight too. I've got my phone light."

"Thanks." Ella flipped on the flashlight, tore apart the granola wrapper, eating the bar hungrily. Gray watched as she washed it down with a long drink. Ella nodded her head toward the rocks. "Over there, Grayman. Before I change my mind and shoot you."

"You're calm for someone who committed a murder," Gray said as he started to walk away.

"I'm sad. I'm afraid for my future. My heart hurts." She sniffled. "And my ankle is killing me." She tried to laugh but failed. "But it was inevitable, Gray. Bad things always happen in fours for me, and the fourth is a death I'm responsible for. It was either him or me. I chose him. There were no other options."

Gray turned his phone light app on and finished his walk across the trail. He only said three more words. "I know. Goodnight."

***

There once lived a Polish man in the late 1800s to mid-1900s by the name of Frank "Rocky" Fiegel. He lived in Chester, Illinois, the hometown of Elzie Segar. It was said Elzie created the character, Popeye the Sailorman, based on Frank Fiegel. The chief of police in Byrdstown was named Rocky Frank. Ironically, Chief Frank had a prominent chin, smoked a pipe, and had a history of tall tales of his physical strength and legendary fighting skills. His barrel chest and huge biceps added to the picture, and behind his back, nearly everyone called him Popeye. Reese always thought it strange "Rocky" wasn't a good enough nickname, since Rocky was a famous fighter with the same physical attributes.

Reese knocked on his door early Monday morning with a file in his hand. Chief Frank invited him in, and Reese sat in front of his desk. "Morning, Chief."

"Morning, Carlton. What can I do for you?"

"I wanted to run a few things past you. I'm hoping to visit the DA today to get charges pressed against a man named Beau Struthers. I'd also like to ask a judge for a search warrant for his home and truck."

"What's in the file?"

"Details of the Angie Phipps case. She's been missing since last Tuesday morning. Her son is dying of brain cancer, and her husband is certain she would've never left. Things were packed, but things were left behind in her father-in-law's home she would've taken if she left for good. A plane reservation was made to Hawaii, but she never boarded the aircraft. At her home, more things were taken but not a swimsuit or pictures of her son, which, of course, is odd as well. A letter was left, explaining she was leaving, but there were grammar errors her husband claims she'd never make. The place was wiped clean of prints except on a Coke can, on the letter on white copy paper—that didn't exist in the house—and on the envelope it was stuffed in. Her car was found at a rest stop, but she never got out of it—the dog got no sniff of her whatsoever—so someone drove it there to abandon it. It was made to look like the car was robbed, but the whole car was also wiped down except for two buttons for the seat that was lowered and moved way back. All the prints match a man named Beau Struthers. I would like to arrest him for the kidnapping of Angie Phipps."

"You think you have the guy?"

"This is a bad guy, Chief. He works for Kingston Phipps. As you know we found two dead bodies in Dale Hollow Lake out in front of Phipps's house. They belonged to two men who went missing twenty-three years ago—men I was convinced Phipps murdered, but I didn't have evidence. In the autopsy, we matched the bullets to a gun Beau Struthers owned. He's a bad guy, Chief, and I'd like to bring him in and prove it."

"Well, besides the fingerprints, it's a lot of circumstantial evidence for a kidnapping, but with the gun evidence too, I think it's enough to take to the DA. Good detective work, Carlton. Go for it."

"Thank you, sir."

Reese stood and left the office. The moment the door closed Popeye made a call to the DA. "DA Morrison's office. How may I help you?"

"Morning, Carla. This is Chief Frank. I need to speak with your boss."

"Yes, sir. Hold please."

The chief was on hold briefly, listening to Kansas sing "Carry On My Wayward Son" when the chorus was interrupted by DA Martin Morrison. "What can I do for you, Chief?"

"Good morning, Marty. My lead detective is on his way to you to seek an arrest warrant for Beau Struthers. I'd appreciate it if you didn't give it to him."

"Yeah, I already received a call about that. I'll put a stall on it as long as I can. Is there something to the warrant that's concerning?"

"There is, but Detective Carlton is retiring Wednesday. I assume it'll all go away once he's done."

"Okay. That's good to know. Have a good day, Chief."

"Yeah…you too." Popeye replaced the phone on the cradle while the song repeated in his head. "Hmmm, 'carry on my wayward son; there'll be peace when you are done.' Sometimes I wonder." He picked the phone back up and called Judge Judy Swanson.

"Pickett County Circuit Court. How may I direct your call?"

"Good morning. This is Chief Frank. I'd like to speak to Judge Swanson."

"One moment, please."

Almost immediately, Judge Swanson answered. "Hello, Chief. I thought I might hear from you."

"Yeah, well, I'm sorry to bother you, Your Honor, but my lead detective, Reese Carlton, might stop by to see you today in hopes of getting a search warrant for Beau Struthers's home and vehicle. I told him to go for it, but I would appreciate it if you turned him down." Popeye took a swallow of his cold coffee and nearly gagged.

"I assume you encouraged him, then?"

"Oh, yes. He's an excellent detective. His file is full of evidence and clues, but he's retiring Wednesday, and I'll put his investigation to rest after that if he doesn't come up with something new and better, like possibly an eyewitness."

"I'm sure I can delay a warrant until your detective finds more evidence. Will he find more evidence?"

"Remains to be seen. But if he does, favors or not, we'll have to charge Struthers."

"That's the law," said Judge Judy. "Thanks for the call."

"You bet. Have a good day."

Popeye hung up the phone, carried his tepid coffee out of his office, and dumped it into the kitchen sink. He knew his detective. If Beau Struthers kidnapped Angie Phipps or killed two Willow Grove property owners, Reese Carlton would likely figure it out.

Chapter 24

When Ella woke up, Gray sat ten feet away, looking into the gurgling stream. "Well, you didn't hit me with a rock or branch in the middle of the night. That's a good start."

Gray smiled. "Good morning. I won't hurt you. We need each other's help."

Ella's ankle looked better than she expected. The stream was cold enough to limit the swelling. She wiped the water off with her blanket and tried to stand. Tried. The pain dropped her back to the ground. Gray rushed over. "Are you okay?"

"No. I'm sure I tore a ligament. Will you help me get my sock and boot on?"

Beside her, Gray located her shoe with the sock stuffed inside. He took it out and rolled it up so he could pull the fabric over her toes. "Point your toes out. I'll be careful." Once the sock covered her foot, Ella gingerly inserted it into her boot. Gray took two granola bars from his backpack and shared one with Ella for breakfast. "Will you tell me what happened?...With my dad, I mean."

"He bound me in the chain like a mummy and locked me to the workbench. Then he tased me because he was a psychopath. While everything was going on upstairs, I managed to get a hand free and took a screwdriver from the bench and slipped it inside my hoodie pocket. He told me he was going to kill me after he tortured me. I told a bunch of lies to play to his narcissism, and he decided to lock me back up in the bedroom where I could talk you into accepting him and his business. He unwrapped me, and I stabbed him, broke his leg, and tased him. And then I shot him. A lot. Then I cleaned the place. There are no prints on the chain, lock, or key. None on the gun, taser, or screwdriver. None in the bedroom or bathroom. I collected my things, hid the chain and gun, and left."

"I'm sorry, Ella. I said I'd protect you from getting hurt, and I didn't." Gray looked off into the stream and tore open his breakfast bar. "I'm an accessory to kidnapping. I gave you my gun, so I'm probably an accessory to a murder too..."

"It was self-defense."

"He was stabbed, his leg was shattered, and he'd been tased. You didn't have to kill him. You murdered him. We need to cover it up."

"It'll look like you murdered him."

"Yep, so we need to cover it up."

"I could let you take the fall."

"I'm not going to go to prison for murder, so I would be forced to tell the police about you. You've been missing. You look exactly like Angie. Beau will confirm you were in the house. Maybe I'll spend time behind bars for being an accessory to a kidnapping, but maybe not. This is a dumb conversation though. We need to cover it up and keep our mouths shut."

"And worry about Beau."

"Yeah, there's that. But do you have a better idea? I swear if you come back with me and help me, I'll never say a word, and I'll make sure you're compensated well. I'm the heir to a fortune."

"Before I decide to be bought off," said Ella, "I have an important question for you."

"Okay."

"When I escaped, there was a black Toyota Tundra in the driveway. Is that yours?"

"No, it's Beau's. Why do you ask?"

"Because I saw it following me Friday night and Saturday morning. I saw it following me twice on Monday too. I think Beau was following me. When did Angie disappear?"

"Last Tuesday."

"And then on Wednesday night, your dad kidnapped me...not Beau...your dad. Why didn't Beau do it?"

"Because his arm was broken. Broken on Tuesday. Surgery was Wednesday morning. My dad picked him up from the hospital and took him home."

"Are you doing the math? If Angie disappeared on Tuesday and I was being followed starting Friday, then they planned this out. They didn't kidnap me because Angie disappeared. They made Angie disappear, knowing they planned to kidnap me to take her place."

"Crap. Dad hated Angie because Angie hated him—had him figured out. And he knew she planned to leave after Noah died...and I'd go with her. So he got rid of Angie and got me to play along with you, thinking it was best for Noah. I became an accessory. He planned to kill you all along, and he played me. He's so selfish and in love with himself."

"Narcissism doesn't mean self-love. It's more of a disorder where he was in love with an idealized, grandiose image of himself. That image he created in his mind helped him to avoid deep feelings of insecurity. That self-centered, arrogant thinking led to behaviors like lack of empathy or consideration for others, a need for admiration, and being manipulative, patronizing, and demanding. Your father was worse, though, because he was a psychopath. He willingly lied, hurt people, and acted outside social norms and laws, all without distinguishing between right and wrong and without remorse."

"I hate to say it," said Gray, "but I'm not going to miss him."

"I have another question. How do you think Beau broke his arm?"

Gray thought through what he remembered from the evidence at his house, and then it hit him. "Angie could have done it with a softball bat. That would explain why it wasn't under my bed and why it had been wiped down."

"And it would explain Beau's new respect for your wife. If she fought to survive and hurt him in the process, maybe that's why he spoke about her to me the way he did."

"And, you know, if Beau was with her at the house, it would also explain the bad grammar in the letter she supposedly left me." Gray rubbed the bridge of his nose with his fingers. "Could my father really have done that to my wife?" There was a pause as the rhetorical question hung in the air. "But we don't know it was Beau for sure. There are a lot of black Toyota trucks in Tennessee and a lot of Tennesseans with bad grammar."

"But you gave your police friend his prints. Have you heard from him? Were Beau's prints on anything pertaining to Angie's disappearance?"

"I don't know. And I can't call him now. Not until the issue with my dad's body is resolved."

Silence hung in the air as they finished their paltry breakfast and drank Gray's water. He dropped some water treatment tablets from his backpack into the canteen and filled it up from the stream. He put it into his backpack along with Ella's shoe, the breakfast wrappers, and both of their sweatshirts. He'd already put his camping pillow and blanket in, and then he forced in Ella's blanket, the flashlight, and the rope. "We need to head back. It'll be nearly three miles, and I assume it'll be difficult for you, but I'll get you there if I have to carry you."

"My walking stick is over there, leaning against a tree. Will you get it for me?"

When Gray returned, Ella had his gun in her hand. "You aren't going to shoot me, are you?"

"Not yet." Ella smiled though.

Gray relaxed. "Okay, let's head back then." He handed the stick to Ella and helped her to her feet. She slipped the gun inside her jeans at the small of her back like she did with Gray's other gun. The knife was in her pocket. Then she took her first step and grimaced, but she took another step and another, using the cane but making progress. Three miles would take a long time.

***

Reese drove to the DA's office from the police station. He entered the doors and walked directly to Carla, DA Morrison's administrative assistant, and greeted her. "Good morning, Carla. I'd like to see the DA about pressing charges against a man I'm investigating."

"Good morning, Detective. Have a seat. I'll let him know you're here." Carla gave the DA a call and was told to have Reese wait. She relayed the message, and Reese spent the next hour reading from his Kindle app, not able to focus on the story.

Finally, Carla sent him in, and Reese explained his situation and desire for the DA to press charges. It was a newly furnished office with degrees and news articles in frames on the wall and pictures of family on his desk and bookshelf. "Let's talk about the gun first, and then we'll get to the kidnapping theory. Can you prove Mr. Struthers owned the gun at the time of the murders?"

"Prove? Not unless I can somehow find a record of when he sold it or gave it away or pawned it. But he worked for Kingston Phipps, who had a motive for getting rid of those men. They were shot with his gun, dumped in a lake in front of Phipps's house, and I have records proving Struthers owned the murder weapon *and* was the realtor at the closing who made commissions on the sales."

Marty Morrison was a nice-looking man in his late 40s or early 50s with a high-priced haircut yet bushy, brown eyebrows. Reese had known him for a long time. "Would an attorney be able to cast reasonable doubt on the ownership of the gun at the time of the shooting?"

"I suppose."

"Okay, so let me ask you if you know for sure Angie Phipps was kidnapped."

"She's been missing for a week, and I presented you with evidence which suggests she didn't leave on her own."

"Has there been a ransom or an eyewitness to prove she was abducted?"

"I've told you my evidence." Reese didn't like the direction the conversation was leading.

"Here's my third question." Morrison glanced again at Reese's paperwork. "How do you know for sure the prints you ran belong to Beau Struthers?"

"I had a…an informant give me a book with his prints on the cover and bookmark."

"Do you know beyond a doubt they belong to Struthers?"

"Yes."

"Because…how?" Marty arched those bushy eyebrows, which Reese took as a condescending look.

"The person who gave me the book had access to the prints and told me he knew whose they are."

"You want me to have him arrested when I don't know one hundred percent the prints belong to him? For effective courtroom use, fingerprint evidence requires proper authentication, accuracy, and reliable corroboration. I'm not seeing that here…yet."

"When we arrest him, we'll print him, and then we'll know for sure."

"I can't have him arrested when I'm not sure the prints are his. Maybe they aren't. How would that look? You're going to have to find more evidence like an eyewitness. That would be best."

"I have evidence."

"Not enough, Detective. Maybe if you had a search warrant, you could get his prints that way, and then I'd have to agree the evidence is compelling enough for an arrest."

"I don't like this decision, Morrison. I've got the man. I'm sure of it."

"And you're probably right, but it must stand up in front of a jury. It's too early for an arrest at this point."

Frustrated, Reese stood, but he respectfully shook the DA's hand and left without further comment. He felt rushed for time, like the door of opportunity would close soon. He drove off to the courthouse feeling only a modicum of hope for a search warrant, but he had to try.

Once inside the courthouse, he found himself waiting for Judge Judy Swanson. After another lengthy wait, she stepped out of her office and told him he could see her, but she was pressed for time. She had an entire wall of books and a window to a courtyard behind her, filtering in sunshine from a beautiful late Monday morning. Swanson was dressed casually in a short-sleeved blouse and high-waisted, pleated slacks. Her robe hung from a coat rack in a corner opposite the bookshelves.

She directed him to sit, and he presented her with his evidence. He made his formal request for a search warrant, emphasizing he had fingerprints for Beau, but the DA wanted to be certain they were his. They could do that at the time of the search.

"Hmmm. As I'm sure you're aware, the taking of fingerprints doesn't fall within the category of either communication or testimony so as to be protected by the Fifth Amendment privilege." She picked a stray hair off her blouse and dropped it in her wastebasket. "But under protection of the Fourth Amendment, I have to see probable cause to issue a search warrant; otherwise, evidence found in the search could be suppressed and prevented from being used at trial. Your suspicions aren't enough to establish probable cause."

Reese listened patiently and then responded. "Probable cause is defined as an officer's reasonable belief based on circumstances and evidence that a crime has occurred. That can include hearsay evidence, like the fingerprints."

"Did your informant witness the kidnapping?"

"No."

"Do you have a witness?"

"You know I don't. I have evidence Struthers's fingerprints were found on suspicious objects in Angie Phipps's home as well as in her car."

"But you can't prove at this point the fingerprints actually belong to Struthers?"

"If I searched his house and truck I could."

"And what exactly would you be searching for? You haven't confirmed the truth of your accusations to my satisfaction, but what do you expect to find in this search and seizure? You haven't described what you're looking for other than fingerprint confirmation."

"I'll be looking for Angie Phipps or anything tied to her like her laptop or phone or car keys or jewelry or credit cards."

"So you don't know for sure she's been abducted, and you can't prove at this point the prints belong to Struthers, yet you want me to authorize a legal search in hopes you can find evidence for both of those things?" Judge Swanson looked at her clock and yawned. "Listen, this is good detecting so far, but it's not enough. You need more for me to issue a warrant. You don't even know for sure she's been abducted, do you?"

Reese rubbed his temples, stood, and reached for his evidence file. "I'll find out, and I'll be back."

"Okay, and when you do, I'll be glad to help you. Have a good day, Detective."

Reese left the courthouse, wondering what else he could do. When he was taken off the case twenty-three years before, he had no bodies, no murder weapon, no fingerprints, no eyewitnesses like Monica Dale, no additional crimes to tie in, and no closing documents for the sales. He had a motive, a suspect, an anonymous phone call, and some sensible assumptions, but what he presented to the DA and judge should have been compelling. He had legitimate evidence. He had two identified murder victims and sales documents to Pickett County Real Estate with signatures from the selling agent who happened to be the owner of the identified murder weapon. That same agent could be tied directly to the real estate owner's missing daughter-in-law by way of fingerprints both in her home and in her vehicle. What else did he need? Was Ella Dixon possibly an eyewitness to more than one murder so Beau kidnapped her as well to keep her quiet in case Reese tracked her down. He needed to find Ella and ask her if she'd witnessed more than one murder. An eyewitness would get him the warrants he needed.

Chapter 25

The trek through the forest was tediously slow. Ella braved it out and endured pain without complaint, but the first mile took almost an hour and a half, and Ella clearly needed a break. They sat on the trail, drank some water, and ate some nuts. "Are you okay?"

"The same as the other ten times you've asked me. I can't put much weight on my ankle, so I'm using the stick to bear the brunt of my weight, and my arms and shoulders and back are exhausted."

"How about if you put your arm around my shoulders and hop on your good foot? That'll be awkward too, but I'll bet we could set a slightly better pace for a while."

"We could try it."

"Or I could carry you piggyback. Or I could make a sled of some sort and drag you. I've been thinking that's a possible good use for the rope."

"You could spend all day making a sled that wouldn't be maneuverable through this trail, so let's try the others first." Ella lay on her back on the ground to rest. Sweat soaked her hair and sweatshirt. She'd toughed it out and was spent physically.

Gray let her rest. He unscrewed his canteen and took another small sip of water, but as he tightened the cap, he saw something terrifying. "Ella, no matter what, do not scream. Do not move quickly." Gray spoke far more loudly than necessary. "Are you confident to use my gun?"

Ella opened her eyes. "What's going on?"

"Slow movements. Do not scream. Can you promise me that?"

"Okay?" Uncertain, Ella sat up slowly and looked ahead on the trail. A huge brown bear stood, looking their way. "Yes, I can use your gun just fine."

Gray stood erect, waving his arms slowly. "I'm going to squat, and I want you to take the gun out and then climb on my shoulders. We need to get big. I'm talking so it can hear me and see I'm not a predator. When you get on my shoulders, start waving your arms very slowly. Big sweeps. There's a large rock to my left. Once we're balanced, big, and non-threatening, I'm going to step off the trail and shuffle sideways to the rock where we'll look even larger. If it attacks, you'll have to shoot it. Flip the safety off and slide the hammer open to load a cartridge into the chamber. Do you know what I'm talking about?"

"Yes, I've done it before."

"Do that now. It's a semi-automatic, and it has twelve rounds. Hold it with two hands and hit that bear as many times as you can."

While Gray spoke, the bear let loose some rumbling growls. Its ears lay back on its head, and it began snapping its jaws and salivating. "It looks hungry."

"Stay calm; those are its own defense mechanisms." He did his best to help Ella stay composed. She clicked off the safety and chambered a round. Gray squatted. "Climb on." When Gray lowered his body, the bear stood on its hind legs and let out a more menacing growl. "It's okay," he said. "A standing bear is curious more than threatening." Ella did as he said. Once on his shoulders, Gray stood. He held Ella's legs with one arm and began waving his other arm slowly. Ella gently waved both arms. Gray took a slow step sideways without taking his eyes off the bear, but he almost stumbled. "I have to watch my feet. Let me know if he charges."

Ella continued waving her arms, talking to the bear. "Hey, big guy, you can leave anytime. You're scaring me. I've never had bad things happen in fives, so you need to go away, okay? Gray's getting us off your trail, and then you can pass if that's what you want. Just don't attack because I don't want to shoot you." By then, Gray had taken a dozen steps and neared the large rock.

"I don't think I can step up three feet with you on my shoulders, so I need to let you off." He turned so Ella could slide off and land on the rock. The bear tilted its head and growled a quieter rumble. Gray stepped up on the rock next, and except for arm movements, he stood perfectly still. "Wide base, Ella. Align the front sight with the rear sight."

"He's moving away, Gray."

"Don't relax. He could charge." Together, they watched the bear wander off the path and into the woods to the north. Ella clicked on the safety and tucked the gun back into the waistband of her jeans. Then she sat on the rock and trembled. Gray sat beside her and held her hand. They didn't talk for several minutes, gazing into the woods, looking for any sign of the bear. Finally, Gray spoke. "It's been a tough week, huh?"

"The worst, and believe me, I've had bad weeks before."

"You keep mentioning that. Do you care to tell me about the bad things that happen in fours?"

"You really want to hear my childhood trauma?"

"If you're willing to share, I promise to listen." Gray handed his canteen to Ella, who took a drink and sighed before she started. "Do you remember anything from when you were six? I remember five things, and they all happened in the same week. I had a Zoe doll, you know, from Sesame Street. She would talk when I rubbed her belly, and I took her everywhere. One day, I was playing with her in my dad's truck, and she fell out the window. The highway was busy and there was nowhere to turn around right away. We went back to look for her and never found her."

"Bad thing number one?"

"Yep, for a six-year-old, it was, but my neighbor's dog had puppies and she offered me one. I begged my parents, so they agreed to let me have it to replace my doll. But it was my birthday, two days later, and I was expecting my first two-wheeled bike. I didn't get it. My parents said I got the puppy and puppies were expensive, so they didn't get the bike for me."

"Bad thing number two."

Ella's eyes teared up. "He was so energetic. I couldn't decide if I wanted to name him Taz or Sonic. But he slept with me, and I felt better about losing Zoe. Next, my grandma got hit by a car. She was hurt seriously, and during the surgery, there were complications, and she died."

"Bad thing number three."

There was a catch in her voice. "I loved my grandma. I cried and cried, and my puppy sensed my sorrow. He wouldn't leave my side. The day after the funeral, my mom took me and my puppy, who I still hadn't named, to the elementary school playground to play. I was swinging on the swings and decided to jump off like the big kids did, but when I jumped, I landed on my puppy. I squished him. I killed my dog."

"I'm sorry. That's a bad week for a six-year-old."

"Each one was traumatic to me. It's like they overshadowed every other memory of my childhood until then, and the pain still gnaws at me occasionally."

"My happiest times as a kid were when I lived with my mom and when I was at college. Once my mom left Dad, I was stuck in between. I did my own thing, but my dad made me feel guilty. He helped me start my construction business, so I always owed him, and he always took advantage of it."

"I'm sorry he was such an awful person...really. I learned while I was his prisoner he was mostly responsible for my other series of traumatic experiences."

"How so?"

"Until I was nine years old, I loved my childhood. My mom was a strong role model for me. She taught me I could do anything I wanted. My dad was almost like my best friend. He worked hard, but he always had time for me. Hunting, fishing, trapping, raising food in our garden. He taught me to never give up and if need be, sometimes to take things into my own hands. My mother modeled that philosophy for me."

"Sounds like a terrific childhood to me."

"It was. Until the dam ruined everything. The first bad thing was the state shut down our elementary school. It was the best school, but making your lake and creating electricity trumped all that, and your father took advantage. He convinced nearly everyone to sell. Threats, bribes, extortion, lies—whatever it took. And my three best friends moved away. That was the second bad thing. Then your dad's henchmen harassed us, and one, a man named Paul Miller, threatened to kill me if my dad didn't sign the sale papers. He signed, but then he attacked Miller. Took things into his own hands. And Miller murdered him right in front of me. He made my mom sign, and then he dragged my dad's body away. We didn't even have a funeral. That was the third bad thing—death of someone I care about like always."

"Let me guess. You're somehow responsible for the next death?"

Ella picked some moss off the rock she sat on and flicked it to the ground. She tied her left tennis shoe tighter. Checked her walking boot. "You really want to hear this?"

"I'm sticking with you through thick and thin from now on. What you say to me, stays with me. I promise."

"My mom found out where Miller lived. We broke into his house and waited for him. Mom found his gun, the same gun he used to kill my dad, and she gave it to me. I knew how to use it better than she did. We waited in his garage until he came home. I was behind his second car, near the doorway to his house. My mom was hidden on the other side of the garage. When Miller got home and headed for his door, I stepped out and pointed the gun at him to distract him. My mom came up from behind him and threw a noose over his head and yanked on it so hard, he fell to the floor. He hit his head on the cement and it knocked him out, I think. He didn't move long enough for my mom to throw the other end of the rope over a rafter. I stood over him, pointing the gun at him, but when he started to move, she hanged him. She was much bigger and stronger than he was, and she was so strong and so angry she lifted him off the floor. He struggled. Clawed at his neck. I watched his eyes bulge and his tongue hang from his mouth....I watched him die. We took justice into our own hands, but he got what he deserved. And then she made it look like suicide.

"She lowered him to the floor and moved two step ladders under the rope. She climbed one and lifted him again until I could balance him seated on the top step of the other.

She wrapped the rope around the rafter to hold him and then tied it while he sat there with me holding onto him. She climbed back down, pushed him off the ladder, and he just hung there dead. We put the ladders away and knocked over a stool to make it look like he kicked it over to kill himself, and we left him hanging there. That's the fourth bad thing. I helped murder my father's murderer."

"And this past week you sprained your ankle, got kidnapped, watched Noah die, and killed my father to save your own life. Bad things definitely happen in fours to you."

"I want you to know how devastating it was to lose my grandma and dad, and Noah's death broke my heart. But they're nothing like being responsible for the death of others—my dog, Paul Miller. Your dad is a whole other kind of pain. Those events will haunt me the rest of my life." Gray nodded but said nothing. What was there to say? He would keep her secrets even if it meant he'd go to prison himself for them. But that wasn't his plan.

"What would you like to do with your life, Gray? I can't imagine it's to run your father's business."

It was Gray's turn to pick moss. He tossed a stick to the ground. "When Angie vowed to leave, it got me thinking again of my dream of living in Montana or Wyoming, maybe. I could buy some land, build my own cabin, hunt, and fish. I'll have access to my dad's money now, so I could retire from the construction business and be a handyman for neighbors, friends, church projects maybe. I could live my life on my own terms. I'll need to start my life over on my own. Maybe Angie will show up again, but I have a bad feeling she won't. What are your goals?"

"When my grandma died, I decided to be a surgeon and save lives, but once I got to school, I never really gravitated toward that. I ended up focusing on cancer, specializing in treatment for kids. I feel like saving lives is my duty since I've taken them. And then I wanted a peaceful house on a lake with a great view and privacy, so I could leave my work at the hospital and go home to relax."

"Then that's what you'll do."

"What do you mean?"

"The lake house. I'll give it to you. It's yours. It's what my wife wanted, and it's what you want too. It's too much house for you, but maybe you'll find a good man and start a family. Maybe you can find happiness like when you were a child. For me, I need to get away. For you, you need peace."

"I don't know what to say. I want to say yes, but I think we have more pressing issues. I'll think about it." Ella re-tied her shoelaces and tightened the strap on her walking boot. "We should get going. Piggyback?"

Gray smiled. "It has to be faster than the progress we were making before, so let's try it."

"I'm heavier than I look. I can't imagine you'll last long."

Gray slid his backpack off his shoulders. "Put this on. We'll walk over to the path and give it a try." He helped her off the rock, and she put her arm around his shoulders and let him help her back to the path. Then he squatted. She climbed on his back and crossed her legs in front of his body, and they resumed their trip back to the house.

Chapter 26

Reese sat in Dale Hollow Tacos, eating his favorite comfort food. Without a witness or some new revelation coming to light, he was at an impasse. Monica Dale-Dixon hadn't answered or called back. Shaggy Rogers reported there were no other clues found in Angie's car. His best option he could think of was getting verifiable fingerprints from Beau Struthers. And then an idea struck him. Why he hadn't thought of it before irritated him.

The copy of *Jurassic Park* had been borrowed from the Pickett County Library. The head librarian was Rebecca Myers. She'd quit the police force eight years before after being shot and spending months in rehab, but she'd been a terrific cop, and occasionally, because of her sharp mind, Reese would discuss a case with her. She could tell him who checked out the book. That ought to be proof enough the fingerprints belonged to Struthers. Reese left the restaurant and drove to the public library on Pickett Square Drive.

He entered the building and wandered around, looking for his friend. Reese spotted her as Rebecca pushed a cart of chairs down a hall toward a meeting room. He hustled over and gave her a hand. "Hey, Becky." She wore jeans and a t-shirt saying "I just want to read my books and ignore all of my adult problems."

"Thanks, Reese. Long time no see. What have you been up to?" Her glasses sat on her head, nestled in her curly, red hair.

"Funny you should ask," he said as he unloaded a couple chairs and opened them up for Becky to arrange in rows. "I'm working on a case, and I'm at a standstill. I think you can help me."

"Okay, I'll trade you favors. You help me with the chairs, and I'll take a break to help you. We have a poetry reading this evening I need to set up for. Is it about the bodies you recovered from Dale Hollow? It made the news and I've heard people talking about it."

"Yes and no," said Reese. "The bodies belong to two of the missing Willow Grove men and forensics in Nashville recovered the bullets and matched them to a gun seized in a domestic violence incident. We traced the serial number and found the original owner. He's a suspect in the murder."

"That's great. So that's the yes part, what's the no part?" Becky sized up her row of chairs and straightened a few.

Reese continued to unload the cart. "The same man is a suspect in a kidnapping, and we have fingerprint evidence, but the DA and judge both think the manner I got them isn't verifiable. It finally occurred to me the prints were on one of your library books. The book was delivered to me, and I was told who they belong to. The DA says it's not good enough to have an unidentified source tell me whose prints they are. But *you* can tell me who borrowed the book. I'm certain I have the guy, but I've been told I need more evidence. If I can prove he checked out the book, that should get me my arrest warrant."

"Help me with one more cart of chairs, okay? I can look it up by the book or by the individual who borrowed it, but if I don't have a court order, it's illegal for me to give you the information."

Reese nodded in understanding, set aside his urgency, and pushed the empty cart down the hallway. The two old colleagues did some catching up. After the second cart of chairs was set up, Reese left the library and headed back to the courthouse.

He announced himself to Judge Swanson's receptionist and sat in a seat once again, waiting to be ushered into her office. When she appeared, Reese stood. "Forget the search warrant for now. I need a court order instead, Your Honor."

"Come in, Officer Carlton." Reese entered the office but didn't bother to sit. "You must have discovered something new."

"Actually, no, but it dawned on me I already have what I need. The DA said I needed proof the fingerprints I procured belong to Beau Struthers. I can prove it with a court order."

"Explain."

"I was given a book which had Struthers's prints on the cover and bookmark. We have prints both from the missing woman's home and vehicle, and they match the ones assumed to be Mr. Struthers's. What dawned on me is the book came from the public library. There are records as to whom checked it out. If it's Struthers, the prints can be verified, and warrants can be issued. But I need a court order to see the records at the library. You told me when I find more evidence, you'll be glad to help me. This is the evidence I need."

Judge Swanson seemed to be in a quandary. She seemed hesitant. She picked up a pen, put it back down, picked it up again, twisting it for the tip to come out of the casing. Finally, she said, "You're right. Knowing the book belonged to Mr. Struthers would be the evidence we need. I'll grant you the court order."

"Thank you, Your Honor."

Judge Swanson picked up her desk phone and called the clerk's office. "Detective Reese Carlton will be coming to you. Fill out the appropriate court order for him and then bring it to me for my signature." She listened for a moment. "Yes, right away. He'll be right there." She hung up the phone. "There you go, Mr. Carlton. Bring me proof the book belongs to Struthers, and I'll issue a search warrant. The DA will most certainly be on board as well."

Once the court order was prepared and copied and the clerk, the judge, and Reese had signed it, the detective headed back to the library. Judge Swanson made a warning call to Kingston Phipps, but he didn't answer. She wasn't willing to leave a message on his phone, so she hung up and went back to her work.

***

Gray carried Ella on his back for a half hour. They stopped three times for him to rest his arms. Ella walked during those breaks, but her pace was painstaking, so Gray determinedly hurried the hike along with her riding piggyback, though carrying her was slow as well. The sky grew dark and overcast, and he hoped to make it home before the inevitable rain. He knew the woods well enough to know they had barely more than a mile to go, but he was sweating, and his arms ached. He stopped for a breather and pointed. "Somewhere around here is where you left the trail and buried your bags under the leaves. I found them and moved them. They're buried in the dirt now, under a fallen tree. And I covered our tracks."

"Your determination encourages me."

"Hopefully it encourages you enough to not shoot me. As sad as it'll be, I'd like to attend my son's funeral."

"Do you want your gun and knife back?"

"No, you keep them."

"You're not afraid I'll assassinate you?"

"I've given it some thought, and I don't think you're evil. Plus, I'm your ride out of here. Hop on again." A loud thunder boomed, and immediately the sky darkened. Gray looked up as dark clouds rolled in. The wind picked up, and the first drops could be heard on the tree leaves. Ella climbed on his back, and Gray hurried as fast as he could, but the rain increased and started wetting the trail.

Another loud thunder shook the air, and the rain poured through the trees. The path got slippery, and Gray nearly lost his footing. "Stop, Gray. Let's find shelter. You're going to get hurt." Water rushed down the path. Both dripped from the rainfall, and Ella slid off his back.

Gray looked into the woods and noticed an inverted rock wall, narrower at the bottom than the top, and near the bottom, the rocks were dry. He picked Ella up in his arms and carried her to the wall. They found a depression under a protruding boulder and stepped into it. Gray sat, removed the backpack from Ella's shoulders, and unzipped it. He took out the sweatshirts both had packed as well as the two blankets. Gray removed his soaked t-shirt and put on his dry sweatshirt, so Ella did the same. He stuffed them back in the bag and wrapped both blankets around them, covering their heads. It was there they waited out the storm, bodies touching.

"You didn't even look at me when I took off my t-shirt."

"I was being polite," said Gray.

"You're nothing like your dad."

"I've had my moments of selfishness, but I blame it on always trying to find my footing. My parents argued so much when I was little, I thought winning an argument was the end all of a relationship. I never saw love. When my mom left, she took me, and for the first time I was able to relax some instead of hiding all the time. I did some regrettable things in high school once I had freedom, but I met Angie right away in college. She was different. My *mom* was different too, but she was simply strong and stubborn. She never tried to compromise that I could see. I learned about relationships from Angie, and she learned it from her relationship with God.

"She tried to get along with my dad, but to him, she was competition for my attention and adoration. She figured him out and labeled him like my mother did, but she tried to compromise and navigate my dad. She tried to find love in her heart for him. Compassion. Understanding. But that's not what he wanted. He didn't want someone who understood the real him. He wanted someone to believe he was who he thought he was. Eventually, Angie gave up. She started avoiding him, and in time, she wanted nothing to do with him."

"And your dad hated her?" Ella put her head on Gray's shoulder.

She looked so much like Angie it made his heart flutter. "I think my dad hated himself most. Money didn't make him happy. Prestige and power might have made him happier, but it was false. No one really respected him. They pretended, and I think he knew it. So he became an alcoholic. He would've never admitted it, of course, but he was. And I think he started blaming Angie for the evil he stored up in his heart. Angie was free. Forgiven. Living by God's grace and mercy, and my dad felt none of it. He may have felt judged, or it may have been simply guilt, but Angie was the opposite of him. Light compared to darkness. He may not have hated her, but he resented her."

"That's deep, Gray. You figured all that out?"

"I listen to what people say. I grew to accept it as truth. *You* figured it all out in a couple of days."

"He ruined both of our childhoods, Gray." She held his hand. "And he worked mighty hard to ruin our adulthoods too. When we're done with this, we need to put it all behind us and move on."

The sky remained dark, but the thunder sounded farther in the distance and the rain slowed considerably. Gray leaned his head back against the rock and fell asleep. Fifteen minutes later, the rain had stopped, and the sky brightened. Ella shook Gray lightly. "I think we can go now."

Gray nodded and stood, folded the blankets, stuffing them in the backpack, and helped Ella loop the straps over her shoulders. With arms around each other's waists, they walked back to the trail. Gray squatted, and Ella climbed on. Except for droplets dripping off tree leaves and the sound of Gray's footsteps in occasional puddles, silence dominated the remaining portion of the trek. Finally, Beau's truck popped into view at the end of the trail.

Gray poked his head out of the trees. Though it was cloudy, there was plenty of daylight left in the evening. He took his key from his pocket and unlocked the house door. They stepped inside, and he relocked it. Still without speaking, Gray took off his muddy shoes and headed down the stairs to the lower level of the house. He flipped on the light in the furnace room where Kingston's body lay cold and stiff on the rug.

Chapter 27

When Reese returned to the public library, people had begun arriving for the poetry reading. He found Rebecca Myers in the meeting room. "I got my court order."

Rebecca gave some instructions to an employee and exited the room with her old friend. They went to her office. She sat behind her desk and used her mouse to activate her computer screen. Reese handed her the paperwork. She glanced over it and then asked, "What's the book?"

"*Jurassic Park.*"

"Two copies have been checked out—a paperback and a hardcover."

"It's the hardcover. Tell me it was checked out by Beau Struthers."

"Beau Struthers. Checked it out last Thursday." She looked up at Reese. "I know him. Huge guy, late 50s, early 60s? Big chip in a front tooth and a busted-up nose?"

"That's the guy. Can you print that out for me?"

"Sure." She clicked on her mouse a few times and then spoke to Reese. "He comes in here often enough that I know him. Polite guy even though his looks are intimidating." She rose from her chair and walked to her printer to retrieve the paper. "Interesting, though, he was here earlier last week too. Used a computer. I remember because he looked terrible. Held his arm like he was hurting badly. Typed using his left hand, and it looked like he struggled doing it."

"He typed up a note? Do you have a record of that?"

"Follow me." She led Reese to the computer lab. "Our members can use the computers for two hours if they have a library card and sign in, so we have logs for that." A library employee with pink lipstick and eyeshadow sat behind a desk beside two copy machines. She wore a pink t-shirt that said "That's what I do. I read books, and I know things." Rebecca said, "Laura, I need to see the sign-in logs for the computers last week."

"Sure." Laura leaned sideways, her straight brown hair with pink highlights hanging over one eye, and opened a two-drawer filing cabinet. She thumbed through some file tabs and took out several sheets of paper, paper-clipped together. She handed them to Rebecca, displaying pink nail polish as well.

"It was early last week if my memory serves me correctly." Rebecca sorted through the small pile. She ran her finger down the Wednesday list and then moved on to Tuesday. "There it is," she said. "Beau Struthers. Tuesday at 12:11 p.m."

"He's that giant man with the crooked nose, right?" said Laura.

"Yes, do you remember him?" Gray estimated the pink lady was in her fifties.

"I do. He was sweating he was in so much pain. He couldn't use his right arm, so he typed something with one finger of his left hand. It took him quite a long time to type it out. He struggled so much I couldn't help but watch. When he finished, he asked me to print the note and gave me five dollars for it. Told me to keep the change."

"Did you see the note?" asked Reese.

"Sort of. I mean, he printed it, and I took it off the copy machine and gave it to him. Short note, signed by a woman."

"Angie? Did he sign it Angie?"

"I don't remember. I noticed a short note signed by a woman, and since he's not a woman, I remember that part."

"Hold on." Reese trotted out of the library to his car and grabbed the folder he'd taken to the DA and judge. He jogged back into the building and to the computer lab. He leafed through the documents and then removed his copy of Angie's note from her home. He handed it to Laura. "Did it look like this?"

Laura looked at it briefly. "Yeah, a short note with a woman's name signed at the end."

Reese turned to Rebecca. "Becky, I need a copy of this log, please."

"He has a court order," said Rebecca to her pink employee.

Laura took the paper to the copy machine and printed a copy, handing it to the detective. He smiled in satisfaction.

"Thank you. I thought this was going to be a bad day, but it's turning out all right."

"Can I get back to my event now, Reese? All this boring police work takes a back seat to thrilling poetry readings. You didn't hear me say this, but authors are weird."

"So are police officers and librarians…" said Reese.

"And proctologists and urologists," interrupted Laura. "Why would anyone choose to do those jobs unless they're weird?"

"And with that, I'm out of here," said Reese. "Thank you, both, for your help." As Reese walked through the library, he reviewed Angie's letter. "Grayson" was used, yet Angie only called him Gray. He wondered if Beau called Gray, Grayson. "I'm leaving for Hawaii," but she never got on the plane, nor did she pack her swimsuit. "It don't make sense," yet Angie spoke proper English. He'd heard Beau make grammar errors, though. Missing commas and misspellings might easily be done by someone in tremendous pain, typing with one finger of his weak hand. "Dir" instead of "die." The e and the r were right next to each other on the keyboard. And "father" spelled "fahter." Again, the h and t keys were close, and they transposed each other in the misspelling. "Father" was spelled correctly ten words later. Beau could easily have made all those mistakes.

Beau was his guy. He'd done something to Angie, and under Kingston Phipps's orders, looked to be the murderer of at least two men twenty-three years earlier and possibly three since Reese suspected him of Paul Miller's murder as well. He was certain he had enough for a search warrant, so he headed back to the courthouse.

***

Judge Swanson's receptionist barely looked up when Reese flew through the door for the third time that day. She pointed to a chair. "I believe that's your assigned seat. I'll let the judge know you've arrived. She said you'd be back."

Reese took a deep breath and then seated himself without speaking a word. He observed the receptionist make her call, but the judge made him wait even though he'd been told she expected his return. Inside the office, Judge Judy attempted to call Kingston Phipps, but he still didn't answer his phone. She called DA Morrison, and they agreed if Carlton had evidence, they'd have to cooperate. Finally, she called Reese into her office.

Reese smiled as he entered. "It looks as though the court order helped you as much as you expected." The judge stood and walked to a mini-fridge. "Can I get you a bottle of water, Detective? You look parched." She took two small plastic bottles out and tossed him one.

"Thank you. And it helped more than I expected."

"Do tell."

"The library book was checked out by Beau Struthers." Reese took out the copy from Becky Myers. "This is authentication the fingerprints are his. I've got physical evidence as well as reliable corroboration the prints on the book and bookmark belong to Struthers."

"I see. Good work, Detective."

"But I have other evidence too. Struthers's fingerprints were found in Angie Phipps's car and her house. They were on a Coke can as well as a letter and envelope Angie supposedly left. Angie's husband gave many reasons why he was certain she didn't write the note. I learned Struthers was at the public library on Tuesday, typing and printing a note, so now I have proof Struthers typed it." Reese handed the judge the copy of the note along with the statement from Gray Phipps disputing it. Then he showed her the log from the library showing Struthers was there typing out a short note signed by a female.

"Hmmm. This is compelling."

"I'd like you to approve a search warrant."

"I agree. You will be looking for additional evidence Struthers is involved in the Angie Phipps disappearance?"

"Yes."

"Okay. You've established probable cause and proven to my satisfaction the search is sufficiently limited in scope to elements regarding the Angie Phipps disappearance. I have to agree the evidence points to Mr. Struthers having committed a crime. It's late today. You'll have your warrant the first thing in the morning."

"I'd prefer it this afternoon, but I'll be here in the morning. Thank you."

"You're welcome. I'll need you to sign some affidavits before you leave. My assistant and I will start work on this immediately."

Reese stood, holding his water bottle. "I'll wait outside."

***

Ella wiped her feet thoroughly on a rug at the door and trailed behind, limping in her boot, but when she reached the bottom of the stairs and saw Gray looking into the furnace room, his back to her, she wanted to run away again. He lowered his head as if in prayer and then turned to face Ella. "I don't know how to feel. Sadness? Relief? Fear? What do we do next?"

Ella hobbled over to him and gave him a hug. "I'm sorry."

"If you hadn't done this, you'd be dead. I know that. What do we do next?" He withdrew from the hug, refusing to find comfort in her gesture.

"We have to get rid of the body. Any ideas?"

"I know from just this past week what my dad would do. He'd dump the body in the lake."

"So let's get rid of any evidence and do it." Ella stared at the body, surprised she felt any remorse at all. "He's lying on a good-sized rug. Let's roll him up in it. I don't want to look at him anymore."

Gray grabbed his father's feet and slid him away from the wall, lining him up so he could fold the blooded end over his body. He grabbed the edge of the rug and covered his father. Ella held the end while Gray began rolling him up inside, and then Ella maneuvered beside him and helped with the process. When they finished, the opposite end of the carpet flopped over. "We need to secure that. Rope maybe? The one in the backpack?"

"We don't need rope." Ella went to the workbench, put on a pair of gloves, and tossed Gray another pair. She awkwardly got down on her knees and peered under the bottom shelf. She then lowered her face down to the cement, reaching her hand underneath and grabbed the chain she'd been held captive with. She reached under a second time and came back with two padlocks and a key. "We'll wrap him in this. It'll serve him right."

She slid one end under the rug and looped it around the carpet once before she locked one padlock on it. Then one circumference at a time, Gray lifted the rolled-up body so Ella could slide the chain under it. Once the full length was looped around the rug seven times, she clicked the second padlock onto the chain, securing it tightly.

"To make it sink so there's no chance it'll float back to the surface, we need to weigh it down," she said.

Ella left the furnace room and scanned the entire lower level. Gray followed behind her. There was a second living room, kitchen, and dining room on that level with sliding glass doors opening onto a fabulous deck. Off the living room in one direction was a hallway to other bedrooms and bathrooms, and off the kitchen in the other direction was a hallway to more rooms. Gray headed toward the bedrooms, so Ella made her way through the kitchen. She spotted a laundry room and a movie/entertainment room with poker tables, a pool table, and other games. Next was an exercise room with a treadmill, an elliptical, a stationary bike, and a weight set with some barbells. She picked up two thirty-pound weights and carried them, limping, back through the kitchen. Gray returned with an impatient look, but when he saw Ella, he said, "Bingo. Speaking of irony, that's what was used for the bodies Reese extracted from the lake to keep them under the water." He took the weights from her because she struggled to walk carrying them, and he went back to the exercise room and grabbed two forty-pound barbells.

When he returned, Ella sat in a recliner, waiting, gloves still on her hands. "This evening, we'll take the pontoon boat out onto the lake and dump the body. I'll take these weights down now and put them on the pontoon. We'll have to carry the body down when it's darker. The weather worked in our favor. I don't see any boats on the water."

"Your gun, the screwdriver, and the taser are in your t-shirt drawer."

"Why are you telling me that now?"

"Sooner or later—probably sooner if your detective friend is the person you think he is—he's going to come for your dad, and with him missing, you'll be a suspect. You need to get rid of those things when we dump the body."

"Thank you." Gray put on different shoes and started to leave with two of the barbells but turned back to Ella. "I called your work, saying I was your dad. You're supposed to be with him on a family emergency. Your parents may need to cover for you."

"You're right. I'll call tonight. They'll cover for me." Ella smiled, knowing they both were thinking of each other. "Is there anything else we need to consider?"

"We should clean the furnace room to be sure there's no trace of my dad in there."

"I'll start working on that now." She stood from the chair and headed to the furnace room to assess the situation.

When Gray returned after his second trip to the boat, Ella had bottles of cleaning spray and scrubbing pads to clean up blood spatter on the wall and a spot on the cement where blood had soaked through the rug. He carried a metal lockbox nearly filled with the screwdriver, his gun and ammo, the taser, and rocks. When Ella finished, she put the scrubbing pads in also. He closed it and locked it with a key. "It's time to move the body. It's getting foggy too. Do you think you'll be able to manage down all the steps to the dock?"

"I'll help as much as I can."

Gray lifted one end of the rolled rug and began walking backward, sliding it out of the room. Ella lifted the other end as best as she could to help, ignoring the pain and stumbling along. The body was heavy, but they got it through the house and down the deck steps. Gray went backward. The stairs descended eight steps at a time, followed by a small platform. That's how the couple worked—eight awkward steps at a time and then a short rest. One hundred and fifty-two steps to the dock. With trees filling the surrounding landscape, the cloudy daylight, the fog, and the privacy of the lot, the only possible way to be spotted was from a boat on the lake, and there were none of those. The other side of the lake was too far away to give a clear view in dim light and fog.

Gray pulled the carpet roll through the hinged gate door of the boat and let Kingston's body rest on the floor as he started the engine. Ella undid the knots tying the pontoon to the dock and pushed off for Gray to motor away from the shore.

Gray never turned on any lights. Instead, he drove slowly and quietly across the water while Ella pried the four barbells under links of the chain and attached them securely with zip ties. He drove a half mile before dropping the lockbox into the lake and close to another half mile to the west before he stopped to dump the body. "It's not light enough for me to know exactly, but I remember this part of the lake is considered among the deepest parts. I've never noticed divers near here, so I can't think of a better spot I can navigate to in the limited time we have." He idled the boat and opened up the side gate. The body still lay directly in front of the exit.

Gray lifted the end nearest the gate, and Ella did her best to lift enough weight to help him move the heavy load. He got the body the foot and a half to the gate and then straddled the body, lifting on the chains and pulling. Together, they lifted, pulled, and pushed, and little by little, it slid through the opening. The boat listed under the weight, but eventually the rug dipped into the water and the load lightened. Finally, the last quarter slid off the boat, pulled by the weight at the opposite end, and it entered the water with a splash. "No way

I could've done that alone, Ella. Whoever dumped those bodies in the lake twenty years ago had help. More than one person did the job…and there were *two* bodies."

"It's done though. Let's get back to the house," said Ella.

"We'll call your parents, and then I'll take you home. Tomorrow, I'll draw up papers to transfer ownership of the house to you, and then I have to go to the funeral home and prepare for the funeral on Wednesday."

Ella stepped beside Gray at the captain's chair and grabbed his hand. "I'm sorry for your loss, Gray. Your losses. Don't take this wrong, but I wish I'd never met you." She tried to smile but couldn't pull it off.

"Angie's gone. Noah's gone. My dad is gone. He won't be missed so much, but I think *his* death might haunt me the most, finding him dead like that and then dumping his body…" Gray paused because he didn't like his next thought. "And if we're right, Angie's gone because of Beau—maybe Beau and my dad—but my dad has been taken care of. I'm going to have to take care of Beau."

"Then you're going to need this." Ella handed Gray his gun.

When they arrived back at the dock, there was barely any light, but they tied the boat down and snapped the cover in place. Then Ella hopped on Gray's back, and he carried her up the steps, stopping at each landing for a breather.

They re-entered the house and Gray collapsed in a chair. "I'll give you my phone to call your mom."

She started laughing. "I don't know her number."

"Really?"

"I store it in my phone…which is on my kitchen counter, by the way. Just take me home. I need a bath."

"Okay. I think I have my breath back." He wrote his address and phone number on a piece of paper for her, and she gave him her contact information and his pocketknife. He grabbed his truck keys and drove Ella to her home in Cookeville to her freedom.

Chapter 28

At 8:00 a.m., Reese entered the courthouse again, anxious to continue his investigation. His retirement party in a day and a half would mark the end of a career and the end of the case he pursued. He needed to search Beau's house and find some answers.

He walked out with the warrant and received a call from Shaggy Rogers as he descended the courthouse steps. "I've heard it through the grapevine you've made some progress on the Angie Phipps case. In a way, that's my case. You handed it over to me when you flew off to Arizona. I heard you have a search warrant. I want to come with you."

"Who else knows about this?"

"DA Morrison, Judge Swanson, Chief Frank. Kingston Phipps has his hands in a lot of things around the county, so there's a lot of interest in finding his daughter-in-law."

"I'm going to head to his house now."

"I'll go with you. I'm right here in the parking lot. Hop in."

By then, Reese approached his car and noticed Shaggy in the spot next to his, so he walked to the passenger side door and got in. "It's best to have you there with me," said Reese. "It's 111 Willow Drive. I'll get directions." He punched in the address in the Google Maps app of his phone. "Twenty-three minutes. Let's go."

On the drive, Reese caught Shaggy up on the details relating to the DA and the judge denying the warrants and why. Then he reviewed the library details as well. Before they arrived at the house, he added his suspicions about the murders, explaining how the murder weapon belonged to Beau.

"You never told me how you got the prints. Was it Grayson Phipps?"

"It was someone who was reliable. I knew the prints were legit."

"Yeah, it's too bad the powers that be had to have extra proof."

"Here it is...on the left." They drove up an attractively stamped cement driveway. From their parking spot, they could see the beautiful lake view, and the stunning house was something boaters would surely admire. Beau's truck wasn't present, but the garage door was open, so Reese saw the two motorcycles he knew Beau owned along with a bright yellow Ford truck.

Reese exited the vehicle and made his way to the porch and rang the doorbell, hoping Beau would answer. Shaggy stood on the sidewalk behind him.

On the second ring, Beau answered. He opened the screen door and looked amused rather than surprised. "How can I help you gentlemen?"

Reese handed him the search warrant. "This is a search warrant, giving me and Detective Rogers permission to search your house."

"Regarding?" Beau's casted arm and wrist lay in a sling hung around his neck.

"Regarding the disappearance of Angie Phipps. Please let us pass and look around."

Beau stepped aside, a literal smile appearing on his face.

Reese entered the foyer and marched through the living room area, surveying the incredible home, trying to decide where to start. It was too much of a house for a single man in his sixties, but it was clean, furnished nicely, and well-decorated. "Don't move, Detective Carlton," said Beau. Reese looked at Beau curiously and saw he had a pistol in his left hand pointed at him. He glanced at Shaggy for backup, but he had his arms crossed as he stood in the doorway, his expression grim, but he made no effort to help. "If you're looking for backup, you're out of luck. He's on my side. Thanks for delivering him here, Rogers." Beau nodded at an envelope on a lampstand near the door. "The thousand dollars ought to soothe your conscience, Scooby Doo. You're excused."

Shaggy looked at Reese with regret, but he grabbed the envelope and left. Reese could hear the car back out of the driveway and spray gravel as it roared away. Beau motioned with his gun for Reese to sit in a chair near the hallway. He backed toward the front door, shutting it.

"Your weapon," Beau said next. "Remove it slowly. Two fingers. Yes, just like that." Reese held it dangling from his thumb and index finger. "Set it on the floor, and then kick it over to me."

The gun slid three-quarters of the way to Beau. He left it where it lay. "You know, a lot of people know I'm here today," said Reese.

"Who do you think knows?"

"The chief, the DA, Judge Swanson. Rogers, obviously."

"Yeah, well, Scooby Doo and the other three generally do what Kingston asks of them...for a fee, of course."

"They warned you?"

"Rogers did. He's my man on the police force. We've had a Rogers taking our money for twenty-five years."

"You were paying Chief Rogers? He's the one who took me off the Willow Grove case twenty-three years ago."

"Yeah, you were asking too many questions. The chief was on 'the payroll' ever since we started threatening Willow Grove property owners to get them to leave. He looked the other way, but he profited from it. It was only natural for us to use his son for our benefit too. He's *my* guy. The others are Kingston's. Rogers will say he came with you and you both left when I wasn't home. Rather than break my door down, you decided to come back later."

"I don't see it. The chief, DA, and judge cooperated with me."

"I imagine they slowed you down at least."

Reese thought about that and reached the conclusion they'd done a good job delaying him a couple of days. "The chief though? He encouraged me."

"And then probably got on the phone to tell the others to slow you down. It's how things work." Beau stood perfectly still, except he lowered the gun in his left hand and seemed to relax out of curiosity. "So tell me, Detective, how'd you figure out to come and search my home."

Reese had some questions of his own, so he decided to answer Beau's. "You were sloppy. You drank a can of Coke at Angie Phipps's house and tossed it in the wastebasket."

"Hmmm, I forgot about that."

"Angie doesn't drink Coke, and Gray emptied the trash before he left for his father's house. He knew it wasn't his, and your fingerprints were on the can. They were also on the letter and envelope."

"Fingerprints on paper? I didn't know that was possible."

"The house was wiped down, which only made sense if a criminal did it. You hid most of your prints, but in the process, made the crime scene suspicious."

"That's all the evidence you needed to come to me?"

"Well, no. There was lots more. You left Angie's Bible and computer bag and make-up bag in Kingston's house, and when you forced her to pack at her house, she never packed a swimsuit or took any pictures of her son. That, by the way, was the first big problem. She wouldn't have left her son. The Coke can was another problem, and the letter was a huge problem."

"Because of the fingerprints?"

"Well, it was odd Angie's fingerprints weren't on it and yours were, but the whole letter was an issue."

"How so?"

"Grayson said Angie always called him Gray, yet you used Grayson. Then there was a grammar error and punctuation errors and typos Gray claimed she'd never make. That threw me for a while because that's Gray's opinion—speculation. Angie could have made errors under the pressure or the timing of the situation, but there was no paper in the house to print on, and if Angie had printed the note at Kingston's house, she would've more than likely left it there."

"She was supposed to handwrite it, so I had to improvise."

"Well, we'll get back to that," said Reese. "We found her car. You did a good job cleaning it up and making it look like a robbery—but our police dog got no sniff of her whatsoever outside of the car. She didn't drive it there, so someone else must have. And we figured it to be someone of good size because the driver's seat was lowered, and the seat was back. And that was another sloppy mistake. We checked for prints and could only find them in two places. The buttons that lowered and pushed back the seat. And low and behold, they were the same prints as the ones in the house. We only had to figure out whose prints they were. It's amazing you're such a bad guy and you've never been arrested."

"Pure luck, and deep pockets from my boss." Beau grinned. "So how did you figure out they were my prints? Something illegal, I imagine."

"Actually, no. From a library book. I needed a court order to see their records, but I finally got one. And you know what I found out? You were there the day Angie disappeared, typing out a note with a severely injured arm. You typed it with your left hand. One finger. Easy to make errors that way. But I have the document you signed to log in to the computers. The time and everything. You typed the note and took it back to the house."

"You're a decent detective, Carlton."

"Yeah, but it leads to some questions. Where was Angie while you were typing out the note? And how did you get hurt? So let me guess. Angie hurt you. The softball bat wasn't under Gray's bed like it was supposed to be. You wiped it down and put it in his closet with his other softball gear. But it was out of place there, and when we checked it, it had been wiped down too, which meant you touched it. Did Angie break your arm with the softball bat?"

Beau laughed. "She got me good. Twice. My arm and wrist may never recover."

"So you killed her. Am I right?"

"She's resting peacefully."

"She's your boss's daughter-in-law and your future boss's wife. Why would you kill her?"

"Accident. Self-defense, to be honest. She wasn't swinging for my arm. She swung for my head. I blocked both swings." He lifted his arm in the sling to display her handiwork. "When she wound up for another one, I backhanded her…and she died. I must have broken her neck. It wasn't the plan."

"What was the plan?"

"To make her leave…against her will, but to make her leave on her own, so Grayson wouldn't leave with her."

"But she wouldn't go."

"Not without a fight."

"Where is she? Did you dump her in the lake like all the other ones?"

"You're really focused on the old days, aren't you?"

"I know you killed at least three men."

"And how do you know that?" Beau looked genuinely interested and lowered his gun.

Reese thought about making an escape attempt, but there were things he needed to know for sure. "The gun I asked you about? It was the murder weapon used on both John Hill and Stephen Stone. When the coroner examined the bodies we removed from the lake, the bullets were still there. They matched a gun confiscated in a crime, and we matched the serial numbers to your purchase. DNA and dental evidence identified the bodies—two of the three holdouts Kingston Phipps needed to get to sell. You were the selling agent at closing, so the three signatures of the three missing men and your initials are on each closing document. I know you didn't murder Robert Dale because I have eyewitnesses who say it was Paul Miller, but I believe you murdered Miller too."

"You can't prove I killed anyone. I could've ditched that gun before the murders. There were no witnesses. No jury could decide beyond a reasonable doubt, even though I did it."

"Why? Why did you kill them? You had signatures."

"We couldn't have them going to the police or declaring the contracts weren't valid because they were coerced. And it was easier to strongarm the wives when they thought their husbands were in danger—or if they thought *they* were in danger because we'd already done something to their husbands. Kingston gave them more than double what he gave the other families."

188

"So Phipps was in charge? He gave the orders?"

"Of course. It was his money and reputation on the line."

"I knew that twenty-three years ago."

"And now you have bodies and a murder weapon and still can't do anything about it."

Reese didn't know if the insinuation was that he couldn't do anything at trial or he couldn't do anything because he'd be dead. But he needed to know the truth. "You would've killed Robert Dale too, right? Miller did it impulsively. He wasn't supposed to kill him."

"That's right. He was supposed to try to get a signature on a purchase agreement, but if he couldn't, he was to threaten the family, and then I would step in later and make it clear his wife and child were in danger. Once he signed, like the others, I would've shot him too."

"My guess," said Reese, "is that because Miller did it and there were witnesses, Phipps had you kill him."

"You finally got one wrong, Carlton. Miller committed suicide. When Miller told Kingston what he'd done and that he'd disposed of the body, Kingston fired him. So whether Miller committed suicide out of guilt or because he'd lost his job or because he was afraid of going to prison, it wasn't my doing."

"He was murdered. There was a ton of evidence suggesting it."

"Well, if I didn't do it, who else had motive?"

"Phipps."

"Ha. Get his own hands dirty? It wasn't him."

Reese sat stunned because the next best guess made perfect sense to him. Monica Dale.

***

After a long, hot bath the night before, Ella had a good night's sleep in her own bed. A knock on her door awakened her, and before she could throw on some pajama pants, the doorbell rang too. Too early to be Gray with the paperwork, she stuffed her foot into her walking boot and nervously peeked out of the closed window blinds to be shocked to see her parents on her porch. In her exhaustion the night before, she'd forgotten to call them, and seeing them on her porch didn't make sense. But she hurried to the front door and opened it for them.

Monica didn't wait for any pleasantries. She flung open the screen door and hugged her daughter. "You're okay! We were worried." Her dad, the man who gave her mom and her a second chance at a life of normalcy, hugged her next.

"Come in," said Ella. "I was expecting someone this morning, but obviously, it wasn't you. I meant to call you last night, but I was so tired I took a bath and fell asleep right after."

"You hurt your foot?" Monica seemed more anxious than concerned.

"Yeah, I sprained my ankle playing golf and re-injured it a couple of days ago."

"We need to talk." Monica grabbed Ella by the hand and steered her to the living room and seated her on the couch. She sat beside her, turning to face her. Her husband, James, sat in a chair.

"What's up, Mom?"

"A detective from Byrdstown kept calling me, leaving messages about the bodies of John Hill and Stephen Stone being found. I ignored him, but he came to visit me in Arizona. James was away on business, but I let Detective Carlton in. He asked about your father's murder and about the murderer, Paul Miller. He said he wanted to find you, to hear your version of the story. He said once he found the bodies and confirmed their identities, he knew you were the one who called him after the murder."

Ella took a deep breath in, releasing it slowly while looking down at her hands, embarrassed. She had no idea the police officer she talked to about her dad's murder was the same man Gray talked about. "I'm sorry I never told you about that call."

"It's okay. The call led him to identifying Miller and made him sure Kingston Phipps had him killed. But that's not what I'm concerned about. He tracked you down, and when he did, you were missing. He called to see if I knew anything, but again, I didn't answer his calls. I only listened to his messages. But when he called saying he'd learned you were with your father because of personal family matters, and he wanted to confirm it, I decided we needed to come here."

"We didn't expect to find you here, but it's the first place we came to," said James. "What did he mean, you were with me?"

"That's what I meant to call you about last night," said Ella. "It's a long story, but I need you to say I was with you, both in case I have a problem with work for missing a bunch of days without notice and in case that detective starts asking questions."

"Are you in trouble, honey?" Monica grabbed her hand. It was an odd gesture. Monica took charge of things. She was a woman of strength and action. Compassion wasn't her thing. It was her father's thing...and James Dixon's thing. Ella learned how to do things and how to think for herself from the two fathers in her life. She learned to be strong and confident and assertive from her mother. Empathy and compassion weren't her things.

"It's been an awful week, but it could get worse if you two don't vouch for me. I need your help. I need you to say we've been together, Dad."

"My conference was in St. Louis. That's a five-and-a-half-hour drive from here. That's not too far."

"Detective Carlton came to Arizona on Thursday. I told him James was out of town. I didn't tell him where or what he was doing."

"Good," said Ella. "The fact you didn't give any details is helpful. A friend of mine called the hospital Friday to say I had a family emergency with my father and would be out of work for a week."

"I got a call and message from the detective Sunday and yesterday, asking what I know about you being with your dad.

I never answered or responded, so he has no information except what we decide to tell him." Monica looked at her husband, who nodded his head yes, and then back at Ella. "So what's going on?"

"I'm not ready to tell you yet, but I need you to trust me. In time, I'll tell you; I promise." Ella wiped a tear from her eye. "I'm good, Mom. Just trust me."

"Marriage problems," said James. "We'll say your mom and I are having marriage problems, and I wanted to talk to you."

"And you wouldn't leave him until we agreed to work things out." Monica smiled. "Your stubbornness runs in the family." At fifty-four years of age, Monica still looked like a TV star. James had a slightly receding hairline but otherwise a good head of brown hair. He had a few wrinkles at the corners of his mouth when he smiled, but he was as fit as Monica. They looked good together. And as the story would be told, Ella fought to *keep* them together. The man who saved her family was convinced by Ella to stick it out with her mother.

"My car never left my driveway," said Ella.

"I drove here from St. Louis and picked you up…when?"

"Wednesday after my second shift work shift ended. Here at my house."

"And we drove back to Nashville, where we stayed until…"

"Last night." Ella looked at her mom. "When did you get here from Arizona?"

"My plane arrived at midnight, Central time. James arrived from St. Louis at seven a.m. We drove straight here."

"So Dad dropped me off and drove back to get you at the airport, and you spent the night together and came here this morning." Ella stood and limped into the kitchen. "That's the story I'm telling at work, and that's the story you'll tell if the detective manages to ever talk to you again. Do you want some eggs? Granola? Oatmeal? I'll make you breakfast."

"No, honey, I'll find something while you shower. And then you need to ice your ankle and elevate it and take ibuprofen. We'll handle breakfast."

While Ella showered and James prepared omelets, the doorbell rang again. Monica went to answer it. A well-built, attractive young man stood on the porch with an envelope in his hand. The flecks of gray in his closely trimmed beard made Monica think he must be older than he looked. When he saw Monica, however, he stepped back and looked at the address on the wall of the house. Confused, he looked at Monica again and took out his phone to double-check the address, again looking at the house number hanging on the siding.

"I'm sorry…I'm here for Ella Dixon. Is Ella here?"

"She is, but she's unavailable. How can I help you?"

"I have some papers for her to sign. Uh, it's for the transfer of a piece of property to her name."

James came to the door behind Monica. "We're unaware of any new purchase Ella has made recently. Who are you?"

"My name is Grayson Phipps. It's, uh, a fairly recent development, but Ella has agreed to become the owner of a new house on a lake."

"Is that so, Mr. Phipps?" Monica glared at him suspiciously. "On a lake, you say?"

"Yes. May I come in, please? All I need is a few signatures. We agreed to the real estate deal within the past couple of days."

"How can that be?" asked James. "She's been with me for the past five or six days."

It was then it dawned on Gray to whom he was talking. "Oh, you're her father. I heard about you. I hope the family problems have been resolved. May I come in?" He didn't expect anyone else at the house, but he'd prepared a backstory he would use if Reese asked any questions. He'd say he heard about her from Reese when he called and showed him Ella's picture.

"Of course you can," said Ella, who was dressed but wore a towel wrapped around her hair. "Mom, let him in."

"Ella?" said Gray. "It's nice to meet you. We couldn't do this over the phone, so I had to come here personally." He gave her a casual wink he was sure no one saw. "I'm Grayson Phipps, but you can call me Gray."

"It's nice to meet you too, Gray," said Ella. "Please, come in."

"Grayson *Phipps*, you said?" Monica's glower continued, but Gray waited patiently for any movement away from the door. Ella stepped in, grabbed his hand, and pulled him down the short hall into the living room. Monica followed. "You look familiar. Any connection to Kingston Phipps?"

"My dad. But he's gone missing."

"Maybe they'll find him at the bottom of Dale Hollow Lake."

Both Gray and Ella reacted by turning their heads to face each other, but they quickly looked away, acting casually. Monica, however, noticed the silent exchange in their looks. She held her tongue but asked, "What's this about purchasing a new house?"

Ella found she had no words, so Gray answered. He looked exhausted. Beaten down. "Before my father disappeared, he gave me his house and made me his business partner. Recently, I heard about your daughter from a friend of mine and learned her backstory about living in Willow Grove and losing her father…"

"Her father was murdered…in front of her eyes."

"Yes, I'm sorry. That's what I heard, and I'm mortified about the circumstances. But now I'm making reparations, if you will. This is a quick-claim title stating I'm giving away the house, and Ella's taking possession of it. All she has to do is pay the closing costs and write a check for the first property tax payment. Once she signs, I'll take the papers back to the title company who will issue Ella the deed to the house. Other than personal items, the contents are included." He flipped to another document. "This is a point-of-sale document stating she gets to keep everything left in the house. All you need to do, Ella, is sign a few papers, and write me two checks."

"No strings attached?" asked Ella.

"None. Oh, and your home is one of the few allowed on Dale Hollow Lake to have a dock. That right transfers as well, and you can keep the pontoon boat. Sign here...and here...and here...and here. That's all there is to it other than the checks."

"Done," said Ella as she signed the last paper. She hobbled to the kitchen counter where she'd put her purse on Wednesday evening when she came in to open the disabled garage door. Gray told her whom to make the checks out to, and she did the rest, handing them to him when she finished.

"You can take possession of it on Wednesday morning. Here is a set of keys, but you should change the locks. I still need to move my father's personal belongings out, but I'll get them out today." Gray's eyes teared up. "I have some personal issues to deal with in the next two days, but I'll return the papers to the title company when I get back in town today."

Gray put everything back in the envelope. "It was nice to meet you, Mr. and Mrs. Dixon." He looked at Ella. "It was nice meeting you too, Ella. I'm going to take care of everything." He looked at her as if he needed to make sure she understood the implications of his statement. "Everything."

He turned and went out the front door without looking back.

Once he left, Monica spoke to Ella. "What am I missing?"

"I told you I'd tell you eventually. I need you to trust me."

"What did he mean when he said 'Everything'?" asked James.

"It could mean a lot of things," said Ella, "and I'm worried about him. He told me his son just died of brain cancer, he's awaiting confirmation his wife has been murdered, and I...um...and his father is missing, so he might be talking about any of those things, but it might mean he's about to do something stupid."

Chapter 29

Gray drove back to Byrdstown and walked the paperwork into the title company. He waited impatiently for the processors. Once they gave him the deed, he left, intending to go to the funeral home to sort through final arrangements, but when he saw a black truck sitting in the parking lot, it reminded him of Beau, and his thoughts turned dark.

He stopped his vehicle, reached behind his seat for his toolbox, and removed a pair of work gloves. He stuffed them into his jeans pocket and took out his gun to inspect it. He slid the hammer open and saw the cartridge Ella had loaded into the chamber. The safety was on. He put the gun into its holster and started his truck again, heading out onto the road and a drive to Beau's house on the lake.

***

"Any more questions before you die, Detective?"

"Several." Reese, by then, had analyzed the entire home—at least all that he could see. Beau was right-handed and had the gun, an eight-shot 357 Magnum revolver, in his left. Statistically, from twenty feet, Beau wouldn't be accurate with his off hand, especially if Reese was on the move. Beau blocked the front door as well as the door to the garage. The kitchen to his right had two islands Reese could use as protection against gunfire, but there was nothing to hide behind to help him get to the sliding glass door onto the deck. It meant if he tried to escape, the escape route would have to be behind him and down the stairs to his right or behind him down the hallway to who knew what. He wondered if there was another sliding glass door off the master bedroom.

"I've got nothing but time. It's *your* time that's running out." Beau raised the gun and pointed it awkwardly at Reese, but he lowered it and smiled.

"You killed Stone and Hill and crammed them into a freezer, and then broke a bunch of bones to stuff the bodies into the body bag months later after the lake filled."

"That's not a question, but it was almost a *year* later. It took the lake a long time to form. The bodies weren't dumped until Kingston's house was built and the dock and boat were available."

"Did Phipps help you?"

"Weighted down, the bag was too heavy, even for me, so yes. I couldn't do it alone."

"Do you know where Robert Dale's body is?"

"Not a clue. It's a miracle Miller disposed of it somewhere it's never been found."

"Where's Angie Phipps's body?"

"Someplace for safe keeping until I have use of my arm again."

"Were you following Ella Dixon?"

"She's from Cookeville. When you interrogated me, I couldn't figure how you knew about her."

"She's the daughter of Robert and Monica Dale. I went to Cookeville to ask Ella some questions, and I found she was missing. She mentioned to her friend someone in a black Toyota truck had been following her. So did you kidnap her?"

"Nah. I was fresh from surgery. That one was Kingston."

"Why?"

"For the boy." Reese had more questions about Ella Dixon, but it was during the momentary pause a vehicle entered Beau's driveway and parked. When Beau turned his head briefly to see who it might be, Reese darted for the stairs. Beau saw the movement in his peripheral vision in time to raise his gun and get two shots off, both missing. Reese dove down the steps, sliding on his stomach and then tumbling down the stairs. As he reached the bottom, Beau fired off his third shot, also missing.

The basement wasn't what he expected. He assumed there would be a walk-out on the lower level, but there wasn't. There was a furnished living area with a gigantic television, a wet bar with a microwave and a refrigerator, and a pool table. There were high windows, allowing some light in, but the lights were off.

Beau flipped on a light switch and bounded down the stairs as Reese froze in indecision. When Beau's body became visible, Reese ran for a doorway opposite the wet bar and another shot exploded from Beau's pistol. The bullet grazed his left shoulder, causing a burst of pain as the bullet entered and exited without hitting anything major. He slammed the door shut and locked it and then looked around at his surroundings.

Weight machines for squats, bench press, and leg press made up a sizable portion of the room. Beau jiggled the doorknob. Weight plates and various weighted barbells lined the floor and shelves along the wall. Reese hurried to the traditional barbell on the bench press to use it as a weapon, but it was too heavy to wield easily—it was long, bulky, and fifty-five pounds. Then he saw a curl bar. It was much shorter and weighed only fifteen pounds, and when he picked it up, he recognized he could swing it easily.

Beau shot his fifth shot into the doorknob and rattled it, but it didn't open. Reese ran to the wall beside the door and pressed his back to it as blood soaked into his shirt. Beau fired his sixth shot and the doorknob on Reese's side fell to the floor. The door pushed open, and Beau extended his hand through the doorway, pointing the gun. Reese, with all the strength he could muster, smashed the barbell across Beau's left wrist. Beau screamed in pain but somehow managed to hang onto the gun. He lifted his arm partially and fired the seventh shot, hitting Reese in the left calf. The gun fell from his damaged hand and landed on the carpet.

Beau kicked Reese in the bloodied calf, but he endured the pain and rolled away. The giant kept coming and attempted another kick. Reese met it with the barbell, bashing it on his shin. Beau stumbled, and Reese swung again, slamming it off his shoulder. Neither broke a bone, but they both hurt. Reese groaned as he pushed off with his right leg and stood, facing a raging bull. Beau screamed and charged into Reese, slamming him into the wall, but he had no working arms and Reese fell to the floor and rolled away again. Beau tried to stomp on him as he rolled, but he missed, so he tried again as Reese rolled a second time, banging into the weight bench. He picked up a forty-pound barbell off the floor and groaned as he threw it at Beau, who instinctively blocked it with his left hand, sending agonizing pain through his body.

When he hesitated, Reese swung the curl bar from his knees and slammed it into Beau's kidney, dropping him to the floor where Reese hit him a second time. Beau groaned and gasped, barely able to breathe. Reese dropped the weight bar and used the bench press seat to help him get to his feet. He took the handcuffs looped over his belt at the small of his back and snapped one cuff on Beau's newly broken left wrist. With the cast, he couldn't cuff the other wrist, but with Beau on his stomach, still trying to breathe, Reese yanked his arm to the side and cuffed him to the weight bench. Beau rolled over and sat up, glaring at the detective.

"You think you can convict me of anything based on my confessions? Good luck with that."

"Oh, I'll get you for the kidnapping of Angie Phipps for sure, and maybe the murder. I'll be searching your house. I'll get you for attempted murder of a police officer and all the corresponding charges that go along with it, like conspiracy to commit murder with Shady Rogers. I'll probably have enough violent crimes adding up that you'll be convicted of Stephen Stone's and John Hill's murders too. Then I'll go after Kingston Phipps."

"You killed my wife, didn't you Beau?" Both heads turned to the doorway where Grayson Phipps stood, holding Reese's gun in his gloved hand.

"Grayson," said Beau. "I'm sorry. It was self-defense."

"She beat the crap out of you with my softball bat, didn't she? And then you typed up a note to convince me she'd left me and Noah, but she wouldn't have done that, and she wouldn't have written the note."

"I hit her because she was trying to kill me, Grayson. It was a reaction. I wasn't planning on hurting her...just making her leave town."

"Put the gun down, Gray. I've got him. He'll be going to prison for a long time."

Gray stepped into the room where he could face Beau as he sat with his back leaning against the bench press. "Where is she, Beau? Where's Angie?"

Beau's chin dropped to his chest. His eyes closed. "I'm sorry. She's in the freezer in the garage."

Two shots rang out as Gray shot Beau twice in the chest. He drooped over sideways and died.

"What did you do?" yelled Reese. "You killed him." Reese stumbled. He looked pale. He'd lost a lot of blood.

"No, you did, Reese. It's your gun. My fingerprints aren't on it. He shot you twice. You had to shoot him. You'd better uncuff him though, or it'll look like you murdered him. I drove into the driveway and heard two gunshots. I came in through the front door and eventually heard two more shots. Your gun was lying on the floor upstairs, so I picked it up. I heard two more shots, and then another. That's seven. His gun still has a shot left, and you had to kill him before he killed you. He murdered my wife, Reese. He kidnapped her and murdered her and then had the nerve to look me in the eye and act like nothing happened. And he's killed other people. Someone's husband. Someone's father. He got what he deserved."

Reese dropped to a knee, looking woozy. He took out his cell phone and dialed 9-1-1. "Officer shot. 111 Willow Drive in Byrdstown...Dale Hollow Lake. Another man down." He punched the end button and looked at Gray. "You need to go now."

"I'll leave the gun at the top of the stairs in case you have any ideas about arresting me. You can get it when you check the freezer for Angie's body. Take care of her, Reese. The only thing she did wrong was marry into my family. Good job, by the way. You've solved your mystery."

"Half of it. I'm coming for your dad next."

"You'd better see a doctor first." Gray trotted up the stairs and left the gun on the top step. He got in his truck and exited in the opposite direction as the police and ambulance would be arriving and took a long route to Crestlawn Funeral Home back in town.

***

Moving slowly, Reese removed the handcuffs from Beau and limped up the stairs, holding onto the handrails to retrieve his weapon. He staggered into the garage and opened the large chest freezer where he found the frozen body of Angie Phipps and then made himself head back down to the lower level of the house. Breathing unsteadily, he grabbed two hand towels from a bathroom and managed to return to the weight room where he carefully picked up Beau's gun, using the towel to protect his fingerprints, and laid it on Beau's open left hand. From where Gray had shot Beau, Reese fired his weapon into the wall, assuring he had gunpowder residue on his shooting hand. Then he sat, exhausted, putting pressure on his wounds with the towels to slow the bleeding, and waited for the others to respond to his call.

After the police and paramedics arrived, one officer burst into the room with his gun pointed, but when he saw Beau and Reese, he holstered it and hurried to Reese's side. He called for a paramedic, and the next hour and a half of confusion included the taking of Beau's body away, the temporary bandaging of Reese's wounds, the discovery and removal of Angie's body, and the protocol steps relating to a police shooting. Ironically, Chief Rocky Frank arrived from the police department and DA Martin Morrison arrived from the district attorney's office. Both had interfered with his investigation of Beau, but Reese wondered if they were relieved Beau had died and wouldn't be able to do any talking. Also, Carl Donaldson arrived to review the crime scene.

Donaldson took pictures and then collected each of the seven bullets from Beau's gun. He bagged them and the gun to study in his lab. He detailed evidence from Reese's gunshots also and collected his weapon as well. He did a gunshot residue wipe test on Reese's shooting hand and clothing, and then Chief Frank let Reese know he was relieved of field duty until the review board had an opportunity to investigate whether the shooting was within department policy and until Reese met with the police psychologist. And then Reese rode in the ambulance to the hospital in Cookeville.

At the hospital, his wounds, neither of which were life threatening, were treated and stitched. Reese took note of his life and realized other than fellow officers, he had no one to call—no family, no close friends. All he had was his job. His job defined him, and there was nothing else. No one else. Working with Grayson Phipps had served a two-pronged purpose. It was a way to keep tabs on Kingston Phipps, and it satisfied the police psychologist who thought it was unhealthy for him to have nothing and no one else in his life. He'd witnessed the best friend he had commit a murder, so calling him for a ride was out of the question. He knew he needed to leave, so he called Ashvi Patel, who volunteered to come to the hospital. The doctor recommended he stay overnight for observation, but instead, he got dressed and left as soon as Ashvi made it to the recovery room.

She drove him to his car at the courthouse. "Please don't criticize me for this, Ashvi, but I have some police business to take care of. You can come with me or wait someplace for me to finish or go back to your home. I'd like you to stay, though."

"You've been shot twice, and you've been temporarily relieved of duty. You're being an idiot. Is that criticism enough?"

"It's the truth…so are you coming with me?"

"I *am* a doctor. I have your health to consider. And I took an oath."

"Good. I'm about to ignore Chief Frank's command and head out to make an arrest. You can watch an expert at work." Both smiled as they got into his car. They became serious when he reached into his glovebox and took out a different gun to slide into his holster.

"You expecting trouble?"

"It's possible because I know the man I arrest will be armed."

Ashvi opened her purse and took out her own handgun for Reese to see. "It might as well be a dual citizen's arrest. I have your back."

"Where have you been my whole life?" Reese looked at her with admiration.

"Waiting around for you, apparently. Don't get yourself killed, okay?"

Reese felt his cheeks redden, so as nonchalantly as he could manage, he took out his cell phone and called dispatch.

"Pickett County Sheriff's Department. How may I direct your call?"

"This is Detective Carlton. I need dispatch."

When dispatch came on the line, he asked, "I need a 10-20 on Officer Shady Rogers."

After a short delay, he got his answer. "He's at 1920 Livingston Highway at Moogies Bar & Grill."

"Thanks. I'd suggest you send a squad car over in about ten minutes because there's about to be a disturbance." He ended the phone call and backed out of his parking space. In less than ten minutes, he'd parked at Moogies. "I'm going to confront him face-to-face. I want you to stand in the doorway in case he makes a run for it and aim your gun at him. Don't shoot. Let him by if he keeps coming, but hopefully he'll stop."

"What's this about, Reese?"

"He hand-delivered me to Beau Struthers to be killed. Took a thousand dollars as payment and drove away, knowing full well Struthers planned on killing me. Struthers claimed he's been paying off Rogers for some time. I'm going in to arrest him."

"Okay, I've got your six." She laughed.

In the midst of a dangerous and serious moment, Reese laughed also. "I'll bet that's something you're not used to saying."

She followed him to the door. She kept the safety on but put her hand on her gun in her purse and watched Reese scan the restaurant and bar. He spotted Shaggy sitting on a bar stool watching a Braves game with a beer in front of him.

Reese limped over and plopped down in the stool next to him. "Keep your hands where I can see them, Rogers. You're under arrest."

Shaggy turned his gaze to Reese and his jaw dropped open. He tried to reach for the gun holstered to his hip, but Reese caught his wrist. "He made me do it, Carlton."

Reese stood, still holding his wrist. He reached for his handcuffs, and Shaggy made a run for it. Ashvi yanked her gun from her purse and held it with two hands, feet spread like she'd practiced at a shooting range. "Stop right there!" Shaggy hesitated. And Reese jumped on his back, tackling him to the floor. Ashvi ran to the two men and aimed the gun at Shaggy's head. "Don't move, scumbag."

Reese snapped one cuff on a wrist and yanked Shaggy's hand behind him. He placed his knee in the small of Shaggy's back and then grabbed the other hand, snapping the other cuff on it. "I've got him, Annie Oakley. You can put your gun down. Shady Rodgers, you are under arrest for attempted murder. You have the right to remain silent. Anything you say can and will be used against you in a court of law. You have the right to an attorney. If you cannot afford an attorney, one will be provided for you. Do you understand the rights I have just told to you?"

"Yes."

"With these rights in mind, do you wish to speak to me?"

Another police officer stood beside Ashvi as Reese finished quoting the Miranda Rights.

"You don't say no to that man, Carlton. I didn't want to do it."

"But you did. You took a thousand dollars and left me there to die." He yanked Shaggy's wallet from his pocket. Ten fresh one-hundred-dollar bills with a twenty and three singles filled the billfold. "There it is, Officer," Reese said to Officer Scott Cole. "I know he's a fellow cop, but I called it in beforehand so you could be here to witness the arrest. Rogers is as shady as his name suggests. Take him in for conspiracy to commit murder. He's already been quoted his rights....Oh, and tell Chief Frank that Beau Struthers talked about

Kingston Phipps before he tried to kill me. Tell the chief I specifically said he *owes* me."

Officer Cole helped Shaggy off the floor, walked him out of the bar, and guided him to the backseat of his patrol car. Reese and Ashvi stood in the doorway and watched. As the car drove away, Reese called the station explaining the situation. When he was done, Ashvi said, "Let me take you home. You're bleeding all over that shirt. You've hurt yourself again."

Without saying anything, he shook his head yes, grabbed Ashvi's hand, and walked her to his car.

Chapter 30

Ashvi had Wednesday off and slept in Reese's guest bedroom after she cleaned his wounds again and helped with the stitches. She woke up in the morning and had breakfast waiting for him when he appeared after his shower.

"At a time when I feel completely alone, it sure is nice to have you here. Are you willing to run a few errands with me?" Never had he seen someone with so much energy and such expressive, beautiful eyes. The Annie Oakley performance demonstrated traits once again that amazed him. If he wasn't going to be lonely and useless during retirement, it would be nice being not lonely and not useless with her.

Not only was breakfast delicious and appreciated but the dishes were done. Ashvi wore the same clothes as the evening before and somehow looked better. "Will I need to keep a weapon handy?"

"Possibly, but I'll do my best to protect you. Otherwise, I won't have a date for my own party."

"Deal. Let's go do some detecting."

Reese combed his hair again, sprayed on some cologne, and brushed his teeth. He gave an unused toothbrush to Ashvi to use, and then they settled into Reese's car and drove to the DA's office. Carla's head popped up as Reese and Ashvi entered. "I need to see the district attorney, please."

"Let me see if I can fit you in this morning."

"No, I'm going in right now. You can warn him, or I'll surprise him, but I'm going in right now."

"Hey, Carla," said Ashvi with a huge smile. "I'm Ashvi from the coroner's office in Nashville. It sure is nice to meet you."

"Well, hello. It's nice to meet you too."

"Thank you. I love your outfit, by the way. Detective Carlton is retiring today. Did you know that? It seems he has a couple of loose ends to resolve before his party this evening, and he needs the district attorney's help. Will you let him know Reese is here to see him?"

"Okay, I'll do that, and I love your necklace. It's beautiful." As Ashvi smiled, Carla called the DA. "You have a visitor. Reese Carlton will be right in to see you."

Reese left Ashvi behind to chat with Carla, and he entered the office alone. "What can I do for you, Detective?"

"You know I got a search warrant from Judge Swanson to search Beau Struthers's home. And you know I found Angie Phipps's dead body. It wasn't easy to pull that off because Struthers had been tipped I was coming, and he tried to kill me. But you know that too because you saw his dead body."

"You're not suggesting I tipped him off, are you?" The surprise and offense were clear in his expression.

"Oh, no. Detective Rogers tipped him off. He's in jail now. I'm sure you'll find conspiracy to commit murder a worthwhile case to try. And since Beau told me Rogers has been taking payoffs for a while now, you'll most likely uncover a few other charges to press. No, you didn't tip him off, but you followed Kingston Phipps's instructions to slow me down. I learned that from Beau, who talked a lot when he thought I'd be dead soon. He also implicated Judge Swanson and Chief Frank." Morrison kept his composure and continued to listen. "Well, you know he's dead and can't do any other talking, so the only person who knows what he said is me, and since I'm retiring today—you're invited to the party if you'd like—I really only care about one thing."

"What's that?"

"Bringing in Kingston Phipps for murder. And that's where you can help me. I'd like you to issue a warrant for his arrest. I know...all the evidence is circumstantial, and the fact Beau told me Kingston ordered the hits doesn't matter because he's dead, but I think I should arrest him anyway, and you should put your full efforts into sending him to prison where he belongs. Struthers also told me Phipps kidnapped a woman named Ella Dixon, so there's that too. So what do you say, Morrison?"

207

"One last favor between friends?" Morrison coolly smiled. "And then you'll retire, and I'll get to have a drink with you at the party and our lives will move on?"

"Exactly. I've waited twenty-three years for this, and I'd like it to end with Kingston Phipps behind bars."

"Okay. Have a seat in the lobby. I'll have the warrant prepared for you."

"The River Grill at 6:00 tonight," said Reese. "No hard feelings unless Phipps goes free. Then I'll have to wonder where your loyalties lie."

"You're bold, Carlton."

"Some of the decisions you people made almost cost me my life, but I survived it, and I'm retiring today, so I've got nothing to lose."

"You'll get your warrant. Good luck."

An hour later, Reese and Ashvi drove away from the courthouse. "You know, I was thinking, without you, I may have been zero for two. With you, I'm batting a thousand. I'm glad you're here."

"I'm having fun watching you blunder around. What's next?" She reached over and took Reese's hand.

"I'm going to arrest Kingston Phipps. I've been right all along. He forced people to sell their land so Dale Hollow Lake could be created, and he had people killed if they refused. I'm taking him in as my last act as a police detective, and then I'll retire in peace."

"What will you do without a career?"

"Not sure yet. I'm not even sure where I'm going to live. I'm thinking maybe Fairfield Glade. I'll take up golf and pickleball and maybe be a volunteer fireman or something like that. Maybe I'll make some friends." They drove silently as Reese contemplated his future.

"You could move closer to Nashville. I'm not ready for retirement yet, but with me, you'll have a head start on making friends. I can play golf and pickleball if that's what you're interested in."

"That's tempting too. What I'm most interested in is getting away from here. Does that make sense? I spend my whole life and career here and then retire and high tail it out of town?"

"You wouldn't be the first or the last. Do what you have the most peace about. But you might want to wait until your gunshot wounds heal. Your competitors probably won't be riddled with bullet holes."

They drove along engaging in friendly conversation until they arrived at Kingston Phipps's home. Together, they gawked at the beautiful house with the incredible lake view before they climbed the porch steps and rang the doorbell. A beautiful, young woman in shorts, a t-shirt, and sandals answered the door.

"Angie?" Reese said before he could think. "Dorella? Dorella Dale?"

"My name is Ella Dixon."

Reese's hand went to his gun, and he lowered his voice. "I'm Detective Reese Carlton. Are you in danger?"

"I'm sorry. I don't know what you're talking about."

"Please, step out of the house." Ella didn't move. "Ma'am, I'm ordering you to step outside." His hand remained on the gun at his hip.

At that moment, Monica Dale-Dixon appeared and stood beside her daughter, still looking intimidating. "Detective Carlton. What is going on here?"

Reese directed his eyes over Monica's shoulder, but he didn't relax at all. "I was told Ella Dixon had been kidnapped by Kingston Phipps. I'm here with a warrant for his arrest on another matter, but when I saw your daughter, I thought it might be an opportunity to remove her from a dangerous situation."

"I don't know where you got your information, Mr. Carlton," Ella said, "but I'm safe here in my own home with my parents."

"I don't understand. This is Kingston Phipps's house."

"No, it was Grayson Phipps's house until he heard about me and my backstory, and he sold it to me."

Reese couldn't have looked more confused. "May I come in?"

209

"I don't think so," said Monica. "Ella, this is the man who has been calling me, worrying me about your disappearance and harassing me about your whereabouts."

James Dixon appeared at the door. "She's been with me. I called the hospital and told them that."

Reese stared in confusion. He looked at Ella. "You told your friend, Stacy Howard, you thought you were being followed by a black Toyota truck. That was confirmed to me by a man named Beau Struthers. Do you know who he is?"

"No, sir."

"Mr. Struthers also told me Kingston Phipps had kidnapped you. You're saying that isn't true?"

"I don't know a Kingston Phipps or a Beau, and no, I wasn't kidnapped."

"How do you know Grayson Phipps?"

"He called me about this house, and I met him yesterday when we did the paperwork for the sale transfer."

"Did he happen to tell you where his father was?"

Monica interrupted. "When we met Mr. Phipps Tuesday morning, he said his father and his wife were missing. It's crazy how so many people disappear here in Tennessee."

"Yes, it is," said Reese, "and when the disappearances seem related, I tend to get suspicious. How long have you been in town, Monica?"

"I arrived in Nashville late Monday night, and my husband and I drove here Tuesday morning."

"I thought your husband said he was with Ella."

James explained. "I brought her home Monday evening and went back to Nashville to pick up Monica. We spent the night and came here in the morning, Tuesday."

Thrown for a loop because he believed Beau, he stood on the porch and thought. "Is there anything else we can help you with?" asked Monica.

"Why didn't you answer my calls?"

"I've never answered a single call from you, Detective. You're prying in a part of our lives it took a long time to recover from. My daughter and I thought we'd moved on, and our family issues are none of your business."

"When we talked in Arizona, I asked you about Paul Miller. What do you know about his death?"

"I told you we were told he committed suicide."

"But did he?"

"I didn't investigate."

"Monica, *you* know who Beau Struthers and Kingston Phipps are, don't you?"

"Phipps was the man who forced us to leave our home and Struthers was one of the realtors—the one who told me to keep my mouth closed if I knew what was best for my family."

"He said he didn't kill Paul Miller."

"He told me Miller committed suicide. Murder or suicide made no difference to me."

"It was what he deserved. That's what you said."

"You don't agree?"

"I think he was murdered, and that's a crime."

"Well, go solve it then, and leave us alone. I'm not interested in your theories because I don't care how he died." Monica bumped her way in front of her daughter. "We don't know where you can find Kingston Phipps, and since your warrant is for him and none of us, I think you should leave us. We're taking a tour of my daughter's new home. Have a good day, Mr. Carlton." Monica closed and locked the door.

Reese and Ashvi walked back to the car. Once inside, Ashvi asked, "What was the point of all those questions about Paul Miller?"

"Monica Dale killed Paul Miller. There's no way I can prove it, but I'm certain of it." He backed his car out of the driveway and started driving to Grayson Phipps's house. "She told me it was traumatic for nine-year-olds to witness murders, plural. Ella saw her father get murdered. What was the other murder? Monica told me she learned from her husband to take things into her own hands, and when I asked her about Paul Miller, she told me to leave it alone. When I told her I thought Miller was murdered, she looked concerned. I noticed that, but it didn't mean anything to me at the time."

"I haven't heard a bit of evidence yet, Reese." Ashvi looked at him in confusion.

"Miller clawed at his throat to try to survive the hanging. There were no rope fibers on the palms of his hands, however. Only on his fingertips. If he hung that rope before he hanged himself, there would have been some. The knot was at the side of his head, not the back, which I think is odd if he stood on a stool, preparing to kill himself, and there were frayed rope fibers on the rope going both directions. Someone strong pulled the body up with the rope, and then the body weight dragged the rope back down, possibly more than once. All those things make me think it was a murder.

"When Struthers believed I was going to die, he admitted to everything—everything except Miller's murder. He said it was suicide, and when he asked me who else had a motive, I knew who it was. Did you see how physically impressive she is? Miller was a scrawny guy. She could've lifted him easily. And the rope was tied to the beam and around his neck with two different boating knots. Miller didn't have a boat, but the Dales did. She took it into her own hands, and her daughter witnessed it. I'm sure of it, but I'll never prove it."

"Hmmm," said Ashvi. "You could be right. That's some good detective work."

"I'm in the same spot I was in twenty-three years ago, except I have a different suspect. Nothing has changed."

"You know, if you were playing golf right now, it wouldn't matter so much."

Reese laughed, and when he looked at Ashvi, her smile lit up her face, and he laughed harder yet. "I have another stop to make. Since the lake house doesn't belong to a Phipps any longer, I'm hoping Gray will be at his home in Byrdstown. Maybe he knows where his father is."

***

When Reese drove into Gray's driveway, his truck sat parked on the cement outside of his garage. He turned to Ashvi. "I need you to stay here this time. What I need to talk to him about should be just between him and me." Ashvi agreed and Reese walked to the front door and knocked. Gray answered dressed in a suit, his tie hanging untied around his neck. "May I come in?"

Gray opened the door without a word. Once inside, he asked, "Are you here to arrest me?"

"That was a dumb thing to do, Gray. It was wrong. I had him. He'd have spent the rest of his life in prison."

"He killed my wife. Seems like murder was something he excelled at. It's a miracle he didn't kill you before I got him."

"Well, it wasn't for lack of trying."

"Are you okay? I mean, it looked like he shot you more than once."

"I'll be fine. Are you okay? You've lost your family."

"Nope. I'm not. I'm in a daze right now, and I don't know how to maneuver through it. I know Angie would tell me faith would get me through. She'd tell me she and Noah are fine now, in Heaven with Jesus. How can I get past how God let all this happen?"

"I'm no preacher, Gray, but my best guess is it's the fall of mankind that's at fault, not God. The world started perfectly, and it'll end perfectly. It's the middle part *we've* mucked up."

Gray sat down on his couch with tears in his eyes.

"Where's your dad, Gray? I have a warrant for his arrest."

"I don't know."

"Are you sure? Struthers told me your father kidnapped Ella Dixon. She worked at the hospital, and I'm assuming your father saw her there and plotted a way to both get rid of Angie and make your son's last days less miserable. She looks exactly like your wife. He kidnapped her, which means you knew about it."

"That's not true, Reese."

"You spent time with Ella Dixon…enough time to decide to give her the lake house."

"No. You told me about her. You told me she was the daughter of one of the three missing men from Willow Grove.

Everyone in this town grew up knowing the stories. I grew up with people looking at me like I had something to do with it. I was eleven years old. When you showed me Ella's picture, and she looked like Angie, you told me who she was. Monday, I contacted her and offered her the house. She got the deed Tuesday."

"She was missing from Wednesday night until Monday, and coincidentally, you were the first person to connect with her? That's hard to believe. Where's your dad?"

"I don't know."

"Struthers told me your dad ordered the hits on the Willow Grove men. He told me your dad had a cop, the DA, a judge, and the chief of police in his pocket. He told me what happened with him and Angie...how Angie attacked him with your softball bat and how he fought back and killed her accidentally. He told me he didn't kill the man who killed Ella's father, and I believed him because it makes sense. Ella's mom did it. That makes the most sense. And then he told me your dad kidnapped Ella. I believe him. He thought I was going to die. He had nothing to hide. What are you hiding? Where is your dad?"

"I don't know, Reese. You were getting close. He gave me the lake house. He made me his partner and gave me the right to make business decisions if he was gone. He must have been planning to leave."

"Is he alive, Gray? Did you kill him?"

"Absolutely not. I couldn't have done that."

"You killed Beau for killing your wife. It was your father who orchestrated her kidnapping to send her away. That's why she's dead now. Maybe you killed him too."

"Maybe...but I didn't."

"How about Ella Dixon? Did she kill him? Was it you who called the hospital saying she had a family emergency?"

"What would make you think that?"

"A gut feeling. Where's your dad? I want my last act as a detective to be his arrest. I think you know where he is."

"I can't help you. You're the detective, and I thought you were my friend."

214

"I *am* your friend, or you'd be behind bars right now. And I know you're going through more than I can fathom. So as a favor from you, I'd like to know where your father is. He deserves to go to prison."

"He's gone. All I know is he's gone. I can't help you."

"Okay." Reese sat down beside Gray and put his arm around his shoulders. They sat in silence a long moment before Reese spoke again. "What time is the funeral?"

"Four thirty."

"I'll be there. As your friend. And once Angie's body is released, I'll be there for her funeral as well. I'm sorry for your losses." He stood and extended his hand to shake, but Gray stood and gave him a hug.

"Thank you. Thank you for being a friend."

Reese nodded and walked out the door and back to Ashvi.

"How did it go?"

"Either Kingston plotted his disappearance, which is unlike a man with his ego, or he's dead. And if he's dead, either Gray or Ella Dixon did it. And what's craziest about this whole situation is I'll never know. Nothing much has changed, has it?"

Ashvi reached out and held his hand again. "You're a good man, Detective. I think you know what happened, and I think you can live with it. But one thing *has* changed."

"What's that?"

"I'm here. This time, you don't have to live with it alone."

Chapter 31

The funeral was a simple affair. Gray said some touching words, and the pastor gave a short, encouraging message. Gray's mother showed up as well as some appreciative clients and a lot of Kingston Phipps's employees. Reese and Ashvi listened to conversations as several discussions were held about Beau being killed in a police shootout and about Kingston's notable lack of attendance. No one had seen or heard from him since Saturday or Sunday. News began leaking out Gray had been elevated to full partner, and concern was voiced as to the impact that would have on their jobs. News also began spreading that Beau had killed Angie Phipps.

At the back of the church with her hair tucked under a black hat and with dark sunglasses so people wouldn't confuse her with Angie Phipps sat Ella Dixon, who left during the last prayer. Reese gave Gray another hug after the funeral and introduced Ashvi to him. She said some kind words and while she also gave him a hug, Gray mouthed the words, "You need to keep this one, Reese." He smiled and shook his head yes.

An hour later, Reese and Ashvi entered The River Grill for the retirement party. There was a cake featuring a picture of a thirty-year-younger Reese in his police blues. Besides on-duty officers and required staff at the station, nearly everyone from work showed up, including Reese's captain and the police chief. DA Morrison showed as well.

Reese mixed with the partiers, who ate wings and appetizers and generally drank a lot of beer. Chief Frank approached Reese to discuss business. "Rogers was processed and is behind bars, awaiting a bail hearing. We'll make sure he's prosecuted to the full extent of the law. We're looking into other improprieties. I'm sorry about what happened. Morrison, Swanson, and I had no idea, but we all feel partly to blame. The investigation into the shooting looks good for you, and if you need it, we'll make sure you can talk to one of the psychologists."

"My gut tells me Phipps is dead, but if he reappears, will you promise me you'll arrest him? Phipps is gone. Struthers is dead. I'm retiring. Leaving probably. Just do the right thing, okay, Chief? If he had something on you or threatened you or if you simply made a bad choice, you have a clean slate now to do the right thing."

"You're a good man, Carlton. You'll be missed. I'll do the right thing."

"Thanks."

"And speaking of the right thing, Ashvi is a step in that direction. You might try to not blow it with her."

"Yes, sir. I completely agree."

The partygoers gathered around and made a couple toasts. Reese opened a few cards and some gifts from his co-workers, which ironically included a dozen golf balls, a pickleball paddle, and a three-pack of pickleballs.

And then people started filtering out, some back to work, some to their homes, and some to another nightly hangout. Reese drove Ashvi back to his house to her car, so she could drive back to Nashville. She asked him to wait as she went to her car and brought back what looked like a rolled-up poster held with a rubber band. "You called for a ride from the hospital, so I didn't have time to wrap it, but I thought of you when I saw it, and since you're about to have a lot of free time, I thought it was perfect."

Reese removed the rubber band and unrolled it. At the top, it said "100 Dates Bucket List." Then there were boxes with 100 date suggestions like "Take a walk on the beach…Visit a food festival…Go ice skating…and Go to a comedy show." As Reese absorbed the implications, he smiled. "This is perfect because I won't have to come up with ideas. Now all I need is someone to do these things with." He winked and smiled again.

Ashvi started hopping up and down with her hand raised. "Pick me; pick me." She laughed so loudly Reese had to laugh along with her.

"Thank you for making what could have been a depressing day into one I'll cherish for a long time. He wrapped Ashvi in his arms and planted a kiss on her forehead. She looked up into his eyes, and Reese kissed her lips. It was a

217

soft, pleasant kiss, but it took his breath away. "I could get used to that."

"Me too."

"Well, you've given me carte blanche for 100 trips to Nashville. You'd better clear your calendar."

"It's clear." She kissed him again, got in her car, and rolled down her window. "Congratulations on your retirement. You have so much to be proud of." As he grinned at her, she backed out of the driveway and headed home.

***

After the funeral, the trip to the cemetery, and a dinner put on by his church, Gray had no idea what to do. He went home, walked into Noah's room, and nearly suffocated from grief. Then he walked into the bedroom where he could smell his wife, and he knew he had to leave. He got in his truck and drove without thinking, and when it dawned on him where he was headed, he knew what he wanted to do. He drove to the lake house. No cars sat in the driveway. His truck idled in park, and he struggled with his desire to go to the door. As he finally decided to put the vehicle in reverse and leave, Ella opened the front door and stepped off the porch.

She walked to Gray's side window. "You must be discouraged. Would you like to come in? We can sit on the deck and watch the sun set."

"I'm sorry I came here. I needed to get out of my house, and the next thing I knew, I was almost here."

"Come inside. I'll get you something to drink, and we can talk. You shouldn't be alone."

Gray climbed out and followed Ella inside. After choosing a bottle of water, they went out the sliding glass doors onto the deck. They sat in silence for an uncomfortably long time on deck chairs, one on each side of a glider bench seat. Finally, Ella asked, "How was the funeral?"

"Horrible."

"Yeah, they usually are. But I knew that. I was there."

"I didn't know that. Thank you."

"Your friend, Reese, came here today, looking for your dad."

"He came to see me too."

"He suspects my mom killed Paul Miller."

"He's good," said Gray. "He suspects either you or I killed my dad."

"He's very good. What happened when you left my house yesterday? You said you'd take care of everything, and it felt quite ominous to me. What did you do?"

"I drove to Beau's. As I got out of my truck, I heard gunshots. I went inside and Reese's gun was lying on the living room floor. Somehow Reese had gotten himself in trouble. They were on the lower level. He'd been shot twice, but somehow, he had Beau handcuffed. Beau admitted to me he killed Angie. Her body was stuffed into a freezer in the garage. So I shot him twice with Reese's gun. Beau's dead. I told you I'd take care of everything. You can rest easy now."

"He didn't arrest you?"

"I wore gloves. It was his gun. Beau shot him twice and had another shot left in his gun. It would look like Reese did it in self-defense. There was no way to prove I did it, so he decided justice and friendship trumped the law, and he covered for me."

"I have a friend like that. I miss her." Ella sighed and looked out over the water. "You know, when your dad and his henchmen came to buy our property, if they would've allowed us to have a slice of heaven like this, my dad would've made the deal. Willow Grove would flood often after heavy rains. Those times are my favorite childhood memories because as a little girl, it was a huge lake to me. My dad would talk about how someday we'd have a house on a lake. I never dreamed it would be anything as incredible as this, but being here now makes me happy. I know my dad would've been happy. Thank you, Gray."

"I had a life of ease because of my awful father. Don't get me wrong; he was incredibly difficult to live with, but I had everything a person could want. I got it, though, because he built a fortune by hurting other people. And then you had a life of difficulty because my awful father hurt you. If anyone should have this house, it's you. The only problem is I don't want to be in *my* empty, lonely house."

Ella stood and walked to the deck rail and looked over the water. "Come here, Gray."

Gray came up beside her and admired the view. "It's beautiful, isn't it?"

"Therapeutic. You can come here any time." Once again, she held his hand, and a moment later, she put her head on his shoulder. He released her hand and put his arm around her waist. "I know I look like her, but can you see me for who I am? Can you see me for me? Damaged child who was adopted and healed...healed enough to find a career and one close friend, but not healed enough to ever trust a man to have a relationship with? Could I ever be someone besides your wife's doppelganger?"

"I don't know how to answer that question except it's possible. With everything tumbling down around me and when I was at my lowest point this evening, I was drawn to you. It's a start. I hope telling you that means something."

"It does." She put her arm around his waist as well, and he gave her a gentle squeeze.

Together, they watched in silence from the railing as the sun disappeared below the horizon and the first sparkling stars emerged. They walked together back to the glider seat and sat, shoulder to shoulder, contemplating the pain of the week that had passed. Ella let her head rest on Gray's shoulder again. Gray sighed, but he felt better. Comfortable.

"What's next, Gray?"

"Sooner or later, there'll be a funeral for Angie. I've got some business decisions to make. A house to sell. Maybe some property to buy out West. Time to heal. Time to figure out my life." After a lengthy pause, Gray spoke again. "If I can get through all that and I end up idling my truck in your driveway again, do you think it's possible I can watch another sunset with you?"

"Not too long ago, you told me you hated yourself, and I said I wasn't too fond of you either. A lot has happened since then. Yes, Gray, you're welcome at my lake house any time. I hope it's not a long wait."

Gray closed his eyes, absorbing the moment, and he grinned. Then he rose from the bench and kissed Ella on the top of the head. "Thank you." He slid the glass door open. "Goodnight, Ella. I don't think it'll be a long wait."

Author's Note

In 1942, the construction of Dale Hollow Dam began in the narrow point in the Obey River Valley adjacent to the mount of Dale Hollow. This was nearly 150 years after five families had traveled overland down through the Cumberland Gap from New York in the late 1700s. They purchased land from Chief Nettlecarrier, who tradition claims sold them the land because they treated the Cherokee natives with respect and dealt fairly with them. Chief Nettlecarrier then moved his tribe to Arkansas. It is suspected the five families from New York came from the town of Willow Grove and, therefore, named their new settlement Willow Grove as well, but it may have been named after the prevalent willow trees.

Dale Hollow Dam and Lake was authorized by the Flood Control Act of 1938 as well as the River and Harbor Act of 1946. Its primary purposes were flood control and hydroelectric energy production. The dam was completed by the US Army Corps of Engineers in 1943, sixteen and a half months after the project began. Hydroelectric power generating units were added in 1948, 1949, and 1953. The lake, which borders both Kentucky and Tennessee flooded the valley, and by 1944, the lake was full, creating over 620 miles of shoreline and a recreational mecca for the two states. The town of Willow Grove was submerged in water after residents were forced to relocate.

I found the story of the Dale Hollow Reservoir fascinating and wanted to use it in my book, but it happened too long ago to be used accurately and historically in my book's setting. People who know the history know this, but I decided to change the date chronology to fit my storyline anyway so I could include a setting known to Tennessee and Kentucky natives and vacationers. I also changed how the land was purchased and used a realtor instead of the state to purchase the land—after all, I needed a bad guy for my mystery. There are other discrepancies to fit my storyline, so I thank you for understanding.

Made in the USA
Columbia, SC
03 July 2023